She refused to hurt Mark Griggs, at least physically.

She'd settled on the handcuffs, gambling now that the combination of the bourbon and his lust would weaken his defenses to a level where he couldn't resist the temptations the cuffs implied. "Makes me a naughty girl," she said, reaching for one of his wrists. "And something tells me you like naughty girls."

"You're sure of that, are you?"

"Sure enough, soldier, to ask you to just relax and let me do the work. I guarantee you're going to love this part. You'll be wild and begging before I release you for the real action."

That promise must have been too irresistible for him to question her exact intentions. She locked one end of the first handcuffs around his wrist and the other end around a sturdy vertical rail on the headboard.

When she'd succeeded in cuffing his other wrist with the second pair of handcuffs to another brass rod, she gazed down at him with a pleased smile. "There, you're my slave now."

Dear Reader,

I don't know about you, but I've been accused of being an intrigue junkie. It's true I love stories of mystery, but they're so much better accompanied by strong, sensual romances. There's one other element I look for: a plot that's unique. That's what I hope I've achieved in *The Lieutenant by Her Side*.

I began with an actual situation whose possibilities fascinated me. In the 1990s, just before the Taliban came to full power in Afghanistan, the country was in turmoil. In that time of upheaval, the National Museum in Kabul was looted. Many of its priceless treasures were eventually recovered. Others disappeared forever. These are the facts that gave me the foundation for my plot. Fast forward to the lieutenant and the woman he comes to love. Their present-day story is fiction—but oh, so very real to me. May they and their adventure come to life for you, too.

Jean Thomas

JEAN THOMAS

The Lieutenant by Her Side

HARLEQUIN® ROMANTIC SUSPENSE

Recycling programs
for this product may
not exist in your area.

ISBN-13: 978-0-373-27812-1

THE LIEUTENANT BY HER SIDE

Copyright © 2013 by Jean Thomas

H HARLEQUIN®

Printed in U.S.A.

™ www.Harlequin.com

Books by Jean Thomas

Harlequin Romantic Suspense

AWOL with the Operative #1694
The Lieutenant by Her Side #1742

Other titles by this author available in
ebook format.

JEAN THOMAS

aka Jean Barrett, lives in Wisconsin in an English-style cottage
on a Lake Michigan shore bluff. The view from her office window would be a magnificent one if it weren't blocked by a big
fat computer that keeps demanding her attention.

This author of twenty-six romances was a teacher before she
left the classroom to write full-time. A longtime member of
Romance Writers of America, Jean is a proud winner of three
national awards and has appeared on several bestseller lists.
When she isn't at the keyboard, she likes to take long walks
that churn up new story ideas or work in the garden, which
never seems to churn up anything but dirt. Of course, there are
always books to be read. Romantic suspense stories are her favorite. No surprise there. Visit Jean at jeanthomas-author.com.

To Jack and Sue, whose support I never fail to value.
Or forget.

Chapter 1

Clare didn't want the man seated three stools down from her to know she was aware of him. At least not with any curiosity that might arouse his suspicion, which was why she was careful to avoid looking directly at him.

In any case, it wasn't necessary for her to risk even a casual, sidelong glance. His reflection in the long mirror on the wall behind the bar was all she needed to tell her he was interested. *Definitely* interested, if his dark-eyed, smoldering gaze that kept slewing her way was any indication.

And why not when she had taken every measure to look as alluring as possible? A black, form-fitting cocktail dress with a low neckline meant to make a woman's breasts noticeably enticing. Her sleek, honey-blond hair swinging to her shoulders. A pair of gold hoop earrings and the kind of makeup that emphasized her eyes and her mouth.

The total effect said she was available.

Well, this was what you intended, isn't it? No one said you had to like it.

And Clare didn't like it. Her appearance in that mirror was as alien to her as the situation itself. Not to mention the guilt that had been gnawing at her long before her arrival tonight at the resort hotel.

But necessary, she kept reminding herself. The only way she could free Terry. An outcome, if it worked, that was imperative.

Trouble was, it had yet to work. She had his attention all right, but if he was going to make a move on her he was taking his sweet time.

"Don't worry about it," Clare had been instructed. "This guy's been deployed to Afghanistan for over a year. With your assets, he's gotta be ripe for a cozy get-together."

It seemed, however, that if anything was going to happen, it was up to her to initiate it.

Maybe because he was the kind of guy who never made any move until the woman signaled her willingness.

Inhaling a slow, deep breath meant to steady her nerves, hoping she wasn't being too obvious about any of it, she consulted her watch before turning her head to scan the lounge with its nautical wall murals and soft, piped in music.

"There doesn't seem to be a clock in here," she murmured in a volume just audible enough for her target to hear her.

The absence of a clock was something Clare already knew. She had made it a point to check for one when she entered the cocktail lounge. "Could be that's deliberate," her neighbor drawled in a husky voice that contained a note of humor. "Could be they don't want their patrons looking at a clock and deciding they don't need another drink."

"Yes, maybe," Clare agreed. "The thing is, I don't trust my watch. It's been running slow. And I noticed earlier when I checked my phone that the battery died. I wonder if you…"

"My pleasure." He looked at his own watch. "Going on nine-thirty."

She made a little noise of exasperation meant to convey her displeasure at the lateness of the hour.

"Waiting for someone, huh?"

"Yes."

"Damn rude of him to keep you hanging around like this. Assuming it is a *him*. No, don't tell me." He leaned toward her with a crooked grin. "I'd much rather you consider the offer of my company and another drink while you're waiting."

Clare hesitated, pretending a brief uncertainty before answering his invitation. "Sure, why not."

His eagerness to join her was so swift she barely had time to register his presence on the stool next to her. He'd brought his glass with him. From the level of the bourbon bottle the bartender had earlier left on the bar beside him, this wasn't the first drink he'd been working on.

"You don't waste any time, do you?" she observed.

"Can't afford to. You might get away."

Except for themselves and the bartender currently absorbed in his newspaper at the far end of the bar, they had the lounge to themselves. Evidence that the Pelican

Hotel had few guests. The parking lot outside with its scattering of cars had already indicated as much to her.

As if afraid he might lose her yet, Clare's companion immediately summoned the balding, solemn-faced bartender who, when he arrived, whisked away the empty glass of white wine she had been nursing, replaced it with a fresh one, topped the drink of the man beside her and retreated to his newspaper, leaving them alone again.

"So, how about some introductions? Name's Mark Griggs. And you?"

"Nola."

"Just Nola?"

"Just Nola."

That seemed to amuse him. A low chuckle rumbled up from somewhere deep inside him. "Okay, Nola, guess that'll have to do."

The truth was Clare hadn't been able to think of a last name which, along with Nola, would suggest…well, frankly, a woman of sexual experience. In the end, she'd decided that Nola by itself might sound intriguing to a man looking for a good time.

That was apparent in the way he was boldly admiring her legs. Clare realized they were one of her better features, long and shapely. She'd made certain to display them to her best advantage with a pair of spiked, strappy sandals and the skirt of her dress short enough to reveal a few tempting inches of her bare thighs.

"You live here on the island, Nola?"

She shook her head and smiled at him, hoping the smile wasn't too blatant an invitation for something beyond innocuous conversation. "Just a visit. How about you?"

"Came for the fishing. They tell me it's good again in the Gulf now that the oil spill is history."

Clare had already been informed this was why he was here, just as she knew he, also, had omitted a portion of his identity. He wasn't just plain Mark Griggs. He was Lieutenant Mark Griggs, U.S. Army Ranger.

Maybe, though, on leave like this and out of uniform, he preferred to be regarded as an ordinary civilian. A uniform, dress or combat, would certainly suit him, she decided, but that robust body was just as impressive in what he currently wore. Faded jeans that hugged a pair of muscular legs and a green polo shirt that did nothing to disguise a powerful chest. The army apparently made certain its servicemen remained in top condition, at least his branch of it.

Careful, Clare. You're not here to admire Lieutenant Mark Griggs. You have another objective, and you need to remember that.

She couldn't see that actual objective. But the thin, leather cord around his neck, from which it must be suspended, was proof enough to her that it was tucked out of sight inside the polo shirt.

"He's never without it," she'd been told. "Always wears it."

Which meant, if she was going to get it, she couldn't be caught staring at the open neck of his shirt. She had to focus on her performance.

Clare was having trouble with that. Flirting with him, while exchanging meaningless dialogue between sipping their drinks, didn't come naturally to her. She felt like a fool cocking her head to one side, toying with the ends of her hair, running the tip of her tongue over her lips as if she meant something more than licking off drops of wine.

Her actions were those of an amateur, not a practiced seductress. But if he saw through them, and he must, he didn't seem to mind. He sat there turned toward her, one elbow propped on the edge of the bar, and looking as if he couldn't wait to get her into bed.

Although he refrained from expressing his desire for her, his intention was clearly there in his face. She could see it in the way his eyes glinted as his gaze lingered on her. Could read it in the little smile that hovered around his wide mouth.

Funny how that rugged face had seemed almost homely to her in the photograph that had enabled her to identify him tonight. The slightly crooked nose and wry mouth in the photo gave an impression very different from the man who sat so close to her in this moment that his knee, either by accident or design, brushed her own knee.

Up close and personal like this, Mark Griggs might not qualify as handsome, but he was decidedly attractive. Maybe because in the flesh there was an animation in that face, a total masculinity that no photograph could ever capture.

And you have no business being occupied by anything other than what you were sent here to get.

Reminded of that mission, Clare stirred on her stool with a restless "I've waited around long enough. It's obvious he's not going to show."

"The guy's an idiot for standing you up."

She shrugged, as if she'd already dismissed her fictional date from her mind. "Doesn't matter. I think I'll call it a night and head on up to my room."

It was up to the lieutenant now. To her relief, he didn't disappoint her.

"Not a bad idea. I should get some shut-eye if I'm

going to be aboard that charter boat in the morning. Not," he added meaningfully, "that the prospect of fishing sounds very appealing right now."

She welcomed his observation with a throaty laugh that she hoped translated as her permission for him to consider another entertainment.

Her message must have been clear. He answered it with a confident, "Let's share an elevator."

Producing his wallet, he slapped several bills on the counter to cover their drinks and a tip. Clare picked up her purse and slid off the stool.

It was only when he fell into step beside her as they started for the lobby that she noticed what she hadn't had the opportunity to observe before this. Nor had she been informed of it back in New Orleans. She could only assume the man who had sent her here hadn't known it himself.

Lieutenant Mark Griggs was limping. Something had happened to his right leg. It wasn't much of a limp, but it was just evident enough for her to be startled by her discovery.

He was aware of her reaction, explaining his condition with an easy, "Souvenir from Afghanistan."

"You were wounded?"

"Yeah, something like that," he admitted, as if it was nothing to make a fuss over. "Took a couple of bullets in the leg while shielding this little kid in a Taliban attack on his village. Resulted in a medical leave."

Oh, great! Bad enough that the ribbons on his uniform in the photograph testified he was a much decorated army ranger. Now she had to go and learn he was a damn war hero. And she was about to commit the unforgivable and rob him.

The guilt clawed at her again, this time triggering the

image of another soldier. But that soldier was long gone, no longer any part of her life. She needed to erase him from her mind if she was to get this job done.

Terry. You've got to think only about Terry. Nothing else matters.

They had reached the lobby. Not counting themselves and the young night clerk looking bored behind the reception desk, the place was as deserted as the cocktail lounge.

He had misread her concern. That was why, with another of those cocky grins of his, he assured her, "Hey, don't worry about it. The leg may not be fully recovered yet, but everything else on this body works just fine."

There was no mistaking the significance of that. Lieutenant Mark Griggs was certain that something was meant to happen between them tonight. And why not, when she had given him every indication she was more than willing?

Had to be why, Clare thought, that as they waited for the elevator to descend, he stood so close to her that she could feel the heat of his hard body, smell the clean scent of his soap. The effect of his nearness had her trembling.

The elevator arrived, discharging a woman in pajamas and robe with a toy poodle on a leash. From the way the dog pulled her toward the front entrance, it was obvious it had a date outside with the nearest tree.

Mark stabbed the button for the third floor when they entered the elevator, then raised an inquiring eyebrow in Clare's direction.

"Five for me," she told him.

Somewhere between the closing of the elevator door and the opening of it again on the third floor, which couldn't have been more than a matter of seconds, the hotel caught fire in a sizzling, all consuming blaze.

At least that's what it felt like to Clare who, without knowing just when or how, found herself pinned against a wall of the elevator, Mark's arms around her, his mouth covering hers.

At twenty-seven years old, she was no stranger to kisses. But nothing in her experience, not even Alan, had prepared her for this man's kiss. It was deep, urgent and beyond mere passion. It was that fire she'd imagined, trapping her in its flames, something that lasted too briefly and at the same time too long.

Whatever it was, it left her light-headed, her knees like water, when he released her and looked around, surprised to find the door slid back on the third floor.

"What do you know," he said lightly. "We're here."

She managed a dry "I would say about five minutes ago."

There was no justice. Not with him looking completely at ease while her own emotions were in turmoil.

You didn't expect this, did you, Clare? Not to be susceptible to him like this.

She had to get control of herself, in control of him. It would be fatal otherwise.

"I guess," he said, "you could travel on up to your own floor."

"Yes, I could do that."

"Or since my own room is much closer…"

"Yes?"

"Hey, I wouldn't suggest something like showing your appreciation for a guy who's served in a war zone on your behalf. I mean, that would be downright crummy."

She wondered how many other times he had used

that innocent little stratagem to get a woman into his bed. She ought to thank him for it. It had the effect of snapping her out of the daze that had resulted from his kiss. She remembered now what she had to do and how to do it.

"All right, soldier, suppose you show me the way to your room."

Once the door was shut behind them, Mark's impatience left Clare time to briefly process only two things. She could hear the muted sound of the surf breaking on the shore somewhere beneath his windows. That was unimportant. The other mattered.

She had managed back in New Orleans to pick up a brochure advertising the merits of the Pelican Hotel. Among its glossy photos was one that depicted a typical room in the hotel featuring an elaborate brass headboard. She was relieved now to see that Mark's king-size bed was no exception. It boasted the brass headboard so critical to her plan.

And that was all the opportunity she had before his arms folded around her again, drawing her up snugly against his tall, solid body. His mouth followed, angling across hers in a kiss so searing she could no longer hear the surf, only the thundering of her rapidly beating heart.

The next few minutes were a blur. She had just a vague memory of Mark dragging his shirt over his head, kicking off his shoes, peeling away his socks, shucking his jeans down to his briefs, then casting them all aside in a feverish haste.

Clare had no memory of removing her own high-heeled shoes and the dress, but she must have shed them since she found herself standing there in nothing more than her lacy black bra and matching bikini panties. It was then, vulnerable like this, that the guilt and the fear assaulted her again. The jagged, cruel scars on his right leg, where the bullets had torn into his flesh, didn't help her state of nerves. Nor did the bulge in his briefs, a clear evidence of his arousal.

It was only when she made herself remember again how much Terry needed her to succeed that she was able to recover her courage and determination.

"You are so damn beautiful," he said in a tone closer to a growl than a husky admiration. "Smell great, too," he added, catching her in another embrace.

His observations, together with the contact of his heated, almost-naked body against hers, could have had her weak and reeling. Almost did, if she hadn't steeled herself against them.

"The hell with this," he muttered, backing them toward the bed, falling on it lengthwise with Clare on top of him.

She couldn't have found herself in a better position than if she had requested it. A position that left her in control.

She made use of it by smoothing the palms of her hands slowly, sensually over the slabs of muscles on his chest.

"Oh, sweetheart, that feels sooo good."

She could feel one of his own hands on her back, fingering the clasp of her bra. Given another moment, he would have the bra falling away from her breasts. Clare didn't allow him that moment. This was one part of her performance she wasn't prepared to surrender.

Swiftly lifting herself away from him, she rested on her knees between his spread legs. "I'm going to make you feel even better than that," she crooned. "*Much* better."

"Yeah? Hey, where you going?" he demanded when she scooted off the bed before he could prevent her.

"Not far."

Her destination was the chair where she had placed her dress and her purse. She was back in a second with the purse and a softly teasing "Did you miss me?"

He grinned up at her where his head rested on a pillow. "You didn't need the purse. Not if it was condoms you went for. I've got a supply of them right over here in the bedside drawer."

"Oh, this is something much more interesting," she purred, extracting from the purse two pairs of handcuffs.

His dark eyes widened at the sight of them.

This was her own method for securing the object resting against his chest. She'd been all too aware of it when he'd stripped off his shirt. The man who had sent her here had tried to give her knockout drops. But introducing them into Mark's drink would have been too tricky, along with the risk of dangerous aftereffects. She refused to hurt Mark Griggs, at least physically. She'd settled on the handcuffs, gambling now that the combination of the bourbon and his lust would weaken his defenses to a level where he couldn't resist the temptations the cuffs implied.

"Into fun and games, are you, Nola?"

"Makes me a naughty girl," she said, reaching for one of his wrists. "And something tells me you like naughty girls."

"You're sure of that, are you?"

"Sure enough, soldier, to ask you to just relax and let me do the work. I guarantee you're going to love this part. You'll be wild and begging before I release you for the real action."

The promise of that must have been too irresistible
for him to question her exact intentions when she locked
one end of the first handcuffs around his wrist and the
other end around a sturdy, vertical spoke on the headboard.

When she'd succeeded in cuffing his other wrist with
the second pair of handcuffs to another brass rod, she
gazed down at him with a pleased smile. "There, you're
my slave now. But you're going to have to watch the
moans and the groans," she cautioned him. "We don't
want one of your neighbors calling a complaint down
to the front desk."

"Not a problem," he assured her. "Except for mine,
the rooms all along this end of the hall are unoccupied.
At least that's what the reception clerk told me when I
checked in."

Clare couldn't believe the luck she was having at
every stage of this operation. If only that too-good-to-
be-true luck held just a bit longer...

"Perfect," she said. "You can shout your pleasure
all you want."

He probably *would* be shouting before much longer.
But not with any sexual gratification.

"Whoa, what do you think you're doing," he ob-
jected sharply when her hands went to the leather cord
around his neck.

"Just getting this out of the way," she said, lifting the
cord and what dangled from it over his head.

"That's not necessary. Put it back."

"Sorry, soldier, but I need this," she apologized,
scrambling off the bed with the amulet clutched against
her breasts.

He stared at her in disbelief. But only for a few seconds before his face turned thunderous. Although help-

less to stop her, it didn't prevent him from expressing his fury in terms that made it plain what he thought of her treachery, starting with a biting, "Why you rotten little cheat, you!" and moving on to a string of blistering, far more explicit curses.

The handcuffs rattled with a similar rage as he yanked at them uselessly. Lieutenant Griggs had altered in the space of a few heartbeats from a man welcoming her seduction to a dangerous adversary.

If it hadn't been for those secure restraints, Clare would have been at his mercy. As it was, he had her shivering with the chilling promise of retribution in those stone-hard eyes that followed her around the room.

She did her best to ignore both his gaze and his savage demands for his release as she methodically made the essential preparations for her escape.

Dropping the amulet into her purse, she hastened into her dress and heels before unplugging the phone on the bedside table.

There was always the possibility that, with enough thrashing around, along with the use of his legs, he could knock the receiver off its cradle, an action that would alert the front desk. Which was why she placed the phone well out of reach.

"What the hell is that for?" he barked when, after finding a spare blanket on a shelf in the closet, she moved again toward the bed. "You planning on smothering me with it?"

"Now don't be difficult." She unfolded the blanket, covering him with it. "With no clothes on and the air-conditioning in here, you'll be cold."

"Well, aren't you a considerate little thief."

"You can always kick it off if you get too warm."

"So what are you planning on doing? Leaving me here for the rest of the night?"

"Only long enough for me to get far away from here. Then I'll phone the hotel to let them know you need their help." She produced the two handcuff keys from her purse, moved in the direction of the door and laid the keys in plain sight on the surface of a desk. "I'll leave these here so they can unlock you when the time comes."

"Thought of everything, didn't you?"

She didn't answer him. What could she say? Struggling with remorse, needing to free herself from the gaze of those accusing eyes, Clare slipped out of the room, closing the door firmly behind her.

Chapter 2

Clare had hoped to find the elevator where they had left it. She wanted to make her getaway as quickly as possible. But, of course, it had been summoned to another floor.

Punching the call button, she waited for it restlessly. She glanced repeatedly along the length of the hall in the direction of Mark's room, unable to rid herself of the threat of his pursuit. Silly of her to be uneasy. He wasn't going anywhere. Not for some time, anyway.

Where was the elevator? Someone must be holding it on another floor, she decided. If it didn't arrive soon, she would take the stairs. Meanwhile...

The amulet seemed to be burning a hole in the side of her purse. In the end, her curiosity to examine it refused to wait for a safer moment. She removed it from her purse, turning it over in her hand.

Perhaps two inches or so in length, the wedge-shaped

amulet was curved on its bottom end. A small hole had been drilled in the pointed top through which the thin, leather cord had been strung.

A ceramic piece, Clare realized, with a dull, buff-colored glaze. Designs had been etched in the flat surfaces on both sides before it had been fired. All lines and squiggles, the jumbled patterns had no meaning for her.

This ordinary-looking wedge didn't seem the sort of thing an army ranger of Mark Griggs's caliber would consider important. For that matter, why did the man, who'd referred to it as an amulet when he sent her to steal it, want it so badly?

Was it very old, a valuable heirloom? Without knowing its origin or history, Clare couldn't begin to answer that. Nor did she really care as long as it won her Terry's freedom.

The ping of the elevator signaled its arrival. Stuffing the amulet back inside her purse as the door slid back, she hurried inside. It wasn't the button for the fifth floor that she selected. That had been another necessary lie. Clare wasn't registered in the hotel.

The elevator released her on the ground level seconds later. Hurrying across the lobby, she went out to the parking lot, secured the bag she had brought with her from New Orleans from the back of her compact and returned with it to the lobby.

There were restrooms off the corridor that led to the cocktail lounge. She went into the women's where she scrubbed off the flashy makeup, removed the hoop earrings and clasped her hair back into a ponytail. When she emerged from the restroom, she was dressed in flats, tan pants and a simple blue top.

Nola had vanished. She was Clare Fuller again and

feeling like her familiar self. The whole transformation from parking lot to restroom and out had taken only minutes. Nor had there been any witness to the change other than the attendant at the reception desk, who had spared her no more than a disinterested glance.

Purse in one hand, in the other the bag that now contained the dress, heels and earrings, Clare exited the hotel. She felt blessedly released from surroundings she never wanted to see again, so grateful to be free of them she permitted herself a brief interval to savor the nighttime air.

It was warm and humid, carrying with it on a breeze off the Gulf the tangy odors of salt and weed and fish. She tried not to think about the man back in the hotel handcuffed to his bed. But the image of him refused to go away, spoiling the moment of her enjoyment. She had deliberately aroused him and then abandoned him. Unforgivable of her. But essential, she kept reminding herself.

Checking her watch in the well-lighted area, realizing it was time for her to leave if she was to make the last ferry of the day off the island, Clare headed for her car. A short while later, with the parking lot behind her, she sped off into the night in the direction of the ferry landing.

She couldn't stop picturing Mark Griggs.

Lieutenant Mark Griggs was one royally pissed off soldier. He'd like to think his foul mood was all "Nola's" fault, but the truth was he was as enraged with himself as he was with her.

With his training and experience, he should have seen through her act from the beginning, sensed there was something not right about it. But the truth was he had wanted her too much to question it, unable to resist the lure of that sensational body. Not to mention the bourbon.

Mark was ordinarily satisfied by nothing stronger than beer. But he supposed he'd been missing the guys in his unit, needing the bourbon to take the edge off his loneliness. Big mistake. It had made him careless, something an army ranger avoided even when home on leave like this.

You know what the real trouble was, don't you? Besides you being a prize idiot, that is. You were too long without a woman. So much in need of one you practically invited her to ambush you.

Damn, he hated being suckered like this. Hated her having left him trapped here, as if he were some victim spread-eagled on an altar in a pagan ceremony of sacrifice.

But he wasn't entirely helpless, was he? He still had the use of his legs. Wanting to prove that to himself, he began to kick at the blanket covering him, using his feet to work it down his body far enough to leave it in a heap at the foot of the bed.

Real smart of you, Griggs. Now, if you get cold, like she warned, you won't be able to cover yourself again.

It had been nothing but an act of childish defiance. It had accomplished one thing, though. Having eased the worst of his frustration, he was just calm enough now to think rationally about this whole business.

The amulet. She had stolen the amulet, leaving his wallet and his watch untouched. Didn't make sense. The amulet couldn't be worth much of anything. Except to himself, that is, and only for a personal reason. Then why had she taken it?

Whatever her reason, he wanted it back. And he refused to wait for her phone call to the hotel, which might have been another lie, to get it. He wasn't a ranger for nothing. The handcuffs and the headboard might be strong, but he was strong, too. And just stubborn enough to somehow free himself. Then he was going after his amulet.

Wherever she had gone, whatever it took, he promised himself with a grim-jawed determination, he was going to find her. And when he got his hands on her...

The luck that had been there for Clare all evening ran out at the ferry landing.

Where were the other cars waiting to board? Where were the passengers on foot? More to the point, where was the ferry itself waiting to load at the dock? Her heart sank with the realization that the place was deserted.

She couldn't have missed the last ferry. The first thing she'd done when she arrived on the island was to check its schedule. The last ferry of each day set out for the mainland at eleven-forty-five. No earlier, no later.

Forget what she had told Mark in the cocktail lounge to gain his attention. Her wristwatch was dependable and her cell phone worked just fine. Both registered a few minutes before eleven-thirty, and the illuminated clock on her dashboard verified that.

There had to be an explanation. Maybe a favorable one, and before she panicked she'd better try to learn it. The nearby ferry office was still lighted. Better still, its late-night attendant must have spotted her arrival through one of its windows. Emerging from the office, he headed across the tarmac to her car. Clare lowered her driver's window to speak to him.

The young man wore shorts and a T-shirt. When he

leaned down to address her through the open window, an earnest expression of apology on his face, she could see that the baseball cap on his head was printed with the ferry company's logo.

"Sorry, ma'am, but if you were looking to cross on the last ferry, there isn't going to be one. She developed engine trouble over on the other side and is stranded there until the mechanics can work on her tomorrow."

Clare's response was an anxious "Isn't there a replacement?"

"Will be one, but not until first light in the morning when she's released from periodic maintenance at the mainland dock."

"Isn't there any other way off the island?"

"You could always try hiring a private boat, but at this hour…" He shook his head. "Leastways, even if there was one available, it wouldn't be anything big enough to carry your car."

No choice. She was trapped here on the island.

"Look, ma'am, there's a motel just down the road there. Real handy. You could check into it for the night. It's what the other folks counting on the last ferry went and did."

She thought about that and decided against it. "No, if it's all right, I'll just wait here in my car until morning. I want to be the first in line to board."

He must have thought her choice was a foolish one, but all he said in parting was a polite "You're welcome to do that, ma'am. Area's safely lighted, and the island police cruise by regularly to make sure everything's secure."

Clare thanked him, and after wishing her a good night he departed, leaving her on her own. She probably *was* being foolish, but she didn't want to chance not being aboard that first morning ferry. Her need to escape the island was almost a frantic one now.

And all because of Mark Griggs and her fear that he would come after her.

You do know you're worrying needlessly, don't you? He can't possibly free himself from that headboard until you alert someone at the hotel to go up to his room and release him. And that can't happen until—

The realization struck her then in midthought. She couldn't phone the hotel tonight as she had planned to do. She couldn't call them until sometime tomorrow morning when the ferry had delivered her to the mainland. Which meant Mark would be spending the whole night locked to the headboard.

The guilt that had haunted her all evening intensified with the image of him helplessly lying there through the long hours, his arms gone numb, his shouts unheard and all the while convinced that her promise to contact the hotel had been another lie.

Clare felt awful about it, but what could she do? Nothing until she was safe on the other side and on her way back to New Orleans. Meanwhile, she would be spending her own uncomfortable night here in her car. That, had Lieutenant Griggs known of her situation, might have offered him some small form of consolation.

On the other hand, she thought, remembering the heat of his anger, maybe not.

The little crook had obviously not called the hotel to help him. Probably had never intended to. Another of her false promises. Mark was on his own. Well, he'd been in scrapes before much worse than this one, and he'd always managed to get out of them.

He must have spent a good part of the night straining

every muscle in his right arm to break the vertical brass rod to which the cuff on that side was locked. His effort was accompanied by a considerable amount of grunting and swearing, not to mention a sore wrist where the matching cuff attached to that arm bit into his flesh.

The rod was too strong. No amount of his own strength would snap it. But by applying an unrelenting pressure, he achieved something else. Gradually, and with every exertion he could muster, the rod began to bend in his direction. Once sufficiently bowed out, it popped out of the sockets that held it, enabling him to slide the cuff off the thing.

His right arm was free, but it had cost him a raw wrist, even though he had tried to support the chain binding the two bracelets in order to relieve the tension.

Free, but too worn out to tackle the second pair of handcuffs until he rested. He hadn't intended to drift off, but sleep had been a requirement at that point. Although still dark out when he awakened, he must have slept for hours.

Entirely sober now, he spent what was left of the night attacking the second rod securing his left arm to the headboard. Knowing now what to do, and with both hands able to do it, the work took much less time.

The sky was still dark outside his window when he was a totally free man again. The first thing he did after crawling stiffly off the bed was to stretch every muscle in his body. They damn well needed it after his long night of punishment.

That done, he went straight for the keys on the desk, rid himself of both bracelets, dumped them along with the keys into the wastebasket there and headed for the bathroom and the hot shower his body demanded.

Although he made swift work afterward of getting

into fresh clothes and tossing his things into his two bags, the sky was beginning to lighten with the first suggestion of daybreak on the way.

No time to lose. He had a date with the woman who called herself Nola.

The yawning night clerk, blinking behind his glasses, was still on duty behind the reception desk when Mark arrived in the lobby. After canceling his booking on the charter fishing boat and checking out of the hotel, he questioned the young man.

"The blonde who was with me last night. You know if she's still in her room?"

"She's not registered here, sir."

Now why was that no surprise to him? "You happen to see her leave the hotel?"

The clerk nodded. "Sometime after eleven, I think. Went out to the parking lot and drove off in her car."

"You notice what the car looked like?" The clerk hesitated. "I've got something I need to return to her."

"Well, I've got a view of the lot from here, and it is well lighted, but I can't be sure. I know it was a compact. Possibly a Honda. Light in color, maybe a pale gray."

Good enough, Mark thought. "So, which way did she go?"

"In the direction of the ferry landing." The clerk suddenly seemed to realize he might be offering information he had no business imparting. "Look, maybe I shouldn't be telling you any of this. I mean—"

"Hey, don't worry about it. I didn't hear it from you."

Telling the guy to have the hotel put the damaged headboard on his credit card, he departed with his two bags.

He was limping when he crossed the lot to his black

SUV. His right leg was bothering him a bit, maybe because of the chill dampness in the early morning air. He'd be damn glad when the limp finally vanished, as the therapist back at Fort Bragg's Womack Army Medical Center had promised him it eventually would.

Reaching his car, he unlocked it, heaved his two bags into the back and climbed behind the wheel. There was no question of catching up to her here on the island, he thought as he raced off toward the ferry landing with the intention of making the first of the morning runs to the mainland. She would have crossed last night on the last ferry of the day.

Yeah, long gone by now. Didn't matter. Sooner or later, armed as he was with a description of her car, he'd manage to hunt her down. Like his leg, it was just a matter of patience. Not to mention a healthy supply of stubbornness.

Clare had spent a miserable night sealed inside her car, suffering a stuffy warmth that would have benefitted from a blast of air-conditioning. To achieve that, she would have needed to keep her engine running. Not possible when there was the risk of emptying her tank.

Even though there was never anyone about, as a precaution she kept her doors locked and her windows up. She'd been tempted several times to lower them just far enough to breathe a fresher, cooler air, but that would have been an invitation to Louisiana's voracious mosquitoes.

In spite of all her discomforts, however, she did manage to sleep through much of the night. Enough, anyway, to find herself fairly restored when she sat up and saw the rosy light of dawn tinting the waters of the strait. To her satisfaction, she could make out the distant form of the ferry crawling toward the island.

The low rumble of engines behind her and the louder banging of car doors had Clare twisting around in her seat. Vehicles were already lined up behind her and others arriving, all of them hoping to be on the first ferry of the day.

The curve of the approach to the landing enabled her to view the latest arrival, a black, powerful-looking SUV. It pulled into line behind the other cars.

Her curiosity answered, she was about to turn away when the driver, shutting off his engine, emerged from the SUV. Clare gasped at the sight of the tall, stalwart figure.

Mark Griggs!

What she had feared might happen *had* happened. He'd managed somehow to get out of those handcuffs. A possibility that wouldn't have mattered if she'd been able to leave the island last night as she'd intended, but now…

Clare tried to calm her panic, tried to think. Unless he'd learned of the ferry's failure last night to depart from the island, he would assume she was long gone. Wouldn't come searching for her along the line of vehicles waiting to board.

Fearing that might happen anyway, she kept a taut watch on him, ready to duck down in her seat if he started her way. To her relief, he remained where he was, leaning against the side of the SUV, sinewy arms crossed over his broad chest, gaze interested in nothing more than the progress of the ferry out on the waters of the strait.

She tried to reassure herself she was safe, that if he did glance in her direction he wouldn't recognize her.

Not at this distance and inside her car, not in an outfit so completely unlike last night's sexy one and with her hair pulled back.

But you can't count on that.

As an added precaution, she fumbled inside her purse for her sunglasses, slid them in place and faced forward again. Keeping low in her seat, she used both her side mirrors and the rearview mirror above her head to monitor his position, which remained fixed. When she was not doing that, Clare anxiously checked on the ferry. Its approach to the landing seemed as slow to her as that of a tortoise. Her whispered plea of "Hurry, hurry!" was, of course, pointless.

She had her car started and ready to roll when the ferry finally reached the landing. She could hear all the other car engines behind her come to life as she watched the two deckhands on board spring into action, binding the ferry to the dock, dropping the solid gate that also served as a boarding ramp, motioning the three vehicles on board to disembark.

Only when the ramp had cleared did one of the hands signal Clare to come ahead. After bumping up the ramp, she was directed to the far end of the deck where the other hand waited to make sure she was positioned to his satisfaction, her engine turned off and her hand brake locked.

She was aware of the other cars crowding in behind her. Maybe there wouldn't be room for the SUV. Maybe the line would be cut off before it reached the SUV, and Mark would have to wait for the second crossing of the day.

But the luck that deserted her last night was still missing. She was just able to glimpse in her rearview mirror a corner of the black SUV squeezed in at the other end of the deck. Her only hope now was that he wouldn't leave his car and come wandering her way, that if he did emerge from the SUV he would make his way instead to the upper deck.

The other passengers were already clattering up the narrow, metal stairway and…yes, there was his tall figure among them!

"Ma'am?"

Startled, Clare turned to find the face of one of the deckhands framed in the opening of her lowered window.

"Your ticket, please."

She reached into her glove compartment for the round-trip ticket she had purchased yesterday on the mainland and surrendered it to him.

"There's an air-conditioned lounge off the upper deck, ma'am. You might be more comfortable there."

"Thank you, but I'll wait here in my car."

She had observed on yesterday's crossing that the ferry was both a front-end and back-end loader. That if a vehicle was the first one to board it would also be the first to disembark. That much was in her favor. Before the SUV could leave the ferry on the other side she would be long gone from the landing. And maybe, if prayers meant anything, Mark would never be aware that she'd been within his reach.

The gulls were screaming overhead and the sun above the horizon when the ferry docked on the mainland.

Clare had her engine started and her hand brake released when the gate finally dropped in front of her. Once the ramp was secured, the deckhand signaled that it was safe for her to leave the ferry.

She didn't pause, didn't look back. The solid road waited for her at the end of the dock. Gaining it, she tore off up the highway that would carry her to the inland freeway that led to New Orleans.

Afraid after a couple of miles that her speed was a reckless one, she eased up on the accelerator, giving herself the opportunity to check the highway behind her in the rearview mirror. There were several vehicles back there, presumably other cars from the ferry. They posed no threat, because she could tell that none of them was a black SUV.

With any luck, Mark was still on the ferry waiting his turn to disembark. She was safe. For now at least. Just the same, she kept a wary eye on her mirrors. Still no sign of him. Not, anyway, until several moments later when she spotted it. The black SUV roaring around the other cars, passing them one by one in an effort to reach the front of the parade.

Her heart dropped, ending up in the area of her stomach.

Mark must have somehow learned she'd been aboard the ferry, that she was now somewhere ahead of him. There was no other explanation for his need to leave the other cars behind him.

Clare urged her Honda into another burst of speed. Useless, she knew. The compact was no match for that damn SUV. He would overtake her like a falcon swooping down on a helpless rabbit. Luck had deserted her again.

Or maybe not.

The highway, bordered on both sides by thick woods, was suddenly no longer ruler-straight. It rounded a sharp bend and once into that bend, with the heavy growth now masking her car from her pursuer, she spied a side road that abruptly left the highway off her left side. Clare didn't hesitate to dive into it.

She'd traveled only a few yards along its winding length before realizing the lane was in reality a dirt track. The palmettos that grew on both sides, along with the other vegetation, identified the region as one of lowland Louisiana's countless marshes.

This was no good. The track was clearly leading her nowhere except deeper into the marsh. She needed to find a place to turn around. But the narrow lane over which she carefully bumped, its rough surface beginning to look wet now, offered her little chance of that. Not until a small clearing suddenly loomed in front of her.

It was so unexpected that Clare, in an effort to avoid plowing into a wall of swamp grasses, stomped her foot on the brake. A serious mistake. There was mud here, a mud so slick under her wheels it sent her car hurtling through the grasses and straight into a swamp.

She heard a loud whump underneath the compact, and then nothing. The engine had stalled. Not that she'd be able to back out of the swamp if it hadn't. She could feel the car settling into the mire up to the bottoms of the doors.

Nice work, Clare. You've stranded yourself in a swamp. And from the sound of that thump below, probably with something busted.

There was silence all around her except for the tick of her cooling engine. But only for a few moments while she tried to decide what to do. And then it didn't matter, because the silence was penetrated by the low growl of an approaching vehicle.

She swung her head around just in time to see the dreaded SUV crawl into the clearing. In spite of all her maneuvers, Mark Griggs had caught up with her.

Chapter 3

Clare didn't know which was worse, being stuck in a swamp or being confronted by Mark Griggs. Seeing the hard expression on his angular face as he turned off his engine and climbed out of the SUV was all she needed to tell her he was in a vile temper. Given the choice, she decided she might prefer the swamp.

The Honda had flattened the tall reeds on its plunge into the swamp, giving her a clear view of the man behind her. If she expected a string of shouted curses directed at her, she didn't get them. Whatever he had in store for her, he was in no hurry about it.

Clare watched him nervously as he methodically removed his tennis shoes and peeled off his socks. Only when the shoes were placed neatly on the ground side by side, with the socks stuffed into them, did he carefully roll his pant legs up to his knees. All of it undertaken like a well-disciplined soldier readying himself for an inspection.

Never once during this little performance did he look her way. Nor did she earn so much as a glance from him when he headed purposefully toward the Honda. Wading into the muddy waters without hesitation, he came around to the passenger door, yanking it open with such force that she jumped.

Clare had laid her purse on the passenger seat. Before she could stop him, he snatched it up, turned and tossed it with such amazing accuracy that it landed safely beside his shoes. With the same swift motion, leaning inside the car, he removed her keys from the ignition and thrust them into his pocket.

There was no word exchanged between them during this entire action. Not, anyway, until his hand stretched across the seat to…well, whatever his intention, it had her shrinking back against the driver's door.

"Relax," he growled. "You might deserve a smack, but I'm not known for hitting women. At least so far. All I wanted to do was…"

"What?" she croaked.

"This." He unsnapped her seat belt. "Now scoot across the seat where I can reach you."

Clare stayed where she was, not trusting him.

"Look," he said gruffly, "you can either let me rescue you, or you can wait here for the alligators and water moccasins."

Both of which, she knew, were as common in southern Louisiana as the swamps that bred them. Unfriendly, too, but maybe not as unfriendly as the man who waited for her decision.

"I'm perfectly capable of rescuing myself," she informed him stiffly.

"Yeah? Show me."

She could have exited the car by the driver's door. But, not wanting him to think she was afraid of him, she slid herself toward the open passenger door. "Just get out of my way so I can—"

Clare didn't get to finish. Didn't get to voice a single word of objection. All she could manage was to suck in a sharp, startled breath when his hands, again with that same lightning speed, scooped her up into his arms.

"No sense in both of us getting wet, is there?" he said.

How he managed to back away with his load, nudge the door shut with one knee and carry her out of the swamp without staggering deserved an expression of admiration. Particularly when she remembered the injury his right leg had suffered. But she was silent. They both were.

Once on solid earth again, he lowered her to the ground. Although that wasn't exactly how Clare would have described it. What he actually did, his arms all the while pinning her tightly against him, was to permit her to slide slowly and with a deliberate sensual torment down his length.

The heat of his body pressed against hers had her feeling woozy. And very much in need of putting some space between them.

"All right, you've demonstrated just how helpless you think I am. How about letting me go now?"

He didn't release her. He continued to hold her, both with his arms and his mocking gaze. "I don't think so," he said in a smoky, husky voice. "You promised me something last night, only you didn't get around to delivering it. Seems to me this is a good time to collect on it."

Clare realized she had gotten herself in a bad situation. She didn't know this man, didn't know what he was capable of, and she was alone with him here in the middle of nowhere.

Damn it, dangerous or not, she wasn't going to let herself be intimidated by him. "You can stop testing me," she defied him. "I'm not playing your game."

"That all it is? A test?"

As if to prove it wasn't, his face came down so close to hers that she could feel his warm breath. Could see his parted mouth ready to descend on hers in a savage kiss that, before he was through, would leave her lips bruised and swollen.

Clare experienced all of it before it happened. Except it didn't happen. With a muttered oath, he thrust her away so suddenly she almost lost her balance.

"You can stop worrying, Nola. I'm no more in the habit of forcing myself on unwilling women than I am in smacking them. Or is *Nola* your name? Why don't we find out?"

His leg didn't stop him from swiftly reaching her purse where it had landed, scooping it up with one hand and zipping it open with the other. He found her wallet on top and her driver's license inside.

"Clare, huh?" he said, consulting the license. "Even a last name this time. Fuller. Cute." His head came up, his dark eyes searching her. "Suits you. Different outfit now, different hair. Not all seductive like last night. No wonder I didn't spot you on the ferry."

"Then how did you—"

"Learn you were aboard? I didn't until we were pulling in and some guy on the upper deck asked one of the hands what went wrong with the other ferry that it wasn't able to make its final run last night. That's when

I figured you must be somewhere on the lower deck. Got down there just in time to catch a glimpse of you headed off the ramp." He shrugged, replaced her wallet in the purse and concentrated on its other contents. "So, Clare Fuller, what else have we got in here? Ah, here we go."

Clare knew he would find the amulet. And he did, fishing it out of the purse with a triumphant grin, taunting her with his recovery by swinging it from its cord, as if it were a pendulum. She could feel the bitterness of her loss settling in her stomach like a sour acid.

She watched him with distress as he looped the cord over his head. Once settled again around his neck, he tucked the amulet out of sight inside his shirt, patting the area of its disappearance with satisfaction.

"There, that's better. Back where it belongs."

Clare refused to be defeated. "Look, I know what I did last night was all wrong, but—"

"Wrong?" His laugh was brittle, harsh. "Lady, it was rock-bottom dirty."

She swallowed her pride, prepared to do whatever it took to get the amulet. "All right," she admitted, "it was a rotten trick I pulled on you."

"Why?"

"Because I need the amulet."

"So you said last night. For what reason?"

"I…well, I can't explain it. I just do. I don't know what its value is," she pleaded, "but whatever it's worth—"

"You trying to buy it from me?"

"Yes."

"Forget it. It's not for sale at any price."

Hadn't she already learned that would be the case

from the man who had sent her to steal the amulet? Still, it had been worth the effort.

Zipping her purse shut with the same finality as he'd dismissed her offer, he flipped it toward her with a careless "Here."

His aim, however, was not a careless one. It was as true as his earlier one, enabling Clare to catch her purse with ease.

She watched him as he wordlessly fetched a pair of old towels from the rear of his SUV, took them down to the edge of the swamp, soaked one of the towels and carried both of them back to the SUV, retrieving his shoes and socks along the way. Leaning against the side of the car to support himself, he washed the mud off his feet with the wet towel and dried them with the other one.

Socks and shoes back on his feet and the towels restored to the SUV, he opened the passenger door with a crisply instructed "Get in."

Clare didn't move.

"No? Fine. Then I guess I leave you out here in the wilderness on your own."

There was a long silence.

He glowered at her.

She glared at him.

In the end, unwilling though she was to go anywhere with him, the thought of being left alone with a useless car landed in a swamp was not exactly the wisest of her two options. No, not even if she was equipped with a cell phone.

Trouble was, she'd left that phone back in the Honda, which meant risking those snakes and alligators. Not to mention the mosquitoes, she thought, swatting at one.

"And just where do you plan on taking me?"

"There's a service garage about a half mile up the highway. I stopped there for gas and coffee in the diner next door on my way to the island. With any luck, they'll have a tow truck to haul your car out of the swamp and back to the garage. And while we're waiting to see if it needs any repair…"

"What?"

"We have ourselves a nice cozy breakfast in the diner. And you get to answer some questions, Clare Fuller. A *lot* of questions. And if I like your answers, maybe I won't turn you over to the cops."

They sat at a corner table across from each other. Mark waited until the waitress had taken their orders and departed before he leaned toward her with an I-mean-business tone in his voice.

"Let's start with some basics."

"Such as?"

She didn't trust him. She'd been silent and nervous all the way to the diner, squeezed as far away from him as she could get in the car. He could see she was nervous now from the way she toyed with the spoon resting on the saucer of the coffee cup the waitress had filled before leaving their table. Well, that was all right. He didn't trust her, either.

"Oh, I don't know. Maybe things like what you do when you're not coming on to guys in bars so you can rob them. Or is that a full-time occupation for you?"

"I don't expect you to believe it, but I've never done anything like that before."

"Yeah? Then what is your job?"

She didn't answer him. It was clear to Mark that she didn't want him to know anything personal about her.

"You ashamed of it, Clare?"

"Of course not. It's a perfectly respectable job." She hesitated, and then seemed to decide that it didn't matter if he knew. "I'm a fifth-grade teacher in a private school in New Orleans."

Mark couldn't help the laughter that erupted from him. Laughter loud enough to draw attention from the other tables near them.

Clare frowned at him. "What's so funny?"

"Just wondering what your fifth-graders would have made of you in that high-class hooker outfit last night." He tipped his head to one side, considering her. "Come to think of it, the change in you this morning looks convincing enough to say 'teacher.'"

"Meaning what?" she challenged him coolly. "The prim image of one?"

"I wouldn't go that far," he drawled.

Or anywhere near such an image. Not remembering as he did the terrific body that would be there under whatever outfit she wore. He had certainly found her alluring last night. And although he hated to admit it to himself, he was beginning to find her just as alluring this morning. With her silky blond hair, blue eyes and lush mouth, not even the plainest of clothing could make a difference.

There was something else Mark found interesting, something that hadn't been evident last night under all the makeup. High on her left cheek was a white, crescent-shaped scar. Now why in hell should something as insignificant as that strike him as captivating?

You don't watch it, Griggs, you're going to be feeling things that are only going to end up burning you again.

It was much safer to get back to all those questions he had, he decided, lifting his coffee cup to his mouth, welcoming the taste of the caffeine-rich brew on his tongue. She had yet to touch her own cup. She was watching him with that same uneasiness that had been there since he'd chased her down in the swamp.

"A teacher, huh?" he said over the rim of his cup. "So why aren't you in your classroom?"

"I took a few business days I had accumulated."

"Which you're spending hunting for strange men in bars. Only I wasn't so strange, was I? You recognized me when you wandered in there, even though we'd never met. How was that possible?"

"I—" She paused before admitting it. "I'd been shown a photograph of you."

"This gets more intriguing by the second. Who showed you the photo, and where did they get it?"

"I don't know where he got it or how he knew you were registered in the Pelican Hotel."

"You didn't ask?"

"It wasn't important."

He lowered the coffee cup to his saucer with a decisive click. "I think it's time we got to the particulars, Clare. Like you telling me just why it wasn't important."

She didn't answer him. There was a mulish expression on her face now. Mark dug his cell phone out of his back pocket and slapped it down meaningfully on the table in front of him.

"I suppose," he said, sitting back in his chair, "I could still let the cops handle it for me. I think they'd listen to a soldier who served his nation in battle, don't you?"

"That's blackmail."

"Yeah, it is. Wonder where that falls in the category of crimes. Somewhere below robbery, I imagine."

Mark could see that his threat worked. Although she plainly resented him for it, she was ready to talk to him again.

"It just didn't matter. Helping Terry was all that mattered."

Whoever this Terry guy was, there was a strong emotion in her voice when she named him. And why, Mark wondered, should that bother him?

"Boyfriend?"

She shook her head. "Sister."

The relief he experienced, slight though it was, also bothered him. He had no business experiencing it. What did it matter whether she did or didn't have a boyfriend?

"Terry is in trouble. *Serious* trouble."

"What kind of trouble?"

Before she could explain, the waitress arrived with their orders. There were scrambled eggs, bacon and buttered toast for him. Clare was having a health-conscious bowl of oatmeal and a bran muffin. Maybe her method for maintaining that sexy figure, Mark thought.

He eyed her as they ate, envying the food that was going into her mouth, remembering how he had kissed that mouth last night and wanting to plunder it again.

She was eventually conscious that he was watching her. Did she guess what he was thinking? Is that why she flushed and looked away?

You're an ass. You've got no business getting mixed up with this woman. Not on that level.

That's what his head told him. Another area of his body told him otherwise. However insistent that area was, though, he refused to listen to it.

Concentrating on his eggs and bacon, he prompted her between bites. "You were saying?"

"About Terry. She…well, she's in jail."

"For what?"

"She's been charged with murdering her husband."

Mark issued a long, low whistle of surprise. He hadn't expected something like this. "She do it?"

"Of course not. Even though God knows she did have a reason, Terry was too much in love with Joe to ever hurt him, much less kill him. Besides, she was in New Orleans at the time the medical examiner fixed for his death, which is a good hour's drive downriver from their parish and another hour back."

"Then she has an alibi."

Clare shook her head. "That's the problem. The only one who saw or spoke to her was the owner of the antiques shop she visited. When the police interviewed him, he didn't remember Terry ever being in his shop."

"There must have been a surveillance camera in there."

"There was. Terry saw herself on the overhead monitor with the date stamp counting down the exact time and day of her visit. The police asked him about this. He said there was no tape for that day, that the equipment was out for repair. He even had the receipt for that repair."

"So?"

"He was lying. I knew he had to be lying. I went to see him myself, and he admitted as much."

Mark had finished his eggs and bacon and was working on his toast. As for Clare, she had pushed aside her half-eaten bowl of oatmeal and was ignoring the muffin. No appetite, he figured. Understandable.

"So why should this guy lie? He must have had a reason."

"He did. Me."

Mark dropped the last slice of toast on his plate, no longer interested in food. "I'm beginning to make the connection. He wanted you to go after my amulet."

"He said he would trade the surveillance tape for the amulet."

"Who is this guy, anyway?"

"His name is Malcolm Boerner."

"Never heard of him. How did he know about me?"

"I don't know."

"But he had a photograph of me you said. How did he come to get it?"

"I told you before I don't know."

"And how did he learn I had the amulet?"

"I don't know that, either."

"Seems there's an awful lot you don't know."

"I told you—"

"Yeah, yeah, all you cared about was saving your sister." Mark cocked his head to one side, appraising her face and what he could see of her figure above the table. What was below the table he had no trouble remembering. Not after last night. "I guess this Boerner character must have decided you had all the right equipment for the job. Guess you also don't know why he didn't come after the amulet himself."

Clare shrugged. "He wasn't specific about it, but I think he felt he wouldn't be able to get close enough to you to get it. You're an army ranger, after all. That must make you naturally cautious of any stranger, and probably too well trained to be overpowered by force."

"But *you* could get close to me. And did." She had no answer for that. "What I can't figure is why he wants my amulet."

"I—"

"Don't say it. *You don't know.* Well, it doesn't make sense. These amulets are available all over Afghanistan, most of them cheap junk. It's rare for any of them to be old. Doesn't matter, though, if they're fakes. The

Afghans are a superstitious people. They think the amulets, antique or fake, have the power to protect them from evil."

"But if yours is very old and Malcolm Boerner somehow knows that…"

"Forget it. It's not old."

"Then why do you value it so much?"

"Remember what I told you in the hotel lobby about this gimpy leg of mine being the result of a Taliban attack?"

"Yes, I remember," she said solemnly. "You were protecting a child."

"That's what they told me. All I know is that this kid was out in the street in the direct line of fire. The next thing I knew I was out there myself with both of us hugging the dust, my body wrapped around his and bullets flying everywhere."

Clare had a look on her face that suggested a sudden, deep regret. As if she might be feeling guilty over her theft of the amulet. Well, maybe she actually did.

"Anyway," Mark continued, "this is where the amulet comes in. The kid's father turned up while the field medic was strapping me on a stretcher to be airlifted by chopper to a combat hospital. He had the amulet with him. Told me in fractured English he'd inherited the thing from a cousin who'd died of—I think he said cancer—in Kabul. And that this cousin, who was a very important man, regarded the amulet as something to be revered and that Ahmad, the kid's father, was to keep it always safe."

Mark paused for a swallow of coffee. It was cold by now. It didn't matter. Clare was waiting for him to go on.

"The amulet was precious to Ahmad, but his son was far more precious to him. You understand?"

"He wanted you to have the amulet in gratitude for saving his son."

"Something like that. He insisted on hanging it around my neck under my dog tags. Told me I should keep it close, and it would guard me from any further harm. Hell, what could I do? He would have been deeply hurt if I'd tried to refuse it."

"And you promised him to always wear it."

"Yeah, I did."

"A man who never fails to honor his promises."

"Don't make me out as something I'm not."

"Mark, I—"

"Hey, I get it. You're feeling lousy now for having taken the amulet, but you still want it. Right?"

Whatever response she might have had, he didn't get to hear it. The mechanic from the service garage next door appeared at their table. He was a large man with a mouthful of teeth so white they almost blinded you. Maybe because his skin, in sharp contrast, was so dark.

Those teeth were on full display now as they smiled down on Clare. "Got your car back from the swamp and up on the hoist. That's the good news. Afraid the rest isn't so good. The underside is damaged. Struck this halfway submerged stump on the way in."

"The thump I heard before the engine stalled. How bad is it?"

"Punctured holes in the oil pan. I can flush out the system and replace the oil pan. Only thing is, I don't have me an oil pan for that model. It would take a couple of days to order and get a new one. Then at least, oh, say another day for the repair. You want me to go ahead with it or what?"

"I don't think I have a choice. Yes, go ahead with it."

"Fine." He placed one of his business cards on the table. "Best you call me to make sure it's ready. Oh, there's this here, too. Found it in the glove apartment when I was looking for the car manual. Figured you'd want it back."

He laid Clare's cell phone beside the business card, wished them a good day and, with another of those dazzling smiles, departed. The mechanic's news had Clare looking so miserable he didn't think she could possibly have a good day.

"What now?" he asked her.

"I can't wait around here for the car. I'll have to find transportation back to New Orleans."

"You might do that. Except in a place like this I don't think you'd have any luck in renting another car. Probably not on any bus route, either. Looks like you're stranded. Unless..."

She gazed at him, those terrific blue eyes registering her realization.

"Oh, no."

"Oh, yeah. Face it, you're desperate. You need me to drive you to New Orleans, and I need to go there."

"Why?"

"Only way you and I together can visit this Malcolm Boerner. I want *all* the answers, Clare."

Her alarm at his proposal was immediately evident. "I can't show up there with you in tow! He'd never give me the tape!"

"He will if he wants the amulet."

"You'd do that? Give him the amulet in exchange for the tape?"

"I'm considering it."

"But to sacrifice it when it's so important to you..."

"My amulet, my choice."

What the hell was he doing? He had no intention of surrendering his amulet. All he wanted was an explanation that satisfied him. He certainly hadn't gotten one from Clare Fuller. For all he knew, everything she'd been telling him was nothing but lies. And if she thought he'd forgiven her for last night…well, he hadn't.

Yeah, he wanted answers, but there was another reason for going to New Orleans with her. Mark was a soldier, a career man who'd been idle long enough. He needed action, and fishing wasn't going to do it for him. But here was a challenge that could.

He'd been a ranger too long not to sense trouble. There was something wrong about this whole business and, yeah, he wanted it sorted out.

That all it is, Mark? Go on and admit it to yourself, why don't you? Sure, your arguments are valid ones. Except they don't include your urge to be with her for a very personal reason. Whatever she is, this woman has gotten under your skin.

Mark rocked back in his chair with a casual "So that's the deal, teacher. The amulet goes to New Orleans, but I go with it."

Chapter 4

"Is that all I was to you? Nothing but a target?"

They had left the coast behind them and were traveling north toward the interstate. Neither of them had spoken a word during these first miles to New Orleans. That alone was explanation enough for Clare being so startled by this question of his coming out of nowhere.

Except that wasn't the only reason for her surprise. It was the content of that impulsive question that had her turning her head to stare at him. His own gaze was fixed on the highway. She couldn't see the expression on his face, but there had been something in his tone…

What? Purely the result of a male ego that didn't want to believe she hadn't been interested in him last night on more than one level? Or was it actually possible that under his tough, army ranger exterior, Mark Griggs was capable of something more sensitive than that? That maybe he'd been genuinely hurt by what he perceived as her heartless rejection?

Clare didn't know what to answer him and was relieved by his curt "Forget I asked. It doesn't matter."

She had the feeling it did matter but that perhaps he was too proud to pursue an answer, maybe even embarrassed now that he'd ever introduced the subject.

They lapsed into another long silence. It wasn't an easy silence. There was an uncomfortable strain between them. And why not when he obviously didn't trust her? Nor did she trust him. If that was the only explanation, it would be both understandable and acceptable. But there was something else much stronger than that. A disturbing sexual tension.

Clare couldn't deny it. It had been there from the beginning last night, this awareness of his potent masculinity. How the very air inside the car was charged with it, making it difficult to breathe when she was so conscious of the heat and scent of his body so close to her own.

Was he experiencing something of the same effect where she was concerned? She didn't dare to make any effort to find out. There was too much of a risk in that.

There had been another soldier in her life. He was long gone now, but she hadn't forgotten the ache of losing him. There was a lesson in that.

You don't permit yourself to get mixed up with men in uniform, Clare.

It was a piece of wise advice, only she wasn't obeying it. She was already involved with one of those men now. No choice. As long as there was still a chance of getting her hands on that amulet, she had to endure the company of Lieutenant Mark Griggs, whatever her dangerous attraction to him.

They had reached the interstate now. Clare trained her gaze on the much safer view outside her passenger window as the SUV sped along the elevated four-lane highway, crossing a maze of bayous and cypress swamps. It was a flat, monotonous scene. Or would have been, if its vegetation hadn't been so rich with the new, tender green of spring. There was a promise in that, though she had no chance to wonder what it might be.

Her companion chose that moment to rupture the silence again, his deep voice firing off a brusque "Why isn't she out on bail?"

He had lifted her so sharply out of her reverie that his question confused her. "What?"

"Your sister. You said she was behind bars. Why wasn't she released on bail?"

"Because Joe was a cop in the parish where they lived. Louisiana's origins were strongly Catholic, so parishes are equivalent to counties in other states."

Mark turned his head, favoring her with one of those bold, wicked grins guaranteed to accelerate feminine pulses. "Playing teacher for me, are you, Ms. Fuller?"

Clare wished he would stop sparring with her, but she didn't think that was likely to happen. He was enjoying himself too much. "Just thought you might like to know. Most outsiders don't."

"Uh-huh. So her husband was a cop. Why did that matter?"

"He was well liked by all the other officers, popular, too, with the judge who denied Terry bail. None of them were ever willing to believe there was another side to Joe Riconi."

Clare couldn't prevent the bitter note in her voice, and Mark was shrewd enough to understand it.

"Don't tell me. He was abusive to your sister."

"When he was drinking, yes."

"How abusive? Physically?"

"Terry maintained it was never anything but verbal, but I had my suspicions. She wouldn't leave him, though."

"They never do. Familiar story."

"Anyway, that's why she's waiting for her trial behind bars."

"These other cops and the judge. They must have guessed something about this abuse, if that was the motive your sister was charged with for her husband's murder."

Clare could only shake her head, not knowing how much serious investigation had been conducted in the case, if any.

Mark was silent again for another long minute, but she knew he wasn't finished with his questions. He was testing her, of course. Probably not ready to accept her story or, for that matter, to forgive her for stealing his amulet. Well, she was ready for those questions.

"So what does all this have to do with this Malcolm Boerner character? Anything?"

"Everything." Clare explained the connection to him. "Joe and Terry were down in New Orleans shopping the day before he was killed. She'd left him waiting for her on the sidewalk while she went into a boutique to look at purses. When she came away from the store, he'd crossed the street and was talking to some guy on the corner. Not anyone Terry recognized."

"Boerner?" Mark guessed.

"Yes, Malcolm Boerner. Terry asked Joe about him when he rejoined her outside the boutique. He was casual about the whole thing, said that Boerner had a shop in the French Quarter where he sold antique firearms. They'd known each other in the old days when they were mercenaries in the Mideast. 'Haven't run into him in years,' he told Terry. 'We were just doing a little friendly reminiscing.'"

"But?"

Yes, there was a *but,* Clare thought, and Mark had sensed that. "Terry had the impression their conversation had been too intense to be just some friendly reminiscing."

"So she heads back down to New Orleans the next day to pay a visit to Boerner in his shop. That the way it went?"

The lieutenant was astute all right. Far more so than Clare was comfortable with. "While Joe was on duty back home, yes."

"Why?"

"Because of the drinking that put him in those vile tempers. Joe refused to discuss it with her, but Terry was convinced the drinking was a result of those years he'd been a mercenary."

"So your sister figures what? That Boerner will have answers for her?"

"Something, anyway, that would help her to help her husband."

"Were there? Answers?"

"If there were, Boerner wasn't willing to share them with her."

Mark had no response to that. He seemed to be considering something. "I'm just wondering," he finally said.

"About?"

"Whether all of this could have any connection with the amulet Boerner is after."

"I don't see how that's possible. They're separate issues."

"Maybe. Maybe not."

"Well, if you can think of an explanation let me in on it, because you know all that I know now."

"Do I?"

The man was exasperating. "And just what haven't I told you either now or back at the café?"

"You went to Boerner yourself after your sister was arrested."

"You already know that."

"Yeah, but what I don't know is whether Boerner offered you his deal then and there, the amulet for your sister's alibi."

"As a matter of fact, he was cagey about it. Hinted he might have something that would interest me, and if he did he would call me. I left him my number, and he phoned that night and asked me to come into his shop the next morning. That's when he explained what he wanted me to do."

Mark was thoughtful again before asking her slowly, "Did it ever occur to you, teacher, why Boerner failed to give the cops the alibi your sister needs when they went to him? What did he have to gain by lying to them when he hadn't even met you yet and realized he could use you? And how is he going to explain that lie if he turns around and provides you with the tape?"

"I don't—"

"Right. You don't care. All that matters is getting your hands on that tape. Well, I don't have the answers, either. But I know one thing for sure."

"And what would that be?"

"Something is definitely screwy about this whole business."

* * *

To Clare's relief, Mark had no more questions for her after that. Possibly because he needed to concentrate on the traffic. It had thickened considerably when they left the Baton Rouge area behind them and began to approach the urban sprawl of Greater New Orleans.

No more questions, but he'd left her with plenty to think about. And feel. Like the hope when they reached Boerner's shop that Mark would be satisfied, would agree to exchange his amulet for the tape. And after that? What then? Would she be able to rid herself of the daunting Lieutenant Griggs whose mere presence evoked emotions that confused and troubled her.

"I'm getting confused," he said.

There he went, startling her again. Was he able to read her mind?

When all she could do was gaze at him in bewilderment, he prompted her with an impatient "Directions. I could use some directions here. The route is getting complicated. Too many choices."

"Oh, right. Take the exit after this next one."

The traffic was heavier than usual when they left the expressway, plunging into the heart of the city. New Orleans, Clare realized, was a popular destination again now that Katrina was a thing of the past. All of the out-of-state license plates testified to that. There were as many of them as during Carnival and Mardi Gras.

Springtime in New Orleans, with all of its festivals celebrating the season and the azaleas everywhere in full bloom, was an irresistible attraction.

Clare was no more immune to the charms of New Orleans than the crowds of visitors. She demonstrated that when, stopped at a traffic light, she lowered the window on her side, inhaling the warm, humid air of the city she loved with all its heady aromas of roasting coffee and damp, mossy earth mingling with the fragrance of sweet olive.

"Can you smell it?" she invited her companion.

"Smells old" was his only comment, though he smiled at her with tolerance when he said it.

"That's the flavor of New Orleans."

"Yeah, that and the exhaust fumes. Which way now?" he asked as the light changed.

Clare knew that parking in the Quarter itself was always a problem. Today would be no exception, which was why she directed him to a high-rise garage on Canal Street.

"We can walk from here," she said after they left the SUV on an upper floor and descended to the wide thoroughfare that was Canal Street. "It's not far."

Even Mark was impressed by the sharp, sudden contrast of the modern city and the historic district as she led the way directly into the French Quarter. She was careful to set a pace that wouldn't stress his leg as they headed along the narrow Royal Street with its brick paved banquettes, shuttered windows and lacy, wrought-iron balconies.

The tourists converging on all the shops were out in full force here, along with the familiar, sightseeing carriages and the street musicians wailing a jazz that, though in no way equal to the music heard at Preservation Hall, added to the atmosphere.

They had covered almost two blocks when Clare halted Mark at the mouth of an alley. "Boerner's shop is just a few doors away."

"So why are we stopping?"

"I have a request."

"What is it?"

"You're probably not going to like it." She drew a deep breath to fortify herself before naming it. "I'd like you to wait outside and out of sight while I go into the shop."

Those distinctive, dark brown eyes of his that were capable of registering a seductive ardor in one minute and a disarming anger in the next narrowed suspiciously. "You're right. I don't like it."

"Look," she said quickly, "if you go in there with me, it could ruin the whole thing. Just give me a few minutes to prepare him, and then I'll call you in. Otherwise…"

How was she supposed to explain to Mark that the unexpected sight of him at her side could have Malcolm Boerner so uneasy he might deny he'd ever sent her after the amulet? It was certainly a possibility when Mark Griggs's size and air of authority made him an intimidating figure. One that was making her nervous herself at this moment with those hot eyes boring into her like a pair of lasers.

"You know," he said, "for a woman who's both intelligent and self-reliant, as I've been thinking you are, you're not using good judgment where the subject of Boerner and my amulet are concerned."

"What's that supposed to mean?"

"That you're playing a dangerous game, and you don't seem to realize it. Suppose you had gotten away with my amulet and left me behind, just as you'd planned. What were you going to do? Just march into Boerner's shop and hand the amulet over to him? How could you be sure once he had it in his possession he wouldn't go and refuse to give you the tape? Provide that alibi for your sister that, like I said before, could get him into trouble with the cops?"

"You think I would have been that naive? You're

wrong, soldier, because I had it all worked out beforehand. I wouldn't have gone alone to Boerner's shop. I would have phoned him, told him I had the amulet and that if he wanted it he was to bring the tape and meet me in a very public video store I know and trust over on Esplanade."

"Where you would have proceeded to do what?"

"Had the store run the tape for me to make sure it was genuine. I would have also insisted Boerner sign a written alibi that Terry was in his place at the time of her husband's murder. And then, *only* then, would I have surrendered the amulet to him."

This time Clare could detect admiration in Mark's gaze. A look that, against her will, stirred a warmth inside her.

"Okay, so you're no fool, but I'm still not standing by while you go into that shop on your own. Even for a few minutes. We don't know what you'd be walking into."

The man was impossible. Where did he think he was? In a war zone issuing orders because he was anticipating an ambush? There was no arguing with him. She would just have to hope that Boerner was too eager to get his hands on the amulet to object to Mark's presence.

As it turned out, none of it mattered, neither their argument nor her fear that she was risking a loss of the tape. A moment later, with Mark beside her, she gazed in dismay at the security screen locked in place across the front of Malcolm Boerner's store. The display window on the other side of the steel mesh that featured a pair of dueling pistols and an ancient blunderbuss was unlighted, the shop behind it dark.

"I don't understand it," she said. "With all these potential customers out here on the street, why would he be closed? This has to be one of the busiest days of the season."

"Any chance of getting an explanation?"

Clare thought about it for a few seconds before remembering something Boerner had told her. "Maybe. He did say, if he wasn't in his shop, I could find him in his apartment."

"And where would that be?"

"Through here." She led the way to a wide, vaulted passageway between Boerner's store and his neighbor's shop on the other side.

Leaving the congestion and noise of Royal Street behind them, they entered the tunnel that had once permitted carriages to drive into the heart of the building and now accommodated only Clare and Mark.

They emerged from the dimness that echoed their footsteps into a sizable courtyard. The contrast between street and courtyard was so pronounced it had them hesitating in surprise. Unlike the street behind them, the courtyard was deserted and silent. The only sounds were the soft splash of a fountain and the faint rustle of the leaves on a banana plant.

Clare was familiar with the courtyards of the French Quarter. They were friendly and serene, but this place...

Why did it suddenly make her feel chilled when the day was so warm? As if there was something sinister here? She was being silly. Mark apparently didn't feel anything was wrong.

"Where to now?" he asked her.

She regarded the building across the courtyard. It had the look of a carriage house that had been converted into apartments, one on the ground floor and another above it that had probably once housed slaves. The arrangement was not an unusual one in her Quarter.

"He said his was the ground-floor apartment off the rear side of the courtyard, and that would be over there."

Circling the central fountain, they crossed the stone flags to a door whose nameplate verified this was Boerner's apartment.

Lifting a fist, Mark's knuckles rapped on the door. It obviously hadn't been securely latched because his action had the door drifting open several inches. As if there had been a hasty departure.

"Funny," he muttered.

Not just funny, Clare thought, but disturbing. Like the courtyard, something felt not right to her.

Putting his face to the opening, Mark called out a deep "Hello. Anyone home?"

There was no answer. Mark turned to her, his face wearing a look now that could only be described as a military alertness. "Wait here. I'm going in."

Spreading the door fully open, he entered the apartment. Clare followed on his heels. He was instantly aware of her behind him.

"I thought I told you—"

"I'm not under your command, Lieutenant."

"All right, but stay behind me, will you?"

She controlled the urge to salute him with a brisk "Sir, yes, sir."

It was a sensible restraint, because there was nothing amusing about the situation. If the gloom and the total silence didn't indicate as much, what waited for them in the living room off the small foyer where they stood left no question of that.

Mark's cautious advance into the room was suddenly halted.

"What is it?" she whispered.

There was no need for his explanation. She saw it,

too, when, not waiting for his answer, she peered around him. Murky though the light was, it couldn't hide the body sprawled faceup on the worn, Oriental carpet.

Mark turned to her with a husky "Boerner?"

There was no mistaking the identity of the thickset figure lying there with its fleshy face and grizzled hair. Clare nodded dumbly.

Mark gazed at her, his craggy face registering a grim concern. "You gonna be okay?"

She managed a numb "Yes." Because that's all she could feel, a numbness.

She watched Mark as he hunkered down beside the body, looking at it closely while careful not to touch it.

"Is he—"

She stopped herself there. It was pointless to ask if Malcolm Boerner was dead. What else could he be when, even through the shadows, she could see the round, blood-caked hole in his forehead and his eyes staring up sightlessly at the ceiling?

There was something else she could see. A thin, leather cord around Boerner's neck. A cord identical to Mark's lanyard, from which his amulet was suspended. Whatever might have dangled from Boerner's lanyard was gone, sliced away from the leather ends.

"Mark," she croaked, "do you see it?"

He understood her. "Yeah, I see it." He got to his feet. "Come on, we're getting out of here."

"I've got to find the tape. If it's here in the apartment—"

"Are you out of your mind? If someone heard the shot that put a bullet through Boerner's head, then they probably called the police. There'll be cops swarming all over the place. Do you want them to find us here?"

"But the tape is vital."

"Clare, you're not thinking straight. We can't hang around, and we can't leave any evidence we were ever here. And we certainly can't report the murder ourselves. With you involved as you are in trying to clear your sister of another homicide, you'd be high on the list of suspects for this one."

He was right. She could see that, now that her state of numbness was dissolving. A cold reality was replacing it. The realization that there had been a reason for the sinister mood she had felt in the courtyard.

"The tape probably isn't here, anyway," she said. "He must have kept it in the shop. I don't suppose…"

"No! Even if we were dumb enough to try to get into that shop, there's no way we could manage it. Certainly not from the front and not from the rear, either. You might not have noticed it when we were in the courtyard, but I did. The back door is solid metal, and the one window has bars across it."

Understandable, she thought, when there were valuable firearms in the shop. No choice about it. She would have to forget the tape for now, much as she hated to leave without it.

It was a dismal outcome.

"You touch anything in here?"

She shook her head.

"Me, either, except for the front door. I'll wipe that down on our way out."

She watched him as he did a fast look around the room, wanting to be certain they were leaving no traces of themselves behind them.

"All right," he said, apparently satisfied, "let's move."

Chapter 5

Mark left the front door slightly ajar, exactly as he had found it. Clare was no longer beside him. Looking around, he found her standing by the fountain. She was gazing at the bubbling water, but he had the feeling she wasn't seeing it.

She didn't seem to be aware of him when he joined her. That worried him. A lot. Whatever recovery she had made in the apartment was gone. What was happening here? A delayed shock?

He had to get her away from this place. From the horror back in that apartment. But first—

Had they been seen by a neighbor either entering or leaving the apartment? There were no windows on the high side walls of the courtyard. Nothing but the ivy growing thickly against the old brick.

What about the apartment over Boerner's? His gaze traveled up a curling iron stairway to a balcony, then moved rapidly across the row of French windows there. The windows had a blank look about them, as if the apartment behind them was currently unoccupied. Maybe.

But if someone somewhere close by *had* heard the shot and called it in, shouldn't he be hearing the sound of police sirens from the direction of the street? Not that gunfire necessarily meant murder. It could mean a lot of things, so possibly the cops wouldn't come racing down the street wailing their sirens.

Hell, he didn't know. The only certainty was his need to get Clare and himself to an area of safety.

She didn't react when he cupped her by the elbow and urged her across the courtyard and through the carriage way as rapidly as this blasted leg of his would permit.

He was relieved when they reached the street where they could blend in with the crowds; no one was paying any attention to them. He wasn't satisfied, though, until they reached the mouth of another alley far enough away from Boerner's shop to be secure. He halted them here.

He could see that Clare was still shaken by the scene they had fled. He had to find someplace she could sit down and rest. Not here in the close confines of the Quarter where the oxygen seemed to be sucked up by the throngs. Yeah, out in the open where they could both breathe.

"My leg could use a bench away from these mobs. Any recommendations?"

He wasn't sure she'd heard and understood him. She was silent for a moment before answering him. "There are benches in Jackson Square. It's not far. Just a block over near the river."

Her voice was wooden, but at least it meant she was functioning again. "Good enough. Lead the way."

Jackson Square, when they reached it, was far from deserted. There were strolling vendors here selling souvenirs to the visitors, artists perched on stools doing pastel portraits of anyone willing to sit for them, tourists aiming their cameras at the spires of St. Louis Cathedral and the statue of Andrew Jackson. But the area was expansive enough to swallow the crowds, the air fresh off the river.

They managed to locate a vacant bench, settling on it side by side. Neither of them spoke. Mark listened to the reassuring sound of the rattle of a streetcar along the tracks below the levee. The sight of Clare beside him when he trained his gaze on her was not reassuring. She was shivering.

"I'm cold," she complained. "Silly, isn't it, when the sun is so warm?"

"Here," he said.

He didn't hesitate, and she didn't object when, wrapping his arms around her, he pulled her against him, sharing the heat of his body.

What are you doing, Griggs? You've got no business getting cozy with her like this when you're dealing with a murder and a woman who might not be all she said she is.

Yeah, but she felt so desirable in his arms. All soft and fragrant, and at the moment compliant, melting against him gratefully. His hands couldn't resist stroking her back, his mouth at her ear soothing her with husky, comforting words that probably didn't make any sense but which she seemed to welcome.

When he unwisely started to tighten his embrace,

she stiffened in his arms. He got the message and just as abruptly released her.

Okay, so he had made a mistake. She could have blamed him for his lack of judgment. To her credit, she didn't.

"Sorry to be such a nuisance," she said, shifting away from him a few inches.

"You're entitled. I'm used to dead bodies, but I'm guessing this was your first experience discovering one like that."

"You'd be right."

"You okay now?"

"I'm fine. Or as fine as I can be under the circumstances."

"That's good."

What had been good, he thought, were those moments when she'd fitted herself so willingly against him. A certain part of his body was still slightly swollen from the effects of that intimacy. Had she been aware of that when he held her?

That face of hers that could have a man imagining all kinds of interesting possibilities didn't look like it. The expression on it was reflectively solemn. And her tone when she spoke to him didn't sound like it.

"That leather cord around Malcolm Boerner's neck. The one so identical to yours."

"What about it?"

"You didn't notice then."

"What?"

"The photo of him on the mantel in the living room. I only had a glance at it before we had to leave the apartment, but I could swear he was wearing an amulet in it similar to yours, cord and all."

"Was he wearing it when you met with him?"

"No, but he was in that photo."

"Then why should he go to the lengths he did to get his hands on another one?"

"Because of its value. Oh, I know what you said. That it isn't valuable. But what if you're wrong, Mark? Maybe it's worth a lot. And two of them—"

"Would be twice as valuable, huh?" He shook his head. "This is only so much speculation, Clare."

"There's more. What if he was murdered for his amulet?"

Was she being revisited by the image of Boerner's body lying there on the floor? Was the memory of that why he saw her shudder in that second?

"None of this is doing us any good." He was suddenly restless. "Look, I need to move. There's a walkway up there on the levee, isn't there?"

"Yes, but your leg…"

"Isn't bothering me now." Nor had it been back on Royal Street. The leg had been his excuse to find a bench for Clare.

"But it will give me trouble if I don't exercise it."

Which was the truth this time. Hadn't his therapist back at Womack recommended a routine of regular exercise? Besides, he had to think, and he was better at doing that while on the move.

Had Clare decided that his leg *was* troubling him? It would explain why she began to point out local landmarks as they climbed the stairway to the top of the levee. Her effort to distract him.

"That's the old Jax Brewery over there on our right. The building was converted to shops and restaurants. And that long structure down there on our left was once the French Market. The place at this end of it is the French Call. It's famous for its beignets, which are a kind of square doughnut that…"

She was being considerate, but Mark absorbed little of what she was telling him. His mind was elsewhere, seeking explanations for what they had left behind them on Royal Street.

"Not very helpful, is it?" she asked him when they reached the crest of the levee.

"Uh—"

"My guided tour of New Orleans."

She smiled up at him with that lush mouth that, even in this awkward moment, was a temptation.

"So what has got you so occupied, Lieutenant?"

Other than being relieved that she seemed fully recovered now, a great deal. But he didn't have an immediate answer for her on that subject. Instead, he focused his gaze on the wide walkway that stretched off in both directions. They weren't alone up here. There were other couples, families, too, enjoying the sights and sounds of the river. It didn't matter. The pavement was so broad and seemingly endless it offered a freedom of movement conducive to exercising both the body and the mind. Just what he needed.

"Let's walk," he said.

They fell into step side by side, strolling off to the left away from the best views of the city's most popular attractions. He waited until they'd left behind most of the other strollers before, ready now to talk, he turned to her with an earnest "Two murders of men who knew each other, first Joe Riconi and now Malcolm Boerner. Too much of a coincidence, would you say?"

"I would."

"And if we put aside the subject of amulets, which couldn't have been a motive in your brother-in-law's murder and maybe not Boerner's, either, then the question is who did kill them and why?"

"I guess that's for the police to determine when they get around to discovering Boerner's death. They'll search the apartment and the shop, of course, but if they don't find the tape, I don't have a way to prove Terry's innocence."

"And I don't have the answers I was hoping to get from Boerner. A police investigation won't provide them, either."

He was silent for a moment, thinking about those answers. Clare said nothing. The only sounds were the hoots and whistles from the vessels on the river.

"I've been forgetting about something," he suddenly realized, slapping the side of his head. "I think I know now how Boerner learned about me and where he got my photograph. The internet."

"Go on," she urged him.

"The army posts bios on its sites of its servicemen and women for public consumption. Things like our ranks and decorations, along with our photos and home states and towns. Nothing sensitive, like where we've served or are currently serving. No home addresses or phone numbers, either. They're careful about that."

"But that's pretty general," she pointed out. "It wouldn't have told Boerner you were on leave and staying at the Pelican Hotel."

"No, but I have an idea where and how he got that information, too. Hold on for a few minutes, and I'll let you know if I'm right."

Fishing his cell phone out of a back pocket of his khakis, he powered it up and checked the instrument for a signal. There was one, but it wasn't as strong as he would have liked. Maybe a different location. Leaving Clare with a frustrated expression on her face, he moved away from her along the levee. Ah, much better now. He dialed the programmed number, counting on her being home. To his satisfaction, she picked up after no more than two rings, which meant she had to be in her lounge chair with the phone beside her and the TV tuned in to one of her favorite morning programs.

Mark knew Clare was just far enough away from him that she couldn't overhear even his side of the conversation that followed. The puzzled frown on her face was evidence of that.

"Personal?" she asked him when he returned to where she waited. "Or do I get an explanation of the mystery?"

Shoving the cell phone back into his pocket, he filled her in on his conversation. "I got what I wanted. That was my grandmother. She raised me, the only family I have. Lorelei—that's my hometown in Tennessee—is a pretty small place and Gran the only Griggs in the phone directory."

Clare understood. "Meaning Malcolm Boerner would have had no difficulty getting her number."

"Yeah, and learning just what he needed to know. Seems Boerner passed himself off as an old army buddy of mine who'd lost contact with me, and could Gran tell him where he could reach me?"

"And she told him."

Mark shrugged. "Gran is a simple, country woman. She wouldn't have questioned his identity or his motive. She was happy to let him know I was on a fishing holiday in Louisiana and staying at the Pelican Hotel on Pelican Island."

"All your questions answered."

"Not everything." He patted the area of the amulet

hanging out of sight under his shirt. "I still don't know how Boerner learned I had what he wanted."

"Does it matter now that he's dead?"

"It could, if Boerner's killer somehow learned from him that I have the amulet. Not that I'm convinced this thing, or its mate if there was one, is a motive for murder."

"But it could be, and that puts you at risk. Mark, listen to me. You've got no reason to hang around New Orleans any longer. You should go, get as far away from here as possible."

"Because I'm at risk and you're not, huh?"

"I'm not the one who has the amulet. You do."

"And maybe the killer doesn't know that. If Boerner told him he sent you after my amulet, he could just as easily think you have it and not me. Puts a different spin on it, doesn't it, teacher?"

"But I'm home now."

"And that makes you safe?"

"I can take care of myself."

"How? By going to the police, which you can't do until Boerner's death goes public? And who knows when that will be. Even then, they wouldn't offer you protection, not when they learn you're mixed up in two murders, as they'll be sure to do. All you'll be to them is what is politely termed 'a person of interest.'"

"What's your alternative, Lieutenant?"

"Me."

"I don't need a bodyguard."

"You need someone, and what better than an army ranger? Protection is what we're all about, Clare."

"I don't want someone offering himself as a target on my behalf."

"Don't make it more than it is. I've got my own reason for wanting to stick close to you."

"The explanation for how Malcolm Boerner learned you had the amulet. That's what you still want, isn't it?"

"I don't like loose ends."

Okay, that was true, but he was letting her think it was just as important as being there to protect her. And it wasn't. The only thing that really mattered to him was keeping her safe.

What's wrong with you, Griggs? You're being as gullible as your grandmother.

Was he? Yeah, he was. How else could he define it, when he had yet to believe everything she had told him earlier this morning without a lingering doubt? Had yet to fully trust her?

But, damn it, he wanted her. It was just as plain as that. He wanted her with the same raw need as he'd wanted her last night before she had pinned him to that headboard and walked away with his amulet.

It was only then that Mark realized he had reversed their positions without being conscious of it. That their argument had somehow resulted in his backing her away until she was now caught against the railing that bordered the levee. Was trapped there as she had trapped him last night.

A situation he could take advantage of?

It was a possibility all right. Providing she didn't slip away from him. Nothing to prevent her from doing just that. Like handcuffs. And he wouldn't try to stop her. But she wasn't moving away from him. She simply stood there, gazing up at him with those sweet blue eyes and a parted mouth that was all breathy with anticipation. At least that's how he was prepared to read it. An invitation he was unable to resist.

"Mark?" she whispered.

"Yeah?"

"What are we doing here?"

"Don't know," he said, unable to keep the gruffness from his voice. "Why don't we find out?"

He leaned into her, his hands framing her face. He could feel her trembling as he lowered his head. No objections, though. A good sign. His angled mouth closed over hers.

There was nothing urgent about his kiss. Not at first. He was careful about that, his lips playing softly with hers, nibbling, tasting. It wasn't enough. He needed what that mouth opening slowly under his signified. A welcome.

He answered it by sliding his tongue between her teeth, probing, inhaling the flavor of her along with a fragrance that he could swear was a lingering scent from last night's seductive perfume. It made him as wild now as it had then, commanding his tongue to sweep the interior of her hot, wet mouth.

His arms went around her, drawing her tightly against him as he deepened their kiss. Was he hearing her moans or his own groans rumbling up from his chest? Maybe both.

All he knew for certain was that, if he didn't exercise self-control, this was going to end in the two of them making a public spectacle of themselves right here on the levee.

It was with a considerable amount of effort that Mark lifted his mouth from hers, his arms dropping reluctantly away from her. Oh, hell, he wanted a lot more than just a kiss. But he guessed that would have to wait.

So, okay, he had managed to restrain himself. But

he wasn't ready to surrender all contact with her, which was why he rested his forehead against hers.

That contact lasted until she challenged him with a breathless "That kiss. Was it meant to convince me to accept your protection?"

"Could be," he lied, putting a few inches between them. "Did it work?"

"Something definitely did," she admitted, "but it wasn't that."

"Stubborn, aren't you?"

"I've been accused of it."

"How about being naive?"

"What's that supposed to mean?"

"Just that if you were reckless enough to come after me last night, a man you knew nothing about or what he might be capable of doing, then, sweetheart, you need protection."

"Uh-huh, and if you were dumb enough to fall for my line, what does that make you?"

She smiled up at him.

He grinned back.

"All right," he conceded, "you have a point."

"Look," she said, "why don't we just agree to look out for each other? A question, though. What happens now?"

He figured she meant it strictly in terms of where they were to go from here and not, worst luck, in any further amorous explorations. Scratching the side of his head, he considered her query.

"Well, we don't go to the cops. Not until we've armed ourselves with enough information to convince them to listen to us seriously."

"And how do we get this information?"

Mark had an idea about that. Squinting up at the sun,

then glancing down at his watch, he made a decision for them. "It's just short of noon. We have the whole afternoon left to us. Any reason we can't pay a visit to your sister?"

She looked at him in surprise. "Terry? You want to see Terry? Whatever for?"

"Answers."

"Mark, she told me everything she knows, and I've shared it all with you. What more could you expect to learn?"

"Think about it, Clare. Boerner and your brother-in-law had that connection."

"Mercenaries, yes. But Joe wouldn't talk to her about it, remember?"

"Even so, she was his wife. In all the years they were married, she must have learned something about his past. Maybe just bits of knowledge she doesn't think matter. But they could matter. Enough, anyway, to piece together some explanations."

"I suppose it's possible."

"Yeah, I know. It's a long shot. But it's all we have. You in?"

"I'm in."

"Then let's go for it."

Chapter 6

Not until Clare had directed him across the Huey P. Long Bridge to the other side of the Mississippi, and through the maze of arteries that finally put them on the River Road headed north, was she able to relax sufficiently enough to think about her situation. Or, to be more precise about it, the man at her side.

How had she landed herself in the company of this enigma behind a pair of aviator-style sunglasses? Because that's what Mark Griggs was, a challenging puzzle who in one minute was irritating her with his take-charge attitude and in the next…

Well, there was no forgetting that episode on the bench in Jackson Square when he had so unexpectedly revealed another facet of himself under that tough exterior. There was only one name she could give it. A tender warrior.

As for what had happened up on the levee…that, too,

was unforgettable. How could it be otherwise when her mouth still stung from that kiss of his that had rocked her senses at every level? A kiss every bit as steamy as New Orleans in mid-July.

He thinks you're in danger, Clare. And you are. Of him.

It wasn't any good, their linking up with each other like this. Not when it offered too many opportunities for other intimate sessions. And after Alan she couldn't afford that.

Why did everything have to be so difficult? Why did Mark Griggs himself have to be so difficult in too many respects? And why, oh why, did he have to be so tempting?

Much to her relief, he misread her sober silence. "Don't worry about it, Clare," he reassured her in that smoky voice that did things to her insides. "There has to be an explanation. There's always an explanation, and we're going to learn it and save both you and your sister."

He was talking about their reason for this visit to Terry. He thought she was concerned about nothing but its outcome. Not that she, herself, needed saving. Except maybe from him.

"I hope so," she said, and went on to thank him for caring.

They were quiet after that. He concentrated his attention on the narrow, winding highway that followed the levee on the west bank of the river. This was plantation country, permitting them at periodic intervals to catch glimpses of antebellum homes situated in groves of live oak trees as majestic as the Greek Revival mansions they sheltered.

They must have been a half hour or more on the road when Mark announced suddenly, "I'm hungry."

"There's a village up ahead. It has a café converted from an old sugar mill. We can stop there."

She noticed that Mark wasn't much interested in the quaintness of the structure itself when they reached it. His attention, after they had been seated, was far more occupied with the menu that specialized in Cajun fare.

Clare was content with a chef's salad, but Mark ordered blackened grouper with all the trimmings.

"When you've been stationed in war zones as often I've been," he explained after the waitress had departed to the kitchen, "with sometimes nothing to eat but field rations, you make up for it when you get home."

Since it was past the busy lunch hour, they had the place nearly to themselves, making Mark noticeably grateful when their orders were delivered to their table without delay.

It wasn't until he'd taken the first edges off his appetite that he was ready to talk.

"I guess you and your sister are pretty tight with each other, huh?"

"We're very close, yes. Or as close as we can be living an hour's drive apart as we do."

His broad shoulders lifted in a little shrug. "I wouldn't know how that kind of thing works, seeing as how I don't have any siblings of my own."

"There's no rule about it. There are sisters and brothers devoted to each other, and there are sisters and brothers who just plain don't get along."

This is a funny thing for him to be discussing, Clare thought. He's got to know this himself, whether he has any siblings or not. So what's happening here?

She had a fork loaded with salad halfway to her mouth before she understood what he was doing.

He's testing me. He still isn't entirely convinced that everything I've been telling him is the truth.

Those shadows of mistrust shouldn't be mattering to her, but after what they had shared this morning they hurt. Reasonable, though, she supposed, after her performance last night.

She put her fork back down on her plate and met his gaze. "I'm not hiding anything from you, Mark."

She watched his Adam's apple bob as he hastily swallowed a mouthful of rice. "Hey, I wasn't—"

"It's all right. You're entitled to hear everything you want to know. Yes, I'm willing to do whatever is necessary to prove Terry's innocence. I would in any case, but there is an added reason besides sisterly affection."

"Yeah?"

"Yeah. See, there's this age difference between Terry and me, which made her eighteen and me just a little kid when we lost our parents in a car accident. She wasn't in the car. I was."

"Oh, hell," he growled.

"It was hell. Not for me, not then. I was asleep in the back strapped into my car seat. The only injury I suffered was from flying glass. It left me with this." She touched the crescent-shaped scar high on her cheek.

"I kind of noticed that."

It was hardly the moment for her to wonder what his feelings, if any, were about his observation. But then didn't just about everyone bear facial characteristics, acquired or natural, that made them interesting? He had one himself in the form of that slightly crooked nose. Not something that should be particularly appealing, but in his case...

"Not then, you said," he prompted her.

"No, not then. I was too young to understand what it all meant. But for Terry...well, it had to be a hell for her that we were suddenly without a mother and a father. She could have terrified me with that. She didn't, though. Instead, she explained to me very calmly that it was going to be all right, that I shouldn't worry because she was going to care for me."

"Couldn't have been easy for her," Mark guessed. "Not when she wasn't much more than a girl herself."

"It wasn't, but she never complained."

"So she raised you herself."

"And I'll never forget it, how she was always there for me. Now I have this chance to be there for her."

"Yeah, I get it. Hell, I ought to when I was there myself."

She was puzzled for a moment, until it struck her what he was saying. "You were orphaned yourself."

"Not technically, but it amounted to the same thing. The guy who fathered me was a drifter. Blew into town long enough to knock up my mother and then disappeared. She wasn't much better. After I was born she handed me over to her widowed mother and then moved on. Didn't bother to come back, either. I haven't a clue where she is today, or if she's even alive, and I don't much care."

"Mark, I'm sorry."

"Don't be. If you're going to be sorry for anyone, be sorry for my grandmother. Gran did her best to bring me up, but I was a handful. On the wild side by the time I got to high school. Barely graduated, and afterward...well, a small town in Tennessee doesn't offer many opportunities."

"But the army did," she guessed.

"It was what I needed. As they say, if the army doesn't break you, it'll make you. It did just that. Enabled me to earn a college degree and join the rangers."

And now the rangers own him, Clare thought. She wasn't prepared to examine why that realization saddened her. It was better that she let the subject alone.

"Hey, we're ignoring our food here," he said.

They finished their meals in silence. Clare was careful to express no further sympathy for him. He was the kind of man whose pride wouldn't have appreciated that. As it was, they had already gotten too personal with each other.

Hadn't she already broken her promise to herself not to get mixed up with another soldier? What had happened back on the levee when she had permitted him to kiss her was a blatant evidence of that.

All right, so the histories of their pasts they had shared over lunch did seem to have eased the issues of trust between them. That was a good thing. The emotions they had stirred in her concerning this restless, intense man were not.

You can't allow yourself to end up caring for him on some deeper level, Clare. You just can't.

At Clare's direction, Mark turned off the River Road not long after the café. Unlike the twisting River Road, the route here was a straight one passing through stretches of pecan orchards.

The rural highway was almost empty. It was the reason why Clare, glancing in the side-view mirror on her side of the SUV, noticed the dark blue sedan behind them.

Its presence wouldn't have mattered to her except for two things. She remembered seeing the same car, or one exactly like it, somewhere between New Orleans and the village where they had stopped. Also, like then, the sedan never tried to pass them but slowed when they slowed, increasing its speed again only when they increased theirs. She watched it in the mirror for a moment before calling Mark's attention to it.

"Mark, there's this car behind us."

"I know. I've been aware of it."

"And?"

"Nothing. There's no reason it shouldn't be headed in the same direction."

"I suppose so. It's funny, though."

"What is?"

"If it's the same car I noticed on the road before we stopped at the café, and I'm fairly sure it is, that means it stopped when we stopped and then managed to catch up to us again."

"So?"

Mark wasn't concerned. He thought it was nothing but pure coincidence. Clare didn't, which was why she kept her eye on the sedan, hoping to catch a glimpse of the driver. But whoever was at the wheel—and she had the impression it was a man and not a woman—kept just enough distance between himself and the SUV to prevent her from seeing his face.

They had entered St. Boniface Parish, where Terry made her home, when Clare became conscious that Mark was regularly checking his rearview mirror. So he *was* concerned about the sedan.

Neither he nor Clare tried now to put it into words— that the blue sedan was deliberately following them. If the blue sedan was deliberately following them, then who was it? And why?

It was unnerving, keeping her tense. It was only

when they approached the parish seat where Terry was being held that she felt relief. The sedan that seemed to be shadowing them turned off on a side road and disappeared from view.

"You see," Mark said. "He just happened to be going our way."

Clare supposed he was right, except she'd never trusted coincidences.

The jail was located in a back wing of the St. Boniface courthouse. After explaining to the burly officer behind the desk they were here to visit Clare's sister, they were asked to produce IDs, checked for weapons and required to sign in.

Another uniformed officer was summoned. She conducted them along a corridor into a small, cheerless room that had no windows and was furnished with nothing more than a table and several straight-back chairs.

"Wait here," she instructed them. "I'll bring Mrs. Riconi to you."

After the door had closed behind her, Mark observed dryly, "If she's the matron of this place, she looks too young and frail for the job."

"Don't underestimate her. She has a reputation for being tough when she has to be."

They seated themselves at the table.

"Hard as a rock," Mark complained about the chair under him. "Guess they don't want visitors getting comfortable and staying too long."

Clare worried her bottom lip as they waited for Terry's arrival. "I've been thinking about why Boerner wouldn't provide Terry with an alibi. If he denied she was ever in his shop, then the police wouldn't look elsewhere for Joe's killer, which was exactly what happened."

"How would that have benefitted Boerner?"

"Suppose he was involved himself somehow in Joe's death and that it had to do with your amulet. Maybe his own as well, and if the police started to investigate him and learned about the amulets—"

"Clare, what was I saying back in New Orleans about a lot of speculation?"

"I know, but there's something else. What if Boerner had a partner, and they had a falling out, and that's why he was murdered? If there was a partner, it could also explain why Boerner didn't enlist me right away to go after you. Could be he needed to consult first with that partner before he offered me his deal."

"Again the speculation."

"But don't you see—"

She didn't get to finish her persuasive effort. The door opened. The officer escorted her sister into the room.

The sight of Terry in an orange jumpsuit looking more forlorn than she had on Clare's earlier visit saddened her. But there was more than just the jail garb that troubled Clare. The sisters shared the same coloring, fair hair and blue eyes. Terry's hair, however, had a lankness about it. And surely there were lines in her face that hadn't been there the last time she'd seen her.

She shouldn't be in this place. Clare stood up and the two sisters embraced, clinging to each other for a long moment.

"I'll be just outside," Clare heard the officer say. "Rap on the door when you're finished."

The woman left them, shutting the door behind her. Clare felt Terry stiffen in her arms. When she stepped away from her, she saw that Terry's bewildered gaze had discovered the presence of Mark, who had risen to his feet behind the table.

She's wondering who he is and what he's doing here.

Clare hastily introduced him. "This is Army Lieutenant Mark Griggs. He's a friend who's here to help us."

Terry's puzzled gaze turned to Clare. "How did you come to—"

"Let's sit down, and I'll explain everything."

She led Terry to the table where they settled side by side across from Mark, who seated himself again after reaching over to shake her sister's hesitant hand.

Scooting her chair around to face Terry, Clare launched into the story of where and how she had met Mark. And, of course, why. She tried to lighten the tale without omitting the essentials, but the distressed expression on her sister's face told her that Terry wasn't happy about any of it.

When Clare ended her account with their discovery of Malcolm Boerner's body and their decision to visit Terry, her sister's face registered a look of serious alarm.

"What have you gotten yourself into? And all on my account. No, Clare, *no!*"

"It's all right, Terry. I'm not going to stand by and see you convicted of a murder you didn't commit," she promised her fiercely.

Mark added his assurance that he would look after Clare, do his best to see to it that she came to no harm, but Terry just kept shaking her head. Without waiting for her to compose herself, he leaned toward her with an earnest "Mrs. Riconi—Terry, we need you to help us help you."

She didn't answer him at first, and when she did it was with uncertainty. "How?"

"I'd like you to tell me just what happened that day after you came back from New Orleans."

"I've gone over all of this before."

"But not for me."

Terry's gaze swiveled to Clare, as if needing some form of confirmation from her. Clare nodded her encouragement.

"All right," she complied.

She went on to give Mark what he asked for in a flat, mechanical voice. The kind of voice, Clare thought, that you used to keep your emotions in check in strained circumstances. It was her sister's familiar method for handling stress that threatened to be unbearable otherwise.

"When I got home, I was a little surprised to find Joe's van in the carport. His shift wasn't supposed to end that early. Not that it worried me. Not then. It was only after I parked my car next to his and entered the kitchen from the carport that I started to wonder if something was wrong."

"Why?" Mark asked.

"Why? Because his service revolver was sitting on the kitchen counter. Joe was never careless like that with his gun. That's when it occurred to me that…well, that he might have been drinking."

"What then?"

"I picked up the revolver, meaning to lock it back in the case where it belonged in our bedroom. I never got to the bedroom. I only got as far as the living room. Joe was there on the floor. I thought he might be drunk and passed out. It had happened like that once before."

"Only he wasn't passed out."

"No, he wasn't passed out. He was dead. The police

found me there kneeling beside his body. I still had the revolver in my hand. Joe's revolver that turned out to be the gun that killed him."

"Terry, who called the police and sent them to your house?"

"Oh, that."

She frowned, as if searching her memory. As if, Clare thought, she was in the same dazed state that must have gripped her that afternoon when the police arrived to discover her waiting there next to her husband's body.

When Terry finally answered Mark, it was in that same wooden voice. "The woman next door. Yes, that's right." She went on to explain it. "They told me Joe must have left the hose running out front to water one of our flower beds. The neighbor came home from shopping to find the water spilling over onto her property."

"She shut it off?"

"She's a crank. She wouldn't have done that. She would have done what she did do before I got home myself."

"Which was?"

"Marched up to the door and banged on it to complain. When she didn't get an answer, she looked through one of the windows and saw Joe's body on the floor."

"And rushed back home to call the cops, huh?"

Terry nodded.

Clare remained silent, satisfied to let Mark do the questioning. He was very good at it, handling it smoothly. It made her wonder if he was experienced with interrogation, perhaps with insurgents in combat zones.

She kept her gaze trained on her sister, her concern

deepening. Terry had always been thin, but was she even thinner now? Or was it just the shadows under her eyes that made Clare imagine that?

I've got to get her out of here.

"There's something I don't understand," Mark said. "If, as Clare told me, the M.E. fixed the time of your husband's death approximately two hours before you arrived home, how could you be charged with your husband's death?"

No longer willing to keep still, Clare answered for her sister with an angry "Because they're imbeciles, that's why. They theorized that Terry must have fled the house in a panic after she killed Joe and wandered the back roads for those two hours in a daze before she realized she had to go back and destroy the evidence. They even managed to back it up with a witness who swore he saw her speeding toward home on one of those roads."

"Is that true?" Mark asked Terry. "Were you on one of those back roads?"

"Yes, but only because it was a shortcut home on my way back from New Orleans."

"So, even with your fingerprints on the gun, it's all circumstantial evidence."

But enough to convict her with an aggressive prosecutor and an unsympathetic jury, Clare thought fearfully. That fear must have registered on her face. It's why Terry, playing the big sister, must have placed her hand over Clare's. It was an action meant to comfort her, even though Clare knew Terry had to be sharing the same fear.

Mark had another question for Terry. "You ever learn why your husband came off duty before his shift was scheduled to end?"

"They told me he wasn't feeling well and asked to be relieved."

Mark looked thoughtful for a moment. "What if that was just an excuse?" he said. "What if he had another reason for going home early? Like maybe there was someone he was going to meet back at the house, and he didn't want anyone to know about it."

Now who's speculating? Clare thought. But Mark had a good argument. Someone had managed to murder Joe with his own gun. Someone he must have trusted.

"I don't know," Terry said. "Joe never mentioned anything like that to me, although he did know I was going to be gone all afternoon. But not to New Orleans and Malcolm Boerner's shop. I told him I was going to Baton Rouge to do some shopping."

Clare continued to think about that unknown someone. Asking herself if it could be the same someone who had murdered Boerner. Another possibility began to form in her mind, but she waited to express it until Mark finished questioning Terry.

She listened while he asked her sister about her husband's years as a mercenary, seeking that bit of useful information that had brought them here. The something that could link the past to the present, provide an explanation for two murders.

Mark's effort was wasted, though. Terry could tell them nothing that would spark a worthwhile connection. Joe Riconi had been unwilling to reveal anything to his wife about those years except vague references to his existence then.

It wasn't until Mark sat back in his chair, clearly disappointed, that Clare found the opportunity to introduce her own idea.

"Mark, show Terry your amulet."

"What for?"

"Just bear with me, please."

Mark obliged her by removing the amulet from around his neck and placing it on the table. Clare reached over and slid the amulet in front of her sister.

"Terry, have you ever seen anything like this before? Could Joe have had one like it?"

Terry gazed at her. "This is what you told me Malcolm Boerner sent you to get, isn't it?"

"Yes," Clare said, not bothering to add that Boerner may already have had another amulet either similar or identical to this one.

Terry bent her head, examining the piece for a moment before shaking her head. "There's nothing about it that's familiar. As for Joe having one like it…" She shook her head again. "If he did, I never saw it and he never mentioned it."

Which, as secretive as Joe Riconi was, Clare thought, didn't mean that he didn't have such an amulet of his own and kept it hidden from his wife.

Was Mark thinking the same thing? Was that why, before Terry could seek an explanation for Clare's interest in a further amulet, for which she had no good answer, he abruptly asked her sister, "Any chance of Clare and I getting into your house? I wouldn't mind having a look around. That is, if you have no objection."

"I don't have any objection, but the police would. The house is still a crime scene, locked and yellow taped they tell me. Something about the forensic team being delayed by another crime scene, and until they can get in…"

"The house won't be released," Clare said.

"It was hard enough getting permission for my lawyer to enter with a police escort. She had to bring me the stack of mail that had piled up on Joe's desk. There are bills that need to be paid. I have to know whether there are sufficient funds in the bank to cover my legal fees." She expressed her unwillingness for the job with a soft sigh. "I haven't got around yet to sorting through the bundle, but I've got to do it soon."

"That's too bad," Mark said, "but I don't suppose we would have found anything in there that the cops haven't already discovered." Recovering his amulet and stringing it back around his neck, he pushed back from the table and got to his feet. "I think we'd better call it quits here before that matron out there starts wondering what's taking us so long. Clare, I'll wait for you outside by the car while you say your goodbyes."

Thanking Terry for the visit, he left the room, closing the door behind him.

Alone with her sister, Clare was quick to make a promise to her. "Terry, I'm going to do whatever it takes to win your release."

Including, she thought, helping out with those legal fees if it became necessary. But for now she kept that to herself, knowing Terry would object.

"By doing what? Playing detective on my behalf? I don't like it," she said, wearing the role of big sister again.

"Honey, I'm not going to take any risks."

"That worries me, yes. But there's something else."

"What is it?"

"Your lieutenant."

"Mark? What about him?"

"I'm not blind, Clare. I saw the way you look at each other. The sparks flying between the two of you are pretty obvious."

"That's crazy."

"I don't think so. This guy may be one hell of a man, as hot as they make them, but his kind can also be dangerous to a woman. I don't want you getting hurt. Just watch yourself with him, will you?"

Chapter 7

She found Mark leaning against the side of the SUV, arms folded across his broad chest, an eyebrow quirked as he regarded her.

"A *third* amulet? That's a stretch, isn't it?"

"You were the one who asked Terry about getting into her house," Clare reminded him. "But, of course, it wasn't so you could look for a third amulet," she added dryly, "since we haven't even established that Boerner had a second one. Right?"

Her sister wasn't imagining it, Clare thought as she watched a big grin spread slowly across his rugged face. A grin that had her insides quivering.

He is dangerous, and if I don't watch myself I could end up getting seriously burned.

"Okay, teacher," he admitted, "so maybe I did have something like that in mind. I still want those answers, and an amulet isn't the kind of thing the cops would have been interested in turning up and confiscating."

"No," she agreed, "it wouldn't have been considered evidence. Probably got overlooked. If it exists."

"Not that it matters, since we can't get into the place. Short of breaking in and risking arrest, that is. The army tends to frown on that sort of behavior from its soldiers."

"Yes, I can see how they would. Although," she went on, her tone a casual one, "breaking in wouldn't be necessary."

"Oh? How's that?" His own tone matched hers, but his eyes gleamed with renewed interest.

"I happen to know where Terry and Joe kept a spare key hidden in the carport."

"In case one of them got locked out, huh?"

"It's what people do, don't they? So, if you'd still like to poke around in there…"

"Believe I would."

It was Clare who suggested as they pulled away from the courthouse that they stop at a drugstore and buy a box of latex gloves. "There have to be fingerprints all over the house," she explained, "including mine from past visits, but I wouldn't like to add to them, especially yours."

"Makes sense."

Had something like latex gloves also made sense to Joe's killer? she wondered as they came away from the drugstore.

Clare directed Mark to Terry's home, which was located at the far end of a housing development a few miles from the parish seat.

"We can't park in front of the house," Mark said

when they reached the area. "It would announce us to the whole neighborhood."

She had already planned for that likelihood. "We can reach the house from the back side. There's good cover there. Take the next turn to the right."

That turn took them along an uninhabited country road behind the development where they parked the SUV at the side of a pasture. Clare led the way across the pasture to a hedgerow. Kudzu vines, the bane of the South, grew thickly here, but she was able to locate an opening familiar to her from earlier visits. A narrow path brought them through the tangle to the backyard of the Riconi house, a single-story, brick ranch.

Mark paused to observe a tall, dense yaupon hedge that screened the property on both sides from back to street. "Whoever visited Joe Riconi that day," he remarked, "would have been easily missed by any of the neighbors."

"Especially if he was cautious. Apparently no shot overheard, either. We go this way," she said, rounding the corner of the house to the attached carport where they stopped long enough to sheathe their hands with the latex gloves.

That accomplished, Mark watched with interest as she dragged a metal trash can beneath the roof of the carport, mounted it and ran her hand along the top of a central beam that supported the cross rafters.

"Ah, got it."

Key in hand, she was prepared to step down from the trash can. Before she could do that, Mark's big hands were around her waist and lifting her to the floor. It was an innocent action that should have meant nothing. Then why did she experience this warm sensation of intimacy?

Foolish, she censured herself as she turned away to confront the yellow crime scene tape stretched across the side door. "We'll have to be careful not to disturb it."

"Which means crawling under it. Should be a lot easier than barbed wire on maneuvers."

"Or rescuing a first-grader who's got himself stuck inside a jungle gym."

Wriggling under the tape, with Mark directly behind her on hands and knees, she used the key to admit them into the kitchen. Once inside, with the door shut and locked behind them and on their feet again, Clare was immediately aware of the same dim stillness as Boerner's apartment. A silence that made her jumpy at the prospect of searching the house.

Mark was apparently not affected by it, asking an easy, "Where do we start?"

"If Joe had anything he was hiding from Terry, his office would be the logical place. According to Terry, it was his private domain, off-limits to her except by invitation or when it needed cleaning."

"You're the guide," Mark said, falling into step behind her.

They were careful not to get too close to any of the windows as they left the kitchen and crossed through the dining room into the living room. Trying not to imagine just where Joe's body had lain here on the floor, Clare moved on down a long hallway. They passed the bedrooms on either side and reached the office at the end of the hall. She stopped here outside the office.

"What?" Mark asked her, his voice registering alertness.

"The door is open. Joe always kept it closed."

"One of the cops could have left it that way."

"Or the killer, if he was in here after he shot Joe."

"Also a possibility. Are we gonna go on standing here, or do we start looking?"

Looking was not going to be too much of a challenge, Clare thought as they entered the office. The room was a small one, furnished with nothing more than a desk, a swivel chair in front of it, a tall filing cabinet and a lounge chair facing a television mounted in a bookcase. There were none of the pictures and ornaments here that Terry had so lovingly placed throughout the rest of the Riconi home.

Joe's computer, she noticed, had been removed from the desktop. Probably taken away by the police.

"What do you want?" Mark asked. "The desk or the filing cabinet?"

"The desk, I guess."

"Let's not make the mistake of the open door," he cautioned her. "Try to leave everything just as you find it."

That wasn't going to be easy, Clare decided as she began to search through the clutter her brother-in-law had left behind in all of the drawers.

They worked in silence as the moments passed. It was Mark who finally spoke after clanging shut one of the metal drawers of the filing cabinet.

"All I'm finding are the usual household records. Receipts and canceled checks, that kind of thing. No revealing papers or letters that might connect him with Boerner or his days as a mercenary. How are you doing?"

Clare didn't answer him. Her silence had him swiftly joining her at the desk, where she was gazing down at the coiled, thin leather cord she'd discovered tucked into a corner of the bottom drawer.

"It's the same as yours," she murmured. "Just like the one around Malcolm Boerner's neck."

"And missing whatever was attached to it."

"Joe did have one of his own. Another amulet. You know he did, Mark. This is proof of it."

"It's not evidence. By itself it's just a leather cord. It couldn't have interested the police, or they would have taken it away."

"But someone did take away what was strung on it, and we both know who that someone had to be. Joe's murderer. It's why he came here."

Clare began to tremble with a feeling of uneasiness, as if the killer was still in the house. Silly of her, but she suddenly felt the need to leave. *Now,* before Mark began to argue with her again about the reality of a third amulet and what it might or might not mean.

She closed the drawer on the lanyard. By itself it was of no use to them. "Let's go," she urged him. "It's making me nervous being here."

Did he want to linger long enough to search the rest of the house in case they were overlooking something of importance? She was ready to tell him that Terry was too familiar with the other rooms not to be aware of anything that mattered and to have mentioned it to them.

But Mark must have sensed how much she wanted to be out of here. He offered no objection. After glancing around to be certain they were leaving everything as they'd found it, they left the office. Clare preceded him down the hall.

She was about to emerge into the living room when she halted so abruptly that Mark bumped into her.

"What is it now?"

"The mirror over there where the fireplace wall is

angled," she whispered, pressing back out of sight. "It reflects a view of the street through the front window. Mark, someone is out there coming up the walk."

Before she could stop him, he stepped around her to look into the mirror for himself. "There's no one there now. Are you sure you saw someone?"

"Positive."

"Man or woman?"

"A man."

"Maybe just one of the neighbors nosing around. Or could be a cop checking out the house to be sure it's still secure."

"He wasn't in uniform. Mark, don't!" she pleaded with him, clutching at his arm as he started to move into the living room. "He could see you through the window if he's still there, and if he has a gun—"

"Why should you think he might have a gun, if it isn't a cop?"

"I don't know. Because…well, because there was something furtive about him."

"Clare—"

"All right, so I only had a glimpse of him. No more than a quick flash really. Just the same," she insisted stubbornly, "I didn't like what I saw."

To her relief, Mark didn't try to reason with her.

"Okay," he said, "we'll hang back here in the hall until we know it's clear."

But she could see by the grim look on his face and the taut way he was holding his body that, being the man he was, what he wanted to do was rush out there and challenge the stranger.

They spent several long minutes listening for any sign of someone trying to get into the house. There was no sound outside.

Restless finally, Mark ventured into the living room to check the scene outside. "No movement out there," he reported. "It's clear for us."

They headed for the kitchen where Clare opened her purse. "I can't find the key," she said, searching through the purse.

"Are you sure that's where you put it? Maybe you slid it into one of your pockets."

"No, I'm certain I tucked it into my purse."

She went on looking for the key while Mark stationed himself behind her in the dining room doorway, a position that gave him a view through the front window in the living room.

In the end, Clare located the spare key, which had somehow worked itself down under a loose tissue at the bottom of her purse.

"Ah, I finally—"

"Get down!" Mark ordered her sharply.

Before she could learn why he'd cut her off, he was across the kitchen and dragging her to the floor between an island and an inside wall. "A police cruiser just pulled into the driveway. I'm thinking it's no coincidence. Looks like that guy hanging around the place could have been spotted by a neighbor, maybe across the street, and called the cops," he said in a low voice.

Which would explain, she thought, why whoever it was out there fled the scene. He'd either heard or glimpsed the approach of the cruiser. And now they were the target, trapped in here.

"If the officer has a key," she said in an undertone, "then we're in trouble."

"Doubtful, but let's not count on it."

They were silent then, listening to the slam of the door on the police car. Seconds later they heard the soft rattle of the front door on the house being tested to make sure it was still locked.

They spent tense moments after that huddled on the tiles, squeezed against each other, hearing the sounds of the officer investigating the windows as he circled the house. Clare was afraid to breathe when he reached the back door, shaking the knob so loudly it seemed to match the pounding of her heart.

The officer must have been satisfied, because a minute later they caught the sound of the cruiser departing. Only then was she able to breathe again.

"I don't know which was worse," she said, "the mystery man out there or the cop."

"About equal, I'd say. Let's go before the local fire department followed by a SWAT team arrives next on the scene."

Not so funny, Clare thought, considering the day they'd had.

Unlocking the side door, they crawled back under the tape, replaced the key, shed their latex gloves and cut across the backyard. "You know who our mystery man was, don't you?" she asked as they picked their way through the hedgerow.

"I'm afraid to ask."

"Joe's killer, that's who."

They had reached the pasture where Mark stopped, turning to look down at her. "This ought to be good. Okay, teacher, why would Riconi's killer risk turning up again at the scene of his crime?"

"Because he's after your amulet now."

She watched Mark inhale deeply, as if striving for patience. "Let's suppose," he said after releasing his breath, "that's just possible. Then how would he have known where to find me?"

"Because he followed us." She could see he was already about to lose that patience with her, which was why she rushed on before he could interrupt her. "No, Mark, listen to me. It all makes sense, if you think about it. If whoever this man is *was* Malcolm Boerner's partner, and they did have a quarrel that ended up with him killing Boerner and taking his amulet, which he probably wouldn't have hesitated to do, not if he'd already murdered Joe for *his* amulet, then…"

Clare watched Mark open his mouth with a clear intention again of stopping her there. She didn't give him that opportunity.

"All right, so we don't know how he knew Joe or that Joe had an amulet of his own, but the rest would fit. Like his knowing from Boerner that I was scheduled to turn up this morning at the shop with your amulet. His waiting around somewhere close by, and then when I showed up with you beside me realizing his chance wasn't a good one and that he could have a better one tailing us to someplace that wasn't so public."

Clare ran out of wind by then, finally allowing Mark to make a contribution of his own. "Uh-huh, the blue sedan that seemed to be following us from New Orleans. Only we lost it way back, remember?"

"Or *thought* we did."

She could tell from the expression on his face that Mark was ready to accuse her again of wild speculations. But he refrained from doing so. Maybe because he now saw merit in them. After all, he had elected to come to the house in search of a possible third amulet, and that in itself had to mean something.

As they went on across the pasture, neither of them speaking now, Clare took advantage of their silence to observe Mark's gait. He'd been on his feet and active now for sometime. Had it been too much for his wounded leg? Apparently not, because he wasn't limping. Not noticeably so.

When they reached the SUV, he turned to her, smiling down at her from that formidable height of his.

"Still concerned about this leg of mine, are we?"

So, as careful as she thought she'd been, he'd been all too aware of her eyeing his leg. "I didn't say—"

"You didn't have to. Hey, don't worry about it. I kinda like the idea of you thinking about me. In any terms."

And that, along with the wicked smile, was all it took for Clare to turn to mush. She remembered again his all too potent kiss back on the levee and how strongly it had affected her. Remembered, too, Terry's warning to her there in the jail's visiting room.

Just watch yourself with him, will you?

Too late. She already wanted this man far more than was good for her. Wanted another of those searing kisses of his, his teeth nipping her lips, his tongue inside her mouth. All of it tugging at her senses.

There was something else that maybe did, or maybe didn't, help matters. Something she could read in the softness of his gaze. The lieutenant no longer mistrusted her, no longer questioned her honesty. She could swear it was there in his eyes.

Funny how that in itself made him dangerous.

The drive back to New Orleans kept Mark occupied. Far too unwisely so where Clare was concerned. She had fallen asleep in a corner of the passenger seat, permitting him to glance down at her as often as he liked without being caught.

Yeah, free to…well, for starters to admire her breasts

as they rose and fell with each slow, rhythmic breath she drew. That alone was an enticing sight that had him squirming inside his seat belt.

Better lift your eyes to a safer level, Griggs.

He did just that, snatching glimpses of her mouth at intervals. This wasn't any better. Not when that mouth was slightly parted, feeding his imagination with a longing to bury his tongue deep inside her.

He wasn't just squirming now. His wild need for her had him growing hot and heavy with arousal. Nor did he think that paying attention to any other areas of that sweet body was going to relieve his desire.

When the car swerved, threatening to go off the highway, he realized that if he didn't focus on his driving he was going to get them into an accident.

Not just your eyes, either, lunkhead. Your thoughts could also use some control.

Right.

Obeying his self-command, he turned his mind to the problem that had taken them to St. Boniface Parish. So where were they now? Any closer to some answers?

For one thing, he was ready now to buy the theories Clare had laid out for him. They did make sense. What he wasn't ready to do, and hadn't been when she'd presented them, was admit this to her. Doing that would only encourage her, raising hopes that could easily lead to nowhere. Because the trouble was, they had nothing solid to support those theories. Not yet. Maybe never.

What was it about those damn amulets worth murdering for? All of it seemed to go back to Afghanistan where the amulets had originated. His, anyway. And probably Riconi's and Boerner's as well, assuming they had served there themselves years ago. In their case as mercenaries.

Had their killer been there, as well? Afghanistan. That was the connection. Mark was certain of it.

Yeah, but even if they got the answers, would they prove Terry Riconi's innocence? That was all Clare cared about. Freeing her sister. He wanted that for her, too.

Again, where does all of this put them? Still in the dark, that's where, blindly feeling their way to what could be nothing more than a dead end.

Whatever the odds, soldier, rangers don't give up.

Chapter 8

Clare was awake when Mark stopped for gas and a bathroom break for both of them. She was still in the women's restroom when he came out of the service station. He waited for her alongside the SUV.

This stretch of the highway was a busy one, which he guessed was the reason why there was another service station opposite theirs across the road. He could have easily missed the blue sedan parked there at one of its pumps, if the squeal of tires from a sports car departing from the station hadn't drawn his gaze in that direction.

Mark stiffened to attention at the sight of it.

Not just a blue sedan but the same make and model as the one that had followed them along this route on their way to St. Boniface Parish. Or had seemed to.

Just a coincidence with an innocent explanation? Because he wasn't willing to believe it wasn't the same car.

No, he decided, this time he was ready to trust Clare

had been right. That the blue sedan had been deliberately tailing them. Even that its driver could be their killer and was now after *his* amulet.

The sedan was currently unoccupied, meaning its driver was probably somewhere inside the service station. As Mark watched the door of the station, waiting for his subject to exit, he could feel his hands down along his sides curling into fists. Could feel himself fired with a determination to cross the highway and confront this guy.

If he could just get his hands on him for a few minutes, demand the answers they needed…

Damn it, Griggs! What do you think you're doing? This isn't a combat zone.

And as Clare had warned him earlier, combat field or not, this particular enemy could be armed and prepared to use his weapon. All Mark had were his fists, because his own service sidearm was in an army lockup, which was required of a soldier when he came off duty.

Fists were no match for a gun, and if he was shot, Clare would be alone and defenseless. He couldn't risk it. But he could go on watching that door. Getting a good look at the bastard would by itself be useful.

His effort was rewarded with frustration when, seconds later, a tall truck as long as a boxcar came lumbering along the highway, blocking his view of the other station. He'd exhausted his arsenal of profanities by the time the truck cleared his line of vision.

The sedan was still there, however, and its driver now with it.

Not a sinister-looking figure. Not even male. Nothing more dangerous than a teenage girl sliding behind the wheel and speeding away from the station to the deep throb of a rock ballad at full volume.

This time Mark cursed himself for being a complete ass. He had blue sedans on the brain. How many others could be out there? Same make, same model. A lot of them.

Clare joined him a moment later. By then he thought he had himself fully under control, but she must have perceived some lingering tension in him.

"Something wrong?" she asked.

There was no way he was going to embarrass himself by revealing to her what a fool he'd been. "Just wondering what was keeping you. What do women do in bathrooms that take them so long?"

"Spend the time making sure the men waiting for them outside are good and impatient before they join them."

"Funny," he grunted. "You ready to get on the road again?"

It was late afternoon and New Orleans not far away now when Mark, who'd been waiting for the right moment to approach the subject, made his casual bid.

"I'm going to need to find a room for the night. Any suggestions?"

"Yes, forget it. With New Orleans crawling with visitors, there won't be an available accommodation anywhere this side of Lake Pontchartrain."

"Well, it won't be the first time I've slept out in the open. Unless…"

She gazed at him suspiciously. "Uh-huh, I get it. Unless I have a spare bed I'm willing to offer you."

"Do you?"

"I don't think I have a choice. Yes, I have a guest room, and you're welcome to it."

It was what he'd been hoping to hear. With the situation being what it was, he felt the need to stay close to her. It was imperative that she be protected, although the arrangement did suggest other interesting possibilities.

You've got a low mind, soldier. You're supposed to guard her, not seduce her.

Mark tried to keep that in mind as they neared the first suburbs of the city. With a killer out there somewhere wanting his amulet, and not knowing whether it was still in his possession or Clare's, the threat to both of them was very real.

That much he was convinced of now. He just wasn't ready to believe what Clare, who apparently had started to check the outside mirror on her side again, announced a few moments later, "He's back with us. Pulled out from a side road behind us. He must have been waiting for us there, knowing we'd have to pass here on our way back to the city."

Mark glanced into his rearview mirror. A blue sedan was following them at a safe distance. He wasn't ready to buy it, though. Not this time. Not after the episode back at the service stations.

"And you just know it's the car that shadowed us up from New Orleans."

"I do," she insisted.

"Clare, do you realize how many blue sedans like that one are out here on the roads?"

"I don't care. It *is* him."

Mark didn't bother arguing with her. Her mind was made up. She continued to ride shotgun as they approached the busy urban area.

"Take the next turn left," she directed him. "It'll put us on the expressway."

He did as she instructed.

Twisted around in her seat now, ever vigilant, she reported, "He's still here with us."

"And so are a lot of other cars. It's an expressway, Clare. Why shouldn't he be on the same route?"

She was right. The blue sedan was still behind them. But although he was far from convinced this was their mystery man, Mark decided to humor her. Accelerating, he began to weave in and out of the traffic in an attempt to put other vehicles between the SUV and the sedan. It didn't work. The sedan managed to catch up to them every time.

"You see. He is following us. Maybe it's time we called the police."

"And tell them what? That some guy we know nothing about is stalking us on the southbound expressway? How do you think they'd react to that?"

"You're right. They'll ask us questions we don't want to answer."

"That's after they've already decided one or both of us is paranoid."

"So what should we do?"

He had yet to believe this particular blue sedan was tailing them. But then why take a chance? "Lose him. Hang on."

Without slowing or warning, he swung over to the right lane and zoomed down the next exit.

"It didn't work. He's come down off the expressway with us," Clare said immediately.

Mark no longer questioned her certainty about the car. There was no coincidence here. This guy was definitely following them.

"I'm not through yet," he promised her.

They were in an industrial region. Somewhere near the river, Mark judged. The sprawling area was a maze of narrow streets, train tracks and drab buildings of all descriptions, many of them looking abandoned.

It should have been the perfect place to shake their pursuer, but no matter how Mark twisted and turned, the blue sedan managed to keep them in sight.

It wasn't until a warehouse loomed in front of them that he caught a break. An eighteen-wheeler was pulling out into the street from a loading dock. Reckless and dangerous though his action was, he floored the gas pedal. The SUV responded by leaping forward to the sound of Clare's alarmed gasp.

Squeezing over to the right so far he almost jumped the curb, he managed to clear the nose of the truck by mere inches. Before its startled driver could brake his rig, the truck was blocking the width of the street, cutting off any passage. The blue sedan was left behind them.

Slowing just enough to safely lift his right hand from the wheel, Mark covered Clare's trembling knee. "You okay?"

"That was an awfully risky thing to do."

"Yeah, but effective."

She had no further objection, only a regretful "It would have been useful if I'd just gotten a decent look at him. But I didn't this time any more than I did back at Terry's place."

Returning his hand to the wheel, not satisfied that the sedan couldn't still overtake them, Mark proceeded to execute a series of swift, confusing turns up one street and down another, all of them designed to discourage any further pursuit. In the end, he crawled into a deep alley, parking out of sight behind an enormous storage tank.

"This should do it," he said, switching off the engine.

Except for the ticking of the cooling engine, there was silence between them. He waited a moment before turning to her.

"We can't spend the night at your place, Clare. This guy is determined. He's bound to find us there. Are you listed in any phone directory?"

She shook her head.

"How about Boerner? You tell him your address? Because he could have shared it."

He received another shake of her head.

"Even so, if someone is persistent enough, there are ways to locate addresses. This is the electronic age, Clare."

"Right. Which is why we're not going to spend the night at my apartment. We'll spend it at my house."

"Huh?"

"I realized a dream and bought a small house this past winter. I've been working on it weekends, redecorating and transferring what I didn't need back at the apartment. I was supposed to move all the rest this past weekend, but then, of course…" She spread her hands in a gesture meant to convey that circumstances had intervened.

Mark understood her. Her brother-in-law had been murdered, her sister arrested and jailed and Clare's move put on hold.

"The point is," she continued, "my address is still the apartment. My line phone, too."

"So we bunk down on the floor at your house."

She shook her head. "I bought new beds and mattresses for the house. They're already installed. But I'll need to stop at the apartment for some clothes and a few other essentials."

Mark wasn't sure that was a good idea. On the other

hand, he supposed their pursuer would need time to learn Clare's address, providing he made the effort.

"Should be safe enough," he agreed, "if we make it fast." He started the engine. "Any idea where we need to go from here?"

Clare's apartment was located on the second floor of a nondescript building near City Park. What identity its few rooms had possessed that might have indicated her tastes was largely gone. The walls were stripped of their pictures, the tables their ornaments, the shelves their books.

Except for the major furniture, like a table and matching chairs in the kitchen and the appliances that she informed him came with the apartment, the place already wore a barren, hollow look.

While Clare flew around, packing a suitcase in her bedroom, stuffing a pair of sacks with groceries in the kitchen, Mark stationed himself at a window overlooking the street. There was no sign of a blue sedan down there. Nor did he expect to see one. All the same, he was uneasy about this delay and thankful when she announced she was ready to leave.

He made certain the sedan wasn't following them this time, checking his rearview mirror both when they pulled away from the building and through the streets along which she directed him.

Her house turned out to be several blocks away from the French Quarter. They'd almost reached it when he slowed the SUV to a crawl.

"What is it?" she asked.

"That," he said, nodding off to their right.

"Ah, one of our famous cemeteries."

Mark had heard about these Louisiana cemeteries,

how the deceased were interred in whitewashed vaults above ground because of the high water table. Picturesque, he guessed, if a cemetery could be called that. He decided this one could, maybe because it was bathed in the golden glow of a flaming sunset.

"I'm just up here on the right, third house from the corner," she indicated. "I don't have a garage or a driveway. None of the houses along here do. They were built at a time when few people had cars, and certainly no one in this neighborhood had one. It's different now. Most of these old places have been restored by people with comfortable incomes. You'll have to park at the curb."

Mark wasn't happy about leaving the SUV in plain sight out front, but it looked as if he didn't have a choice about it. Not, he convinced himself, that there was any chance of their pursuer finding it in a city as large as New Orleans.

Clare's own place, he noticed as he helped her to remove her things from the SUV, was a narrow, freshly painted, white frame house squeezed between two others almost identical to it. Its lines were simple, but at the same time it possessed a character about it. Maybe because the long windows, one on either side of the door, were attractively shuttered, and there were potted boxwoods beside the doorstep.

There were no lawns fronting any of the houses. All of them opened directly on the sidewalk, making it easy for them to carry Clare's suitcase and the sacks of groceries to the door.

"Is it my imagination," he asked as she fumbled for the key in her purse and unlocked the door, "or is it growing dark already?"

"That's another thing about New Orleans. We don't

have lingering twilights. It goes almost straight from sundown to night."

Mark realized he was getting an education here from the teacher.

"Here we go," she said, opening the door and reaching for a light switch.

He followed her into what he presumed was the living room. Or would be once it was fully furnished. Right now it was mostly a collection of unpacked boxes, two card tables and a few chairs. "This is a bit smaller than your apartment, isn't it?"

A bit? The place lacked breadth. The house was only one room wide.

"Actually," she said, "it's larger than the apartment. This is a shotgun house, Mark. Something else unique to New Orleans."

"Uh—"

He must have looked baffled, because she laughed softly. "Wait here, and I'll show you."

He watched her cross the room, open a center door to another room and switch on another overhead light. From there she moved on to other rooms, a whole series of them, each one directly behind the one preceding it. When all of them were blooming with light, she returned to the living room.

"Stand here," she directed him. "That's right, where the center doors all line up with one another. Now can you see why it's called a shotgun house?"

Damned if he couldn't. "Yeah, I get it. You stand here and fire a shotgun, and the cartridge travels from the front of the house clear to the back without touching a wall in between. Cool. Anybody ever try it?"

"I wouldn't be surprised. Come on, I'll give you a tour."

She led him through the first center doorway. "This is the only hallway in the house. I'm thinking it was once a third bedroom, but some owner, probably long before me, had walls erected that provided a full bathroom on this side and a laundry room and half bath on this other side."

They went on into the next area, which Clare informed him was her bedroom. After that came the guest room, and beyond it was a spacious kitchen equipped with new appliances.

"Nice," he complimented her. "Very nice, all of it."

And he meant it. It was a snug home, and even though many of the furnishings had yet to be added, it already wore the warmth and appeal of her personality.

What had been completed were the walls. They were covered in every room with the pictures that had been removed from her apartment. Most of them paintings and prints of local scenes that reflected her love of New Orleans. He could see that in these pictures, hear it in her voice whenever she spoke of the city to which she was so attached.

Now why, of all things, should that make him a little sad?

They were retracing their steps to the living room when Mark's attention was captured by an arrangement of framed photographs on the outside wall of her bedroom. He stopped to inspect them. The first one depicted a smiling Clare posed on the front steps of a brick building with children ranged on both sides of her.

"These your fifth-grade kids?"

"My current class, yes. I have photos of my others before this, but I haven't mounted them yet."

"And this one?" he asked, moving on to a photograph of a young, African American woman with a piquant face.

"My friend, Monica. She teaches the fourth-grade class next to my room. We're very close."

But clearly not as close as she was with the smiling, good-looking man in the next picture. Clare shared the photo with him. More than shared. She was plastered against his side, his arm possessively around her waist as they stood at the rail of one of those old, restored stern wheelers that now served as excursion boats on the river. Why Mark should experience a sudden pang of jealousy was something he didn't choose to examine.

"Who's this guy?"

She paused before answering him, and then all he got was a brief "Alan Britten. We'd better bring the suitcase and groceries inside." She turned away and headed for the front door.

Now what was that all about? Mark wondered as he trailed after her. She'd been pleased by his interest before this Alan Britten character. And then when he'd asked about him, she had clammed up. The tone of his question? He'd meant it to sound casual but was afraid it had come out more like a demand.

Maybe, but somehow he didn't think that was the explanation.

Clare faced him in the kitchen, leaning back against the counter after they had unloaded the groceries and put the perishables away in the refrigerator.

"Are you hungry?"

"I can always eat."

"Good, because I'm going to fix us dinner."

"What's on the menu?" he wanted to know.

"A New Orleans specialty. Shrimp Creole. It's better with fresh shrimp, but I'll have to use the frozen. Between here and the apartment it should already be mostly thawed."

"Does the tourist industry know about you?"

"Why?"

"Because you do one hell of a job selling this city. Yep, I'd say you'd easily qualify as their secret weapon."

"I have run on about my town, haven't I?"

"I don't mind. So, how can I help with dinner?"

"Do you know how to cook?"

"I know how to heat up MREs. Does that count?"

"Now it's my turn to be enlightened. What are MREs?"

"Meals Ready to Eat. The army kitchens supply us with them when we're out in the field. They're not bad, either."

"Fascinating. But I'm afraid that's not going to help where Shrimp Creole is concerned. How else can you be useful? Domestically speaking, that is."

Mark stroked his chin, thinking about it for a moment. "I can make beds. If basic training taught me anything, it was how to make a bed army style."

"Think I've heard about that. So tight it'll bounce a quarter, huh?"

"Well, that's the general idea, anyway. Not that I've ever seen it actually tested."

"Great. The beds in both rooms need making up for the night. You'll find clean sheets and pillowcases on the closet shelves. Hop to it, soldier."

He tossed her a smart salute and headed for the bedrooms. "And make sure you do a good job of it," she called after him, "because I'll be inspecting your work later."

Mark had finished with the bed in the guest room

and was moving on toward the master bedroom when he realized he was grinning like an idiot. Had been grinning since he'd left Clare in the kitchen.

There was no mystery about it. He enjoyed her company, the easy banter they'd been exchanging in the first relaxed aura they'd experienced since meeting each other in the bar of the Pelican Hotel.

It was this house. Not just its homey pleasantness but a feeling of security, as if its walls were embracing you in a safe cocoon.

Safe? Not a wise conclusion when there was danger lurking out there somewhere in this vast city. A danger that could find them if he neglected to be on guard against it.

But there was something else he couldn't deny to himself, something equally pleasant. His awareness of Clare and him being alone in the intimacy of her home and where it might lead. An intimacy he wanted very badly. And that also could be unsafe.

It was a long way from Afghanistan, and there was nothing to spoil it. Except for one thing. The memory of Clare and Alan Britten in that photograph nagged at him. They'd looked so damn happy together.

Mark found himself struggling with the desire to make her happy like that himself. Dumb, but there it was.

Chapter 9

Shrimp Creole and cornmeal muffins. Mark didn't know if the combination was a regional favorite or not, and he didn't care. All that mattered was that it was delicious.

"Okay," he said, complimenting her, "so the teacher knows how to cook, too."

"Does that surprise you?"

"Everything I learn about you surprises me."

"Ah, but aren't women supposed to acquire an air of mystery?" she teased him.

"I'd say they're born with it."

It was this kind of harmless dialogue they exchanged while they ate their meal. The gentle light of the torches and candles on the patio, together with the tranquil flow of the electric fountain, was conducive to their conversation. Nothing serious, nothing intense. As if by an unspoken, mutual consent they had agreed that they needed a time-out to recharge themselves. It was why neither of them tried to discuss what their next move might be in this game they were playing with a desperate killer.

Mark knew there was another game on the table. The one he and Clare alone were playing. The game of a man and a woman caught in a powerful current of physical attraction. A current drawing them into deep waters that were capable of drowning them in their own emotions.

They didn't speak of this, either, but he felt they were both aware of it. That it couldn't be shut out like the subject of two murders and the puzzle of some amulets that had presumably triggered those murders. That it sizzled there between them, incapable of being extinguished even though Mark made the effort.

"I'm still seeing that photograph of you and your class and wondering."

"About?"

"How you ended up choosing to be a teacher?"

"I didn't choose education. It chose me. My love of children helped with that decision, of course," she added, pouring coffee for them.

He could certainly relate to that. Hadn't the army chosen him? There had never been any question about his wanting a career in the military. He still did.

There was a lull in their conversation while they drank their coffee. It was the silence of two people who were comfortable with each other. It probably would have remained that way if Mark, no longer able to resist asking the question that had been demanding an answer ever since he'd scowled over the sight of that other photograph, hadn't gone and spoiled the moment.

"The guy who has his arm around you in the picture.

What did you say his name is? Alan Britten, right? Any chance of you telling me about him?"

She lowered her cup to its saucer and stared at him, the expression on her face a guarded one now. His mistake. If he hadn't been so abrupt, if he'd approached the subject in a strictly offhand manner, she might have been willing to confide in him. As it was, he was afraid she would refuse to answer him, that she would consider it none of his business.

In the end, though, her voice grave, she did give him what he wanted. "Alan was my fiancé."

Was. She had used the past tense. He should have stopped right there, not gone and pursued it just to satisfy his need to be certain that Clare didn't belong to some other guy. Which, considering the desirable woman she was, wouldn't have been surprising.

"One of you went and ended the engagement, huh?"

"No, the war did that."

This wasn't good. He could already sense that. Was already regretting he'd ever discovered that damn photograph and asked her about it. She wouldn't be telling him this otherwise, and he wouldn't have awakened what had to be a painful memory. But now that he had, she seemed willing to reveal all of it.

"Alan was another teacher. We had that in common, as well as sharing a lot of other interests, so I suppose it wasn't surprising we fell in love. He was—" she faltered for a second before finding the words "—was such an optimistic guy, always seeing the positive in people, especially the kids he worked with. But the war…"

She paused. Mark waited for her to go on.

"Alan had joined the National Guard. Not just because it made his college education possible, but because he considered it his duty. You understand that, don't you?"

"Yeah, I understand."

"When his unit was called up, he wanted us to be married then and there. I told him no, that it would be better if we waited until he got back when we would have time to plan the kind of wedding we both wanted. I lived with that mistake for a long time."

Mark realized what she was telling him. "He didn't come back."

"No, Alan didn't come back. He was killed in Iraq by a roadside bomb. A lot of them died that way, didn't they?"

"Yeah, they did," Mark said, hating himself for having been such a jerk to be irrationally jealous of a decent guy who, as it turned out, was another soldier, one who had died while serving his country. "Clare, I'm sorry I brought it up. I shouldn't have gone and reminded you of what had to be a really bad time for you."

"It's all right." She got to her feet and began to clear the table. "It happened over three years ago. I did my grieving. Did it for a long while before I was able to recover from his loss. I suppose I shouldn't have that picture there on the wall, that I should put it away. But I was beginning to forget what Alan looked like, and it made me feel guilty. That I owed it to his memory to have something I could look at that would remind me of him and what we had."

"I get it."

"Thank you for that. If we're through out here, we'd better unplug the fountain and snuff out these candles and the torches."

"I'll do it."

That done, he helped her with the tray she had started

to load with their dishes. Carrying it back inside, he deposited it where she indicated beside the kitchen sink.

"The dishwasher hasn't been connected yet. We'll have to do all this by hand."

"I'll wash," he offered. "You dry, since you know where everything gets put away."

As they worked, she talked about the substitute teacher who was standing in for her while she was absent from her class. "I left complete lesson plans for her, so I hope she follows them. I don't want the kids getting behind."

It was an understandable concern, something Clare addressed in a tone that was in no way anything but ordinary. She seemed all right now that she'd permitted herself to tell him all about Alan Britten. Mark hoped that was true.

"I don't know about you," she said after she closed the cupboard door on the last cooking utensil, "but I'm ready to turn in."

He agreed with her plan. Neither one of them had gotten any solid sleep last night, and the day had been a long, tiring one.

Clare made use of the main bathroom while he brought in his two bags from the SUV. After placing them in the guest room, he went around the house making sure all the windows and doors were locked. There wasn't any likelihood of their being invaded in the night, not when their mystery man couldn't have the faintest idea where they had gone or how to find them, but just the same…

Satisfied they were secure inside the house, Mark visited the half bath, said good-night to Clare, shut the connecting door between them, peeled off his clothes and crawled into bed. He expected to fall immediately into an exhausted sleep, but it didn't work out that way.

He found himself awake in the darkness of the room, turning restlessly, sleep eluding him as the minutes passed slowly.

He never slept in anything but a pair of briefs when he was on leave. He shouldn't have been hot, not with the air-conditioning softly humming away. Even when he tossed aside the thin blanket covering him, his body felt warm, like it was about to break out in a sheen of perspiration.

What the hell was wrong with him?

But Mark knew what was wrong.

He wanted the woman next door. From the moment he had sighted her last night in the bar, he'd wanted her. Had been wanting her all day. Except now it was more than just a matter of wanting. It was *need*. A need so urgent his body was raging with the fever of it.

He was conscious of her nearness. Only a wall separated them. Listening intently, he thought he could hear her shifting on her mattress in there. Or was it just his imagination, because he wanted her to be as awake and aware of him as he was of her? Wanted her alluring body flushed with a longing to be joined with his.

A groan rumbled up from deep inside him. He was aching for her, and the ache was no longer bearable.

Clare didn't need the sound of the bed creaking in the guest room to remind her that Mark was only a few feet away. Hopefully, he was just moving in his sleep and not staring up into the darkness as she was.

She should have drifted off long ago. Her fatigue after she'd scrubbed off her makeup, cleaned her teeth, shed her clothes, dragged an oversize T-shirt over her head and climbed into bed had certainly warranted it. But her mind couldn't seem to shut off long enough for sleep to overtake her.

Mark, of course. Thoughts of him kept crowding into her brain. Some of them innocent, some of them downright wicked. Things like how tough he could be. And yet he had this almost boyish capacity to be fun-loving and sweet.

Hard and then gentle. A fatal combination. The danger Terry had warned her of back at the jail.

That was just the innocent. The wicked was her memory of his riveting kiss this morning on the levee and the yearning it had awakened for something far more intimate than a kiss. A yearning that was now filling her head with wanton images of them locked in—

The images stopped there, sharply cut off by the soft sound of the guest room door opening. Her head turned in that direction as the door clicked shut behind the tall figure that had crept into her bedroom. Raising herself on one elbow, Clare gazed at him.

She had left the door to the hall open, as well as the one to the living room beyond. There was just enough light from the street lamp on the corner to faintly illuminate Mark's body, naked except for a pair of briefs, standing there against the closed door.

The sight of him, face in shadow but the muscles of his arms and thighs gleaming in the soft glow, had the breath sticking in her throat. There was a long, taut silence before he whispered her name.

"Clare?"

That was all, just that one word. But his husky voice spoke it with the tenderness of a caress.

She swallowed before managing to answer him. "I'm awake."

"I thought you might be."

She didn't ask him what he wanted. She already knew. The tone of his voice carried an underlying plea that told her why he was here. There was another silence, a brief one this time, before she responded to that plea. It needed no words, only the rustle of her movement as she shifted to the other side of the bed, making room for him.

He must have heard her action and understood it. That was why he padded swiftly across the room, why he was suddenly there beside her on the bed. His body fitting itself to hers, he reached for her eagerly. His arms went around her, drawing her tightly against his hot flesh.

Clare knew that welcoming him into her bed like this was a mistake, but she hadn't the will to resist him. She wanted him too much. Wanted to share not just what her body could offer him but her pulsing emotions, as well.

He held her so snugly that she could feel the hard bulge of his arousal in his briefs. There was another bulge she could feel, a slight one this time that indicated he had a mysterious something tucked inside the waistband of those briefs.

"What are you hiding in there?" she demanded, hearing it crackle softly as she touched the area.

"Later," he murmured. "Right now I have other business that needs my attention."

"Like?"

"Like this."

As dim as the light was, his mouth managed to find his intended target without error. Not her own mouth, not yet. What he wanted, to her surprise, was the scar high on her cheek. She felt the tip of his tongue there slowly tracing its crescent shape.

When he paused at last, it was to confide, "I've been meaning to explore this from the moment I noticed it."

"It can't be that fascinating."

"Oh, yeah, it is."

"Your finger could have done that."

"Not nearly so satisfying as my tongue."

"What else does your tongue want to explore?" she challenged him boldly.

"Everything."

He demonstrated that claim by burning a wet trail across her forehead to her other cheek, then descending slowly. She expected him to settle on her mouth. He didn't. He bypassed that area and instead went to her throat.

What he did there, concentrating on her sensitive pulse, was absolutely erotic.

"Please," she begged him.

"Please what?"

"I can't take this anymore."

"You have to. We've just begun."

That was when he finally transferred his attention to her mouth, when his teeth nipped and tugged at her lips until they were raw with wanting more. Only then did he oblige her with a kiss so demanding that her mouth opened for him. Obeying her invitation, that talented tongue of his entered her mouth where it sought and captured her own tongue in a prolonged duel of sweet sensations.

He literally took her breath away, making her so faint with his searing kiss she thought she would pass out before his mouth finally lifted from hers.

"Where," she croaked when she at last found air again, "did you ever learn to kiss like that? I don't imagine it was something the army taught you."

"You'd be surprised—" he chuckled "—at what a soldier on leave can learn."

"It's a good thing one of us knows what he's doing."

"With a woman as sexy as you, it's no problem."

Clare had never thought of herself as sexy, but she was in no state to argue with him. Not with his hands skimming the sides of her breasts, testing their plumpness. Without her bra, they were vulnerable.

They would be far more vulnerable when the T-shirt was removed, which he intended when he growled an impatient "Let's get rid of this thing. Arms up, please."

She complied by lifting her arms, permitting him to peel the T-shirt over her head and cast it aside. There was no pause to follow that action. His hands were immediately busy, stroking the fullness of her breasts, his fingers teasing the nipples into rigid peaks.

"Like silk," he whispered. "Your breasts are like silk."

His touch was wonderful and at the same time so unbearable that she could scarcely choke out a hoarse "Mark, please."

"I know, sweetheart, I know. But there's more."

He proved that when he bent his head, his forceful lips closing over one nipple and then the other, drawing them deeply into his mouth where his tongue swirled slowly around each of them in turn. It was pure torment, threatening to become even worse had he not taken pity on her and surrendered her breasts.

"Don't plead that's enough," he warned her when he raised his head, "because we're far from through here."

"What—"

He didn't give her time to finish asking what he intended since one of his hands had already smoothed a path down over her belly, coming to rest at the waistband of her panties. He stopped there only for a scant few seconds before that hand dipped beneath the waistband, inching its slow way lower, still lower until it reached the juncture of her thighs where his fingers stirred through the nest of curls there, searching for the cleft he wanted.

When he found it and gently parted its petals, she clutched at his hard shoulders, moaning as he thrust a finger inside her and began to gently rub the wet nub there.

She was so totally lost by then that it took only a moment before she was crying out, bucking wildly as the first spasms seized her in a blissful release. He waited for them to pass, giving her time to rest.

Leaning forward, he kissed her. "You okay?" he murmured.

She wasn't sure, but she gave him what he wanted to hear. It was enough to bring him into action again.

"Time for you to find out what I've been hiding in here," he said.

She heard the faint crackling noise again, realizing he must be extracting what he'd tucked inside the rolled waistband of his briefs. Whatever it was, he pressed it into her hand.

"You do the honors," he instructed her.

Clare could identify it now. A condom. He must have had it, and probably others as well, in his luggage. Although she'd had very limited practice dealing directly with condoms, she was beyond any further objection. Tearing open the foil-wrapped packet, she removed its content.

He'd shed his briefs and was ready for her. Her hand closed around the swollen shaft that rose from his groin.

"Careful," he cautioned her, sucking in his breath as

her trembling fingers rolled the condom down over his length. "You've got me in agony here."

"What are you doing?" she asked. The near darkness revealed nothing more than the quick movement of one of his hands.

"Taking off the amulet. I don't want anything between us for this." She felt him sliding the amulet beneath one of the pillows for safekeeping. "I'm ready now. What about you?"

Having removed her panties, she assured him she was, although she wasn't certain of anything now but her need to be joined with him.

"Good, because I can't hold out much longer."

That was evident when he impatiently levered himself over her, nudging aside her knees. Flattening the palms of her hands against the slabs of muscle on his chest, Clare lifted her hips to accommodate him.

Then, with one powerful thrust, he buried his entire length deep inside her.

He gave her only a moment to adjust herself to him before, his hips pumping out a smooth rhythm, he began to deliver a series of jolting strokes that Clare endeavored to match with her own rhythms.

In a state of delirium now, she was dimly conscious of being swept up in a tide of sensations. The sound of his whispered endearments, the musky scent of his body taking control of her, the lingering flavor of his minty toothpaste when he kissed her repeatedly, the feel of him, damp with a sheen of perspiration, as she raked her hands over the bunched muscles of his back.

It seemed disloyal to the memory of Alan to compare this man in any way to the man she'd lost, but she was unable to deny it. Lieutenant Mark Griggs was a dynamic lover, though admittedly the other lovers she had experienced were few. Still, the joy he gave her was indescribable, ending all too soon when he rocked her into a blinding orgasm.

He followed her into that oblivion within seconds, shuddering with his own climax. Sinking down against her with a massive sigh of gratification, he kissed her one last time before rolling over onto his side.

Arms reaching out for her to hold her close, he confided an emotional, "It's been a long time since I've had sex as fantastic as that." He amended the declaration with a quick "Come to think of it, it never was that fantastic."

Clare didn't have to exaggerate to agree with him. She could imagine the grin he must be wearing there in the almost total darkness. She wondered if he was still smiling when his even breathing told her he'd drifted off to sleep.

She didn't sleep. She kept thinking of the lovemaking they had shared, as steamy as the New Orleans night.

What is this going to cost me?

Heartache, if she'd already fallen for him. Had she? Compelling though Mark was, and he was that and more, it didn't seem possible, not when just yesterday he'd been her enemy.

Yesterday. Had it been only twenty-four hours since they'd been together? A single day, and yet it seemed so much longer than that. And now he was her lover.

You can't afford to let yourself get serious about him, Clare.

There were too many reasons why she couldn't. Chief among them was the temporary nature of their relationship. She belonged here in New Orleans, in this house. Belonged to the teaching career to which she was dedicated. While Mark…well, when the reason for their alliance ended, when his leg was fully recovered, he would go back to his beloved rangers. And that, if she was foolish enough to care about him too much, would leave her grieving over his absence as she'd once grieved over the loss of Alan.

What about Mark? Would he miss her as she would miss him? She wanted to think he would, but she didn't know his deeper feelings where they were concerned. As appealing as he was, there had to have been other women in his life, maybe more of them than she was ready to acknowledge. Was she just another of his short-lived affairs, someone he would dismiss when he was gone from her life?

No, he was better than that.

In the end, though, with her emotions in turmoil as they were, there was only one absolute truth. She couldn't be certain of anything.

Actually, there was one certainty, at least in this moment. It seemed that Mark muttered in his sleep. Not that she could distinguish anything he was saying. She managed to smile about her discovery while wondering at the same time if, along with her other concerns, it was going to keep her awake.

Clare was asleep beside him. Mark wasn't. Something had awakened him. What?

He lay there, listening. Silence. A total silence in the house. He could no longer hear the flow of the air conditioner. The temperature must have dropped in the night, cooling the house to such a degree that the thermostat had shut down the system.

He decided that the complete stillness must have roused him. Not so unusual. He had a nature as alert to silence as it was to unfamiliar noises. It was something most rangers possessed, a necessity in war zones where surprise attacks could occur at any hour under any conditions.

What time was it, anyway? He couldn't see his watch. It was too dark to read it, but he sensed that daybreak wasn't far off. Too early to get up. All the same, his feeling persisted that something wasn't right.

His mounting uneasiness was verified a moment later by a glimmer of faint light. Not from the street. From the opposite direction.

Turning his head, he located the source. There was a thin bar of light originating from beneath the connecting door to the guest room. A shaft that brightened slightly, then dimmed as it swept away. Too weak to be anything but a flashlight. Not a big flashlight, either. Something more like a penlight.

He and Clare were no longer alone in the house. They had a visitor.

Chapter 10

Whoever was lurking around Clare's house was being damn furtive about his presence. Except, that is, for the necessity of the light, which had to mean he was looking for something. Otherwise, Mark could detect nothing else from that other bedroom. Not even a whisper of movement.

He wasn't an ordinary thief. He was searching for something in particular. Mark had no proof of that, just his instinct telling him that the something was his amulet. And if that was true, then it meant their pursuer had somehow managed to find them.

All this went through Mark's mind as he slowly eased himself off the bed, careful not to disturb Clare and just as careful not to betray his action with any sound that would alert the enemy.

He didn't try to retrieve his briefs. It was imperative that he not waste any time, which was why he was still naked when he padded silently on bare feet to the connecting door, where he paused to listen. He heard nothing on the other side to tell him that the intruder in there was aware he was on the move.

He was safe. For the moment, anyway. Mark knew, however, that when he burst in there, if his opponent had a gun, he was risking his life. Hell, it wouldn't be the first time.

Surprise was his one advantage. Hand on the knob, he crouched over as low as possible to minimize the chance of his being an easy target. Then, taking a deep breath, he twisted the knob, flung the door wide open and propelled himself into the other room.

The glow of the penlight was enough to locate the dark form holding it. Before he could swing it in Mark's direction, he launched himself at his startled objective, catching him off guard just as he intended.

Mercifully, there was no bark of gunfire, which meant he either didn't have a gun with him or was unable to reach it. The impact of Mark's body slamming into his was enough to send the penlight clattering to the floor, where it rolled away and shut off.

But as hard as Mark struck him, it didn't bring him down as he'd hoped. Using whatever means were available to them both, the two of them locked themselves in a fierce battle in the darkness.

Mark swiftly realized that his opponent was an equal match for him. He also realized the bastard was a dirty fighter, not just punching with his fists but attempting whenever he could to deliver nasty chops with the sides of his hands and gouging Mark with his thumbs.

These weren't the techniques of a usual combatant but those of someone who was, or had been, a professional. It was the style of fighting onetime mercenaries Joe Riconi and Malcolm Boerner must have used.

They were of minimal value in this instance, though, because Mark had learned those same techniques in his training as a ranger. He knew both how to break them or elude them.

Mark was sure that in the end he could have defeated him, had their weapons been nothing but their hands. He was less certain of that when his adversary managed to produce a knife.

Clare came awake with a start, alarmed by the sounds coming from the guest room. Sitting up, her hand reached for the lamp on the bedside table. Even before she had its glow, she realized that Mark was no longer at her side.

What on earth—

Managing to find her sleep shirt on the floor where it had been discarded, she pulled it over her head. She didn't bother with anything else. Fearing the worst, she left the bed and rushed through the open door into the guest room.

The lamp behind her wasn't sufficient enough to reveal anything more than two figures in the shadows, their struggle accompanied by grunts, curses and heavy breathing.

Her hand was groping for the light switch on the wall when one of those bodies staggered against her. The force of what she presumed was an accidental connection, and not a deliberate attack, was so hard and heavy, robbing her of air, it sent her sliding down the wall. She landed on the floor, back against the wall and legs stretched out in front of her.

Whoever it was had to have immediately recovered

himself and fled toward the kitchen. By the time Clare could breathe again, the overhead light was on and a totally naked Mark, who must have found the switch, was hovering over her in concern. He held out a hand to help her up, but she waved it away.

"Did the SOB hurt you? My fault, actually. I slugged him such a good one there at the end I guess he fell into you. He must have had enough, because he ran out back."

"No, I'm all right."

"Then I'm going after him."

"Mark, no! You don't have a stitch of clothes on!"

But he was already gone. She could hear his bare feet slapping against the kitchen tiles as he raced toward the patio.

By the time he returned, Clare was on her feet again and closing the cell phone she had just used.

"He got away over the fence before I could catch him," Mark reported. "I would have scrambled after him, but—"

"And maybe made your leg worse, if you'd tried it!"

"I was going to say I didn't, because I was still worried about you."

"Even going after him like that was a damn fool thing to do."

He looked down at himself, seeming to finally realize that he was naked. "Yeah," he said sheepishly, "I guess if any of the neighbors were up and their outdoor lights on, they would have gotten an eyeful."

She didn't know about the neighbors, but she was getting that eyeful herself. It was scarcely a moment for her to be feeding her treacherous libido over the nude sight of him in all his male splendor. But she couldn't seem to help herself as her gaze traveled from his wide shoulders, down his powerful chest to his exposed manhood, where she tried not to linger, and on to his muscular legs.

It was when she reached his feet that she discovered what she had overlooked until now. There was a knife on the floor. A very wicked-looking knife. She stared at it in horror. Was that blood she was seeing on its sharp blade? Mark's blood?

She had been so intent on searching his body she hadn't bothered examining his face. Her gaze shot up, noticing for the first time the wound on the side of his jaw.

"You're bleeding!"

His hand went to his jaw. "It's nothing. Just a scrape where his knuckles grazed me."

"But that knife—"

"Never touched me. I managed to smack it out of his hand before the tip of it ever got near me."

She'd imagined the blood on the knife then, and thank God for that. "Just the same, that scrape needs attention."

"Later." He frowned, suddenly aware of the cell phone in her hand. "Who were you planning to call?"

"The police, and I already have. And don't give me all the reasons why I shouldn't have called them. Not when I didn't know what was happening to you out back. Did you ever manage to get a look at him?"

"Not as dark as it was in here, no."

"But we both know who he was, don't we?"

"Yeah, and what he was searching for."

"He didn't get it, though." She hadn't forgotten that Mark had removed his amulet and tucked it under the pillow in the master bedroom. "All the same, he found us here. Not just managed somehow to find us but to get inside the house."

That whoever had been shadowing them had now violated her home made Clare not just sick over the realization but deeply angry.

"And that," she added, "is another reason why I called the police."

"Clare," he reminded her, "we can't tell them we think this is the same guy who murdered Malcolm Boerner, not when as far as we know his death still hasn't been made public."

"No, but we can report an intended theft. I can't take any more of his watching us and waiting for another chance to strike. I want him caught and behind bars."

"And how do you think the cops will be able to do that?"

"His fingerprints. They must be everywhere in here, certainly on that knife. And if his prints are on file..."

"Forget it. He's too cunning for that. He was wearing gloves. I could feel them. Probably the same kind of latex gloves we wore at your sister's house."

Mark's disclosure was a disappointment, but she wasn't ready to abandon her hope in that direction. "The police may have other methods for identifying him. Speaking of which, one or more of them is going to turn up here at any minute."

"Meaning you'd like me not to be naked when they do." He nodded in her direction with a wide grin. "How about you? Wouldn't you, uh, like to greet them in something more than that sleep shirt, sexy though it is?"

Clare took his advice. When a police cruiser pulled up in front of the house, she was ready for it, having traded the sleep shirt for jeans and a Saints T-shirt. Mark had managed to get on nothing more than his pants and his amulet strung back over his head, resting on his bare chest where he insisted it belonged.

When the buzzer sounded, they went together to the front door. The solitary, uniformed officer they admitted into the living room was a tall, darkly handsome man.

"Officer Martinez." He looked from Clare to Mark. "And you?"

They gave him their names, which he jotted down in a small notebook, along with Clare's information that she was the owner of the house. He looked so young, as if he was fresh out of the police academy. She couldn't help wondering how helpful he would be to them.

"I understand you folks have had some trouble here. Suppose you tell me about it, and I'll see what I can do."

Clare let Mark do most of the talking since it was he who had discovered the intruder and tangled with him. It was unfortunate that his explanation omitted all previous knowledge of the subject. But, as they had both agreed, the circumstances of their involvement made it necessary. Otherwise, they would have been suspects themselves. Besides, anything they had learned so far was still just conjecture. There wasn't any actual evidence that their intruder was a killer after Mark's amulet.

"Any chance you can describe him?" Officer Martinez wanted to know when Mark had finished with his account.

"Too dark."

The policeman nodded regretfully, closing his notebook with a brisk "Let's have a look at the scene where this confrontation happened."

Clare led the way into the guest room. Martinez glanced around, noticing a chair that had been overturned in the fight before paying particular attention to the knife they had left where it landed on the floor.

"Yours or the thief's?" he asked Mark.

"His."

"Well, there should be plenty of prints here, especially on the knife. I'll have to get the techs in to dust for them."

Mark shook his head. "No good. He was wearing gloves."

"That's too bad. Still, the knife might tell the lab something. You never know."

Clare was impressed by his efficiency as she watched him carefully handle and bag the knife. He then took a flashlight out of his utility belt.

"I'm going out back to see if I can learn how he broke in. Some of these burglars have MOs that help us to identify them." He looked pointedly at Mark. "While I'm doing that, you might want to take care of that wound on your face."

There had been no time for Clare to play nurse before Martinez's arrival, but she was determined now to make sure Mark obeyed the officer's advice. When he went through to the kitchen, she turned to Mark.

"Into the main bathroom, please," she directed him brusquely.

She was prepared for an argument, but to her satisfaction she got none. He preceded her with an uncharacteristic meekness into the master bathroom where she kept her first-aid supplies.

"Where do you want me, teacher?"

She glanced at him suspiciously as she removed a clean wash cloth and a face towel from the cupboard.

"On the stool."

He was seated and ready for her by the time she had

wet and soaped the face cloth. Bending over him, Clare washed the caked blood away from his jaw, as well as along the side of his neck where the blood had trickled.

She was blotting the area dry with the towel when, meeting his gaze, she noticed what she could swear was a glint of amusement in those dark eyes. He's enjoying this, she thought.

"How bad is it?" he wanted to know.

Now that she'd cleaned the blood away and exposed the wound, she could see it was shallow, nothing more really than the scrape he'd earlier insisted it was.

"It will probably need stitches," she informed him dryly. "Maybe even surgery and a stay in the hospital."

"Uh-huh."

Dropping the wash cloth in the sink and slinging the towel over her shoulder, she rummaged through the medicine cabinet for the tube she wanted. Finding it, she bent over him again.

"Turn your head. No, the other way." Uncapping the tube, she squeezed a liberal amount of ointment on her finger and began to apply it to the scrape, observing as she worked, "You can't say our Officer Martinez isn't thorough."

"Yeah, for what must be a routine break-in, he is that. Ouch, that stings."

"Don't be such a baby. It's just an antibiotic ointment. You don't want to risk infection, do you?"

Slight though the injury was, she supposed it was tender to the touch. And, admittedly, her treatment of it hadn't exactly been a soothing one.

"You're done."

"Hey, don't I need a bandage?"

"You don't need a bandage. You'll heal nicely without one."

He's trying to prolong this, she thought. And there was that light again in his eyes, something far rawer than the scrape on his jaw. She knew without asking, *just knew,* that he was thinking about their lovemaking.

She lowered her gaze from his, but that was a mistake. She found her attention riveted now on the sight of his naked chest. Could actually feel the heat rising from him, wrapping around her like an embrace, triggering her own memory of last night's incredible sex.

There was no question of it. She was far too susceptible to this compelling man.

Relief came in the form of Officer Martinez calling to them from the vicinity of the kitchen. "Folks, if you've got a minute there's something I'd like to show you out back."

They joined him in the now lighted kitchen.

"This way," he said, leading them through an open French door onto the patio. "Careful, there's glass down here. You don't want to step on it in those bare feet of yours."

Flashlight in hand, the policeman aimed its strong beam down on the bricks. A rectangle of glass lay flat on the pavement off to one side of the door.

"This is how your burglar got into the house. He used a glass cutter to slice out one of the door panes. You can still see the suction cups he attached to the outside of the pane. They allowed him to remove the pane from its frame without breaking the glass and making a racket. All he had to do then was reach inside and unlock the door. It's a familiar method for thieves to gain entry, which makes him no amateur."

Clare shivered. She wasn't sure whether to blame the chill of the early morning air or the realization that her snug home was vulnerable. That whoever wanted to get inside could find a way to do it.

"And I went and overlooked all this," Mark said regretfully.

"Understandable," Officer Martinez said. "You were chasing him, and it was dark."

They went back into the kitchen where the policeman advised Clare, "You'll want to call a glazier to replace that missing pane. And you might think about installing a burglar alarm."

"I will," Clare assured him. "Is there anything else?"

"Yes. Do a careful look through the house to see if you've got any missing valuables. I doubt he had time to lift anything and pocket it before Lieutenant Griggs jumped him, but it's always possible. If you should find you're missing any items, let us know. We keep an eye on the pawn shops. Stolen goods sometimes turn up there."

Clare didn't need to concern herself with recovering any missing valuables. She knew there was only one thing their intruder had wanted, but she couldn't tell Officer Martinez that.

"I'll file a report, of course," he said, "but don't be surprised if we don't catch him. I'm afraid crime of this kind is no rarity in New Orleans."

They walked the officer to the front door where he told Clare he would ask their police patrols to keep an eye on her place. They thanked him for his concern. When he'd departed, Clare locked the door behind him and turned to Mark. He had his hands in his pockets and a sober look on his face.

"What?" she asked him.

"Nothing."

"Yes, there is. You're thinking his visit didn't accomplish anything. Well, I think it did. If our mystery man was out there nearby watching the house and saw the arrival of the police cruiser, there's a chance it will discourage him from coming back here and trying it again."

"If you say so."

Fair of her or not, his reaction irritated her, and for a good reason. She knew without either of them saying it that she was wrong and Mark was right. Their enemy would do anything to get Mark's amulet. Hadn't he already killed twice to get his hands on the other two amulets?

"For heaven's sake, will you please put on a shirt?"

"It bothers you?"

Regretting she had barked at him, Clare softened her response. "No, why should it?" She added a hasty "I just thought you might be cold, is all."

"It's still dark out there. Must be plenty of time before sunup. Maybe we should go back to bed," he said, changing the subject.

"After all that's happened? I don't think so. I would never be able to go back to sleep."

From the way he was gazing at her, Clare had the feeling his interest in bed had nothing to do with sleep.

"It's too early for breakfast," she said, "but I could use some coffee."

If he was disappointed in her alternative, he didn't voice it. "Yeah, maybe that's a good idea. It will give us an opportunity."

"For what?"

"The serious talking we need to do."

Chapter 11

Mark found a scrap of plywood in one of Clare's closets just large enough to fit over the opening in the French door where the pane was missing.

It would have to do until Clare could get a glazier in here, he thought, tacking the piece to the frame. Mark would also recommend that she add some sturdy bolts to all the doors and windows, ones that couldn't be easily reached from the outside no matter what panes of glass were removed.

By the time he was finished covering the opening, Clare had the coffee made and ready to pour into the mugs she'd set out on the breakfast bar in the kitchen. The eastern sky was brightening when they perched on stools across from each other.

"Thank you for fixing the door," she told him.

She didn't thank him for the polo shirt he'd pulled

over his head, but he could see her eyeing it with a certain relief.

Lecher that he admittedly was where this woman was concerned, it pleased him the sight of his naked chest apparently disturbed her on a level that—

Stop it right there, soldier. You've got other business to attend to here.

He hadn't forgotten that, but he waited until he'd swallowed his first satisfying mouthful of the steaming coffee to engage in the serious talk he'd promised her.

Lowering his mug, Mark leaned toward her with an earnest "The plywood might keep the squirrels out, but it isn't going to prevent that bastard from getting in here again."

"You think he'll come back."

"He wants my amulet, Clare, and from what we know about him, he'll go to any lengths to get it."

"But he wouldn't try to enter the house in broad daylight."

"Not likely, but even with the patrols Martinez promised us we can't spend another night here. It's too dangerous."

She nodded solemnly. "You're right. I knew it even before I called the police. I just didn't want to admit out loud that I would have to leave my home, find somewhere else to stay until this whole mess is cleared up."

"We have all day to decide where we'll go."

She was quiet for a moment. He watched her over the rim of his mug, wondering what she was thinking. She started to lift her own mug and then stopped, shuddering visibly.

"What is it?" he asked her.

"I just had an image of that brute stabbing you with his knife."

"But he didn't."

"No, you prevented that. But he came close to killing you, and if he'd had a gun instead of a knife— Mark, why didn't he have a gun?"

"Probably got rid of it after killing Boerner to avoid the possibility of it being traced back to him."

Clare nodded, silent again. This time she was relaxed enough to drink her coffee. He could tell, though, that quick brain of hers was busy again between sips.

"You know we could go back to my apartment tonight. Even if he did learn that's still my current address, being on an upper floor makes it secure. Plus it has a stout lock and—"

She went blank again in midsentence.

"Now what?" he asked her.

"I just realized how he must have found us here. You said yesterday that, this being the electronic age, our stalker could have learned my apartment address. He must have eventually done just that, and no matter how late the hour went there and roused the super in my building. He's the kind of jerk who wouldn't be opposed to accepting a healthy bribe, and he knew where I was moving."

"And after accepting a bribe," Mark surmised, "the super tells our bad guy just where to locate us. Yeah, it makes sense."

They were silent after that, each with their own thoughts as they drank their coffee. Mark didn't feel that spending the night in Clare's apartment was a good idea, no matter how safe she promised it was. But there was plenty of time to discuss that.

Aware of the light strengthening outside, he glanced through the window over the kitchen sink. The sky above the neighbor's roof was tinted the color of a maiden's blush. Not that he'd ever been poetic, but it did seem to be a fitting description for a sky that was heralding another sunrise.

Clare checked her watch. "It's much too early to try calling a glazier. I'll wait until after we have breakfast to do that. Meanwhile, if you don't mind holding the fort, I'm going to take a shower."

Mark watched her slide off her stool and head in the direction of the main bathroom, his gaze pinned on her shapely bottom. He didn't want to be left holding the fort. He wanted to be in that shower stall with her.

He couldn't stop them. The lusty images that swarmed through his mind. He could picture that sweet body of hers under the hot spray, could see the water sluicing over her full breasts, pouring down her belly to the curly nest below before cascading down her long legs.

He remembered last night's incredible sex in her bed, how she had felt under him, all soft and compliant. How she had responded to his lovemaking with low moans and a restless body longing for everything that he could provide.

Mark wasn't fully conscious of his actions. They seemed to be automatic, taking him from the stool to the French doors that opened onto the patio. Making certain they were locked, unable to resist his intention or to question the wisdom of it, he left the kitchen and sauntered through the bedrooms, pausing only long enough to find a condom in his luggage before moving on into the main bathroom.

He was helpless by the time he closed and locked the door behind him, driven by a primitive force he could no longer control. Or wanted to control. He had to answer the fire in his loins.

She didn't challenge his presence in the bathroom. Maybe because the noise of the water pelting down on her made her unaware of his arrival. Or maybe because she didn't mind his unannounced arrival. He hoped it was the latter.

Either way, it didn't stop him from removing his clothes and strewing them carelessly onto the floor. He was already hard and aching when, fully naked, the condom in his hand, he opened the frosted glass door, stepped into the stall and shut the door behind him.

He found her rinsing shampoo from her hair. If she was startled by his sudden appearance, she didn't react to it, other than to go very still. Had she ordered him out of the stall, he would have complied. Thankfully, she said nothing. She simply stared at him.

"I decided I needed a shower, too. Hope you don't mind my sharing the hot water before it runs out," he said gruffly.

"It never does. Or hasn't so far. I have an extra-large hot water heater."

"Let's test it to see if it holds."

"Yes, let's," she said with a little smile he chose to read as an invitation he gladly welcomed.

It was all Mark needed to place what he carried on the same ledge that held the shampoo bottle and the soap dish. Her eyes widened at the sight of the foil-wrapped condom, but she made no objection.

She must have expected him to scrub himself when his hand closed around the bar of soap. When, instead, he pressed toward her and began to lather her own, already slick body with long, slow strokes, she gasped.

She was receptive, though, to his sensual attentions. *Entirely* receptive. He could tell that when she squirmed in delight as his soap-enriched hands encircled her and began to massage her back, moving onward to caress her silken smooth buttock cheeks.

"Hold still," he commanded her.

"I'm trying, but you don't make it easy."

Nor did he want to make it easy on her when his hands slid around to her breasts where he spent some time before, satisfied, he worked his way down over her hips.

"Good?" he asked her.

"Very good," she murmured.

"More?"

"Yes, please."

Slipping a hand between her legs, he began to rub the super sensitive area of her groin until, bucking with release, she fell against him weakly.

He held her for a quiet moment while the steam rose around them in little wisps. He didn't try to kiss her. Didn't make any effort to fasten his mouth on the tips of her breasts. There could be no lengthy preliminaries, as there had been last night. His need to be joined with her was too urgent for that.

When he separated himself from her, it was only long enough for him to scoop up the condom where it waited on the ledge, tear it open and roll it down over his swollen length.

"I hope you're ready for me," he pleaded. "And even if you're not, please say you are because…oh, hell, I can't wait."

"I can see you're suffering," she said, her gaze lowering to his rigid shaft that was throbbing almost painfully now with wanting her. "So don't wait."

He didn't. Hands grasping her hips, he lifted her onto himself, driving his full length into her with one powerful thrust. Her legs locked around him, clasping him tightly as he supported her there against the tiled wall.

The water from the shower head rained on them, streaming over their bodies in concert to their own performance that followed.

Mark loved the way she mewed with pleasure when he rocked her. Loved the way she responded to his strong strokes with a series of little whimpers as the wisps of steam coalesced into a cloud.

There was no prolonging the culmination. Although he managed to hold back long enough to make her come once, then still again, his own climax swiftly followed, his body shuddering with gratification.

They clung to each other for a moment. Even when he let her slide down his length until her feet touched the floor, he continued to hold her.

"We did get a long time on the hot water," she said, "but I think it's beginning to cool off."

One of his hands released her only long enough to turn off the shower. By now it had washed away the lather that had managed to transfer itself from her body to his. It had rinsed her off, as well. There was no telling where the bar of soap had gone. He couldn't see it in all this steam.

His hand went back to join the other one at her waist. But only for a second. He wasn't finished. His hands shifted to frame her head on either side. There were drops of water leaking down her cheeks. Leaning into her, he began to lick them away.

She managed a sigh of contentment just before his mouth settled on her own in a kiss that lasted only long enough for both of them to realize they were growing cold.

Clare opened the door, preceding him out of the stall.

After handing him a bath towel, she provided one for herself. By the time Mark rid himself of the condom, disposed of it and rubbed himself dry, she had her own towel wrapped around her body.

"I need to blow-dry this hair before I think about breakfast," she said.

And he needed to get dressed. Gathering up his clothes, he left her in the bathroom and strode toward the guest room. Guilt set in even before he put on fresh underwear. By the time he was in jeans and a shirt, the guilt had intensified into a conviction that he'd been irresponsible. He shouldn't have joined her in that shower stall. After what had happened earlier, he should have stayed out here and remained vigilant, even though it was daylight now.

What the hell was the matter with him?

That should be an easy question for you to answer, Griggs.

Yeah, he knew all right. The truth was, he just couldn't get enough of Clare Fuller. She was in his blood.

His carnal desire for her was a certainty. How he felt about her emotionally was not. Or maybe he was just afraid to acknowledge those feelings. Afraid of the complications involved in something beyond the pure sex she seemed to enjoy as much as he did.

Mark was in too much of a hurry to bother with socks or shoes. He was barefoot when he went from room to room checking all the windows and outside doors. They were still tightly locked, of course. There was no one in the house but Clare and him, and no sign of anyone lurking outside watching the place.

Was he being unreasonable, even extreme with this need to safeguard her at every turn?

* * *

The mirror over the sink was misted from all the steam they had raised in the shower stall. Clare lifted the hand towel off its rack and began to wipe the mirror dry. When it was clear again, with her reflection there in the glass staring back at her, she went very still.

What are you seeing, Clare? What is it you suddenly don't like?

But she knew the answer to that question, didn't she? It was the expression in her eyes. Something close to panic. Panic about what?

Come on, you know the answer to that one, too. It's because of Alan, isn't it?

Yes, it was because of Alan. Hadn't she promised herself long ago not to get involved with another soldier either emotionally or physically? So why did she have to keep reminding herself never again to risk the possible consequences of such a relationship? The kind that could end with death in a war zone, leaving her struggling with an unbearable anguish.

Now look what she had gone and done to herself. Not just last night, but again this morning. She'd invited Mark Griggs into her bed, which afterward should have ended it then and there. But, no, instead she had repeated her mistake, welcomed him recklessly into her shower.

She hadn't learned her lesson. Why? The explanation was a simple one. Because the man who was sharing her home was, on the most primal of levels, irresistible.

It wasn't enough, of course, to justify her weakness. There should be more than just the sex. Maybe there was, at least for her. But she couldn't be sure of that. And until she was, with Mark feeling it, too, and letting her know as much…well, she would have to deal with it somehow.

Impatient now with herself, she picked up the blow-dryer in one hand and a hairbrush in the other and resolutely began to work on her damp hair.

When Clare arrived in the kitchen, dressed in cotton pants and a shirt, her honey-blond hair clasped back in a ponytail, she found Mark restlessly pacing the room like a sentry on patrol. That can't be good for his leg, she thought, and probably hadn't been last night when he'd struggled with his assailant, but he seemed oblivious to it.

"Something the matter?" she asked.

"No."

His answer was too brief, too curt, and he was frowning. He was in a bad mood. Why? Was he regretting their interlude in the shower? She hoped not, but she didn't ask him. She feared the answer.

And what right do you have to be hurt if he is regretting what happened in the shower, when less than twenty minutes ago you were punishing yourself in the bathroom with the same self-reproach?

She didn't.

The kitchen was bright with sunlight, giving her an excuse to change the subject. "What would you like for breakfast on this sunny morning?"

"You choose."

"I can manage an omelet."

"Fine."

For a man with an appetite as healthy as his, his reply lacked any enthusiasm. She didn't pursue it. Moving from refrigerator to stove, she busied herself making the omelet and a fresh pot of coffee. He didn't offer to help. Fine. Let him sulk.

She had a small television set on the counter. Grabbing up the remote from where it lay on the breakfast bar, she turned on the TV. "The news should be on soon," she remarked. "Maybe there'll be something about Malcolm Boerner's death."

"Could be, unless his body is still waiting to be discovered."

They didn't talk after that. Mark finally roused himself long enough to place plates and mugs on the bar, adding cutlery and paper napkins to the settings. Clare poured coffee and dished up the divided omelet and slices of buttered toast.

Perched on their stools, they ate in silence as they listened to the news. To Clare's disappointment, there was no mention of Boerner. When the news went to a commercial break, which was to be followed by sports and the weather forecast, she decided she'd had enough of Mark's dark mood, whatever his revelation cost her.

She muted the TV and bent toward him across the bar. "Okay, that's enough. I want to know what's eating you, and don't tell me I'm imagining things because I know I'm not."

"Yeah," he admitted, "I'm being a crappy guest, aren't I? Sorry about that."

"So?"

"You want an explanation."

"I think you owe me one, yes."

"It's just that after I left the bathroom, I got to thinking…"

He can't bring himself to say it, she thought, a lump in her throat because she knew what it was. But she had to hear now what she couldn't find the courage to hear before.

"Tell me," she demanded.

"I decided what happened in the shower was a mistake."

She sat back on the stool, stung by his disclosure, even though she'd anticipated it and after her own doubts earlier deserved it.

Her face must have registered her disappointment because he went on with a swift, understanding "No, not that. The sex was great, and I wanted it as much as I think you did."

She felt a sense of relief, although she was still puzzled. "Then what is it?"

"After what happened last night, I should have been on watch. I shouldn't have let my guard down. It's something a ranger never does when there's been an attack, and the danger could still be near."

"Mark, this is my home, not a battlefield."

He shook his head, unwilling to be convinced he wasn't at fault for what he must perceive as a lapse of vigilance. "It might have been better if I'd let him have the damn amulet. That way you wouldn't be at risk any longer."

"Look, I appreciate this need you have to protect me. But you're forgetting something. Without the amulet, I lose the only chance I have at this point to help Terry."

"You're right, and I realize that now, which is why whatever comes I intend to stay the course."

It was a promise for which she was grateful, but she didn't like how grim he still looked. We need something cheerful here, she decided. And she knew what that something was.

Without preamble, she launched into a sudden "Did you know that you talk in your sleep?"

"Huh?"

"It's true. I heard you last night. And I have to tell you I learned some very interesting things."

"Oh, my God! Don't tell me it was about Amber and Valerie."

"I'm afraid it was."

"Look, they never meant anything to me."

"Maybe not, but it was pretty lurid stuff. Frankly, I was shocked by it."

"You're saying you heard it all?"

"Every word."

He considered her for a few seconds before that wide grin she loved spread across his face. It was a relief for her to see it, even though he followed it with a cocky "Liar."

"You can't accuse me of that. You were asleep. How would you know what I heard?"

"Oh, I know all right. I've been told by guys I've shared barracks and bunkers with that I have an annoying habit of muttering in my sleep. Thing is, not one of them could make sense of it. It was all gibberish, and I never had a memory afterward of what I could have been chewing over."

"Are you saying there never was an Amber or a Valerie?"

"Oh, I'm not admitting to that," he said, a teasing glint in his dark eyes. "All I'm admitting is that I sometimes talk in my sleep. Your turn now."

"For what?"

"Confessing what annoying little habit you have. It's only fair. And don't tell me you haven't got one. Everybody does, usually more than one."

"Well, since you insist, there are these occasions when I get a song into my head and can't seem to shake it. Then I go around humming or singing it and driving myself and everyone near me crazy. So, now that you've heard the worst about me—"

She broke off there. Mark was no longer paying attention to her. He was pointing a finger in the direction of the TV on the counter.

Chapter 12

Clare swung around on her stool to find the television screen filled with an image that was familiar to her. Mark had to have recognized it, too, which was why he'd directed her attention to it. A message traveled across the bottom of the screen announcing a special news report.

Snatching up the remote, she activated the sound as the camera moved in close on an attractive young brunette with a microphone in her hand.

"Deborah McCord here reporting to you live from the French Quarter. I'm standing on Royal Street in front of the shop of antique firearms dealer, Malcolm Boerner, whose murdered body was discovered in his apartment a little over an hour ago by a concerned neighbor who called the police. It looks like they're about to bring out the body now."

The camera moved back, revealing the mouth of the

passageway to the courtyard, where a uniformed officer was lifting aside one of the barricades the police had erected to prevent the public from entering the courtyard.

Leaning forward, Clare watched as a gurney bearing a sealed body bag was wheeled out of the tunnel. *Malcolm Boerner is in that bag,* she thought, remembering the horror of how she and Mark had discovered his body long before reporters had arrived on the scene.

The TV camera, which had followed the journey of the gurney into the ambulance, resumed its coverage of Deborah McCord, who had stationed herself at the mouth of the tunnel. She knew her business, because a hefty-looking plainclothesman was emerging from the courtyard, chewing on a toothpick. The reporter seized the opportunity to intercept him.

"Would I be correct in telling our viewing audience you're one of the homicide detectives investigating the murder?"

He clearly didn't like having the microphone thrust into his face, answering her with an unfriendly "You would."

"Detective, could you comment on the murder? Was it connected in any way with the firearms the victim sold in his shop?"

"It's too early for that. When we have something, we'll issue a statement."

Without any further remarks, he brushed by her. The reporter was left with nothing more to say except a final "Tune in to our six o'clock newscast when we hope to have more details for you on this tragic murder."

The station returned to its regularly scheduled program. The remote was still in Clare's hand. Using it to turn off the TV, she faced Mark again, expelling a long breath.

They had watched the broadcast in silence, but she was eager now to express herself. "This is it! We can go now to the police!"

"No, we can't."

"What do you mean we *can't?* You said that when Boerner's body was discovered—"

"I know what I said. That we couldn't have any knowledge of his murder until it was made public."

"Which it has been. That means we can no longer be considered as suspects. Not when they have no reason to believe we were anywhere on the scene."

"So what are you going to tell them?"

"Everything. All that's been happening, including the business of the amulets and how this mystery man has gone to such lengths to get his hands on your own amulet. We don't have to let them know we were anywhere near Boerner's apartment. We can say that when I tried to deliver your amulet to him yesterday and found his shop closed—"

"What? That we just left it at that and walked away?"

"Yes. Why not?"

"Clare, they're not dummies. They may not connect us directly with Boerner's murder, but they could consider us as persons of interest. You, especially, because of your need to help your sister."

She had heard a version of this same argument before from Mark, and in her present mood she didn't need to hear it again. Angry with his resistance, she threw the TV remote down on the breakfast bar. "I can't believe how you've gone and done a one-eighty on me!"

"I've just told you why."

"All right, then I won't say anything about the amulets. All I want is that tape to prove Terry was in Boerner's shop when she said she was."

"It's too early for that. Yeah, they'll go through both the apartment and the shop looking for evidence. They'll probably find Boerner's security tapes, but it will take time to run them, maybe even days. And in the end the one you want might not be among them, not if he's tucked it away somewhere else."

"And what are we supposed to do until then? Just sit here and wait?"

"No, there's still my amulet. It's all we have now."

"I don't care about that damn amulet! The only important thing is—" She caught herself there, suddenly realizing what she'd been saying and ashamed of herself for saying it. "Mark, I'm sorry. All you've been doing is trying to help me, and I go and explode on you like a temperamental kid."

"You're forgiven, as long as you agree that this little trinket of mine—" his forefinger poked at his chest where the amulet rested under his shirt "—matters."

"I do."

"Good, because I happen to think it's the key to everything, along with the other two amulets we think Boerner and your brother-in-law had before their killer got his hands on them. I'm more convinced of that now than ever."

"Okay, the amulet matters. Because?"

"Because if that tape never turns up, our only alternative is to win the cops over to our side. Get them to start believing like we do that whoever murdered Boerner also murdered your brother-in-law, and that your sister had nothing to do with her husband's death."

"Just by showing them your amulet? That isn't going to work."

He shook his head. "No, it wouldn't. That's why when we do go to the cops, we need to go armed with knowledge."

"Like what?"

"Like why those amulets matter so much that someone was willing to murder to get them."

"How? Just how do we get that kind of knowledge?"

"I don't know, but there has to be a way. Like we say in the rangers—"

"There's always a way," she finished for him. "Yes, I remember."

"Right."

He let it rest there. They were stalled with nowhere to go. Clare was frustrated by that. She wanted results. Mark seemed to realize that.

"Don't worry, teach. We'll come up with something."

He rose, cleared off the breakfast bar and began to methodically wash their dishes at the sink. She sat there for a moment watching him. There was something downright sexy about the sight of this big man with a towel draped over one shoulder and his hands plunged up above his wrists in sudsy water. Not the kind of domestic thing you expected from a tough army ranger, who had to be more familiar with his rifle than a scrub brush. But pleasing nonetheless.

Clare joined him at the sink. Plucking the towel from his shoulder, she started to dry the dishes he'd stacked in the rack in the other half of the double sink.

It was when she picked up the first of the two coffee mugs she and Mark had used at breakfast that inspiration struck. The mugs were part of a set she had purchased from a potter last year at an outdoor art fair at Riverbend. *Ceramic* mugs. That memory, coupled with another memory from the past, gave her what she and Mark were looking for. Possibly.

"Mark, listen to me," she said. "I think I know where we can get the information we want about the amulets."

The excitement in her voice won his immediate attention. "Let's hear."

"To understand this, you need first of all to know that I earned my degree here in New Orleans at Tulane University."

He had withdrawn his hands from the sink in order to face her, ignoring the water he was dripping on the floor. "So what are you telling me?" he said, one of his eyebrows arched skeptically. "That we can research Afghan amulets in the library there?"

"Now don't get ahead of me. This is nothing to do with the university library. It has to do with a man who taught at Tulane before retiring. I believe he lived in the Garden District, and with any luck still does."

"Who?"

"Professor Duval. He was the head of the art department there. I had only one course from him in art history and wished I could have taken more, he was that impressive an instructor. But art history wasn't the field he specialized in. *Ceramics,* Mark. He's an authority on ceramics."

"I'm beginning to catch on," Mark said. Realizing he was shedding water on the floor, he helped himself to another towel and began to wipe his hands. "My amulet is a ceramic piece, as the others must be. And you think by examining mine this Duval could identify it, maybe even give us more than that?"

"It's worth trying."

"Let's go for it. You know how to reach him?"

"I don't have his number, but unless he's unlisted he

should be in the directory. Oh," she remembered, "my phone book is still in the apartment."

"You've got a laptop here, haven't you? Didn't I see it set up on a card table in the living room?"

"You did." She could access a New Orleans directory on the internet.

Recovering her cell phone from the counter, Clare headed for the living room with Mark behind her. It took her only a few moments after seating herself in front of the laptop to locate what she was searching for.

"Here it is. Etienne Duval, the only Duval whose address is in the Garden District."

Reaching for her phone, she called the number listed. It was answered after a few rings by a male voice a bit creaky with age but making up for that with a robust cheerfulness.

"Duval here."

"Professor, this is Clare Fuller. I don't suppose you remember me…"

"Ha, I never forget my students, especially the pretty ones. What can I do for you, Clare Fuller?"

She explained why she was calling.

"Sounds intriguing. Of course, I'll see you and that amulet. I'm free now. You know the address?"

She told him she did, thanked him and added before she rang off that they were practically on their way.

"We're in," she reported to Mark.

There was a grim look on Mark's face as the SUV carried them in the direction of the Garden District. She suspected that his mind was occupied with last night's bold invasion of her home and his promise to keep her close to him and safe.

It was why, out here in the open like this where they

could be a target, he kept checking his rearview mirror. She, too, was on the lookout for the blue sedan, but there was no evidence of it this morning.

"You don't need to be so worried, Mark. There's no sign of his following us."

"But he's out there somewhere waiting for another opportunity. I can almost feel him."

Like Mark must have sensed the enemy waiting to strike in places like Afghanistan, she thought. It wasn't just because he had been trained to that, either. It was his innate ability to perceive danger that made him the ranger he was.

There was no point in arguing with him about it. This role of protector was something he was determined to fulfill. She just wished he didn't have to be so intense about it.

Not until they reached the Garden District did Mark relax a bit. Maybe because this area of the city was too interesting to ignore.

"More streetcars," he said, eyeing one of the restored trolleys rumbling along the center of the broad thoroughfare that was St. Charles Avenue.

"They used to be more commonplace in New Orleans," she told him. "Now there are just enough of them to please the tourists."

"And, man, the houses!"

Clare knew what he meant. The homes here in the Garden District weren't just residences. They were grand mansions equal in splendor to the antebellum plantation houses along the River Road, and made even more imposing by some of the city's oldest live oak trees that surrounded them.

Playing tour guide again, she explained to him, "A

good many of them were built before the war by wealthy Creoles."

"I take it we're talking about the Civil War."

"Please, if you are a true native of the Deep South, you refer to it as The War Between the States."

Her correction won a chuckle out of him. "Are you a Creole descendant, teacher?"

"Sorry, I can't claim that distinction. But I'm willing to bet, from his name alone, that our Professor Etienne Duval can."

The professor's home, a dignified Greek Revival behind a waist-high iron fence, gave weight to her supposition when they turned into its driveway behind the house a few moments later.

The professor must have been watching for them, because he appeared almost instantly on the back porch, bounding down the steps like the young man he no longer was to welcome them as they exited the SUV. Whatever his heritage, there was nothing formal about the rotund little man. He greeted them with exuberance, pumping Mark's hand when Clare introduced him.

"I had the old carriage house converted into a potting studio," the professor said, indicating a handsome building toward the rear of the property. "Everything I might need to identify this amulet of yours is there."

He led them along a brick path and into the former carriage house where he switched on a battery of lights that revealed a spacious studio occupied from end to end with all the required implements of a potter. Among them, Clare was able to identify a potter's wheel, a massive kiln and open shelves along which were ranged a variety of ceramics in their raw state waiting to be fired.

Noticing her interest, the professor explained to her, "I've never lost my desire to have my hands in clay. Sell most of my pieces, too. A shop on Magazine Street carries them for me. But that isn't why you're here."

They followed him to a long work table.

"Now if I can have that amulet, Lieutenant."

Mark removed the amulet with its attached cord from around his neck and handed it to the professor, who turned it over in his hand.

"Afghan in origin, is it?"

"That's right."

Mark went on to tell him how he had come to own the talisman, what he had been told by the man who had gifted him with it and of the magic powers it allegedly possessed. None of which he believed himself, Mark hastened to add.

"Yes," the professor said, "I've heard the Afghans can be a very superstitious people. Well, let's see what this piece can tell us."

He turned on a gooseneck lamp positioned above a large, powerful-looking magnifying glass on a stand. Placing the amulet under the glass, he bent over the table and began to examine both sides of the wedge-shaped piece through the glass.

With a tension that, given their situation, Clare regarded as understandable, she and Mark waited for the professor's verdict. When at last he stood erect and turned to them, the amulet back in his hand, there was a grave expression on his round face.

"I'm afraid I have disappointing news for you, Lieutenant."

Chapter 13

"We're ready to hear whatever you have to tell us," Mark assured the professor.

"To begin with, this is not an old piece. Therefore, it has no value as an antique."

Mark exchanged looks with Clare. She knew from the what-did-I-tell-you expression on his face the message he was conveying to her: that all along he'd maintained the amulet was not a valuable antique.

"How can you tell?" Clare asked the professor.

"The buff-colored glaze alone indicates that. It has no age on it. There are other signs, but I needn't elaborate on them. Added together, they mean that this amulet was created using modern techniques and materials."

"How long ago?" Mark wanted to know.

"Difficult to say. I would estimate no more than twenty years, if that. That's as close as I can get without a lab analysis."

"There's more, isn't there?" Clare guessed.

The professor nodded. He turned to Mark with an apologetic "I'm sorry to say, Lieutenant, that your amulet isn't, in fact, an amulet at all."

"Then what is it?" Clare asked.

The older man shook his head. "Beyond being nothing more than a ceramic pendant, I have no idea. I've seen many amulets in my time, both new and old from various countries, but never anything like this. For one thing, the characters that were etched into both sides before the piece was fired are all wrong. Can you see what I mean?"

They moved in close to him, Clare on one side, Mark on the other, in order to have a better look at what he was indicating to them.

"They don't represent a language," he continued. "For want of a better definition, they're some kind of crude symbols. By themselves, they mean nothing. Possibly because they end so abruptly on both ends of the wedge."

"As if they were meant to go on from there," Mark surmised.

Clare had noticed this herself that first night when she had briefly inspected the piece after coming away with it from Mark's room at the Pelican Hotel.

"Exactly," Professor Duval said. "There's some evidence for that, too. Look here. Can you see how the rounded bottom of the wedge is smooth, but the edges of both ends are slightly rough? As if the wedge started out as part of a much larger piece and then at some point was cut away from that piece."

Leaving the rest to be divided into those other amulets? Clare asked herself. Or whatever they were meant to be, because all of this still remained a mystery.

"Let me illustrate for you what I think might have happened. Although, of course, it's only a theory."

Taking paper and pencil from a drawer, the professor placed the sheet on the table. He laid the wedge over it, with its pointed end facing up and its curved bottom facing down, and began to outline it with the pencil.

Clare and Mark watched in fascination as, once he had its shape on paper, he lined the wedge up against the side of his drawing and repeated the process. Moving onward from there, like a hand on a clock counting out the hours one by one, he ended up with the last outline exactly meeting the other side of the first one, with neither a gap nor an overlap. What he'd formed was the closed circle he must have visualized.

Was she the only one, Clare wondered, who saw it as a pie divided into five equal slices? The three of them gazed down at the drawing in silence. It was Professor Duval who roused himself first from his reverie.

"Your wedge could have started out as a disc like this, locked together with the others until they were cut apart from each other one by one."

"And if they were available to be fitted together again?" Mark asked him.

"Creating what was intended when whole, I suppose. Perhaps a meaningful pattern or design. That's entirely possible."

"Or," Clare suggested, "maybe a kind of code. Even, say, a picture map?"

The two men turned their heads to stare at her.

"Yes," the professor said, "that's a thought, too. But," he added, elevating his shoulders in a little shrug, "without the other wedges, there's no way of knowing. In any case, it makes for a highly interesting riddle. I just regret that I wasn't able to provide you with more information."

"No apology necessary, professor," Mark said, taking the pendant the older man handed to him and looping it back over his head. "You've given us new information, and we thank you for that."

Mark was quiet when they left the carriage house and climbed back into the SUV. She waited until they were driving away from Professor Duval's home to ask him the first of all the questions that were chasing through her mind.

"Are you disappointed your amulet isn't genuine?"

"Pendant," he corrected her.

Mark hadn't answered her question, though. He was silent again and remained silent until he pulled over to the curb on a side street, where there were no other vehicles in sight.

"Why are we parking here?"

"We need to talk, and I don't want to be distracted by a bunch of traffic."

A credible reason, she thought, but not his only one. She understood that when he failed to look at her. Instead, he checked the street both ahead of them and behind them.

He's making sure we're safe here, she realized. *That our mystery stalker hasn't managed to find us.* Which, after what they had learned from the professor, could very well mean Mark's pendant was far more valuable than an antique amulet.

Satisfied the street was deserted except for them, that there was no one else in evidence either in a blue sedan or on foot, he answered her question.

"No, I'm the one who insisted all along it was a fake, remember?"

"But the Afghan who wanted you to have it considered it was genuine."

"Because the cousin he inherited it from," he reminded her, "somehow communicated it was a powerful amulet and to always keep it safe."

"And if instead it's part of a code or a picture map..."

"Then it explains why the guy who's chasing it wants it so badly. Because, unless he's able to reassemble all of the pieces, mine included, then he probably has no way of reading the whole thing."

"There's something more, Mark. When Professor Duval divided that circle, there were *five* wedges."

"Yeah, I didn't miss that."

They were silent again, gazing at each other. Clare couldn't help noticing the scrape on his jaw and remembering how he had gotten it.

It maybe didn't make sense in this situation, but she experienced a strong urge to lean over and plant her mouth on it. She didn't. Not because she thought he would object to her sensual action. Knowing his sexual appetite, he would probably want to get intimate right there in the car. Or would have, if he didn't have the need to remain vigilant.

She didn't ask him about the injury. He wouldn't have welcomed that. Besides, it already seemed to be healing nicely.

There was something else, however, she couldn't ignore. Mark was slowly, maybe unconsciously rubbing the upper part of his leg where it had been wounded in Afghanistan.

"Is it aching again?"

"Like I told you the other day, it sometimes does

that. Nothing to worry about. Let's get back to the subject of the pendants and how we can account for there being five of them."

"Well, we're fairly certain because of the lanyards that both my brother-in-law and Malcolm Boerner each had one. And if our unknown killer already had one of his own before he went after Joe and Boerner, that, along with yours, makes four pendants."

"Unless one of the others had two of them, which would add up to five pendants. But somehow…"

"You don't think so," Clare pressed him.

"No, I don't. What I'm thinking, even if I don't have any solid reason for thinking it, is that there were five players in whatever this game is they were playing and that each of them was given a pendant. Mine we know I got from Ahmad, who inherited it from his deceased cousin. And if this cousin was the fourth player—"

"Then," she said, completing the thought for Mark, "there's a fifth pendant out there somewhere."

"Yeah, in the possession of someone who's as much a mystery as our unidentified killer. And if that suggestion of yours about a picture map or a code is at all accurate, the question is a map or code to what and where. We've still got a hell of a lot of missing pieces in this puzzle, Clare."

"But enough to go to the police now," she said anxiously. "You do agree with that, don't you?"

"Okay, we go to the cops."

Mark knew that Clare wouldn't be put off any longer in her quest to enlist the police to aid her in clearing her sister of the murder of her husband. But he was far from convinced they would seriously listen to them as she directed him to the department's headquarters on Broad Street, although he hoped for her sake they would.

The headquarters for the New Orleans police department turned out to be housed in a five-story, modern building. When compared to so many other structures in the historic city, Mark considered this one to be of no particular architectural merit. Not that it mattered.

Parking in an area reserved for visitors, they made their way into the ground floor lobby where two uniformed officers, both female, were on duty behind the reception desk. It was the elder of the two, an African American woman, who greeted them with a courteous smile.

Mark had decided this was Clare's scene more than his. He let her state their business.

"We'd like to see the homicide detective in charge of the Malcolm Boerner murder investigation. We believe we have information pertinent to the case."

"That would be Detective Myers," she was told. "Let me see if he's available."

The officer picked up a phone at her elbow. They waited while she explained their errand. Ending her call, she informed them, "He'll see you. I'll need your IDs before I can send you up."

Satisfied after examining their driver's licenses, she issued them visitor tags, which were to be clipped to their shirts.

"Homicide is on the third floor." She handed Clare a key card, instructing her, "This is to be inserted in the slot inside the elevator. It will only allow you to be carried to the third floor and back down again when you're ready to leave."

No question of the security in this place being as tight as the latest practices can make it, Mark thought.

Something that as a ranger he both understood and appreciated.

"Detective Myers will be waiting for you when you arrive," they were informed. "You use that elevator there."

Mark's reservations about this errand were emphasized a moment later when the elevator door rolled back on the third floor. He recognized the beefy man who confronted them. It was the stern-faced detective the reporter had tried to interview this morning on TV. He had the same bushy eyebrows that needed grooming and was chewing on another toothpick.

What's with the toothpicks? Mark wondered. Could be they were substitutes for cigarettes if the guy was trying to quit smoking.

"Detective Myers," he introduced himself. "And you?"

They gave him their names.

"All right, let's see what you've got for me." Wasting no time on pleasantries, Myers led them across a bullpen where other plainclothesmen were busy in their cubicles.

They ended up in an interview room. After shutting the door behind him, the detective pointed to a pair of chairs. Once Clare and Mark were seated in them, Myers settled his bulk on the other side of the table.

"I'll be recording our conversation," he said, indicating the machine in front of him. "It's standard practice in an investigation."

"Understood," Clare said.

She was smiling. Mark wasn't. He had yet to decide whether Myers was going to be on their side or not.

There was one thing he was sure about. He wasn't impressed by this guy, even if he had finally gotten rid of the toothpick.

The detective started the recorder, stated his name and the purpose for the interview, paused for a second to consult the clock on the wall, told the recorder the time and went on to give Clare and Mark's names.

The essentials fed into the machine, Myers continued with a brisk "Now what is it you have to tell me?"

"It's complicated," Clare warned him. "If I could start from the beginning…"

Having already decided downstairs this was more Clare's story than his, Mark was prepared to let her do all the talking.

"I'm here to listen to you," the detective said. "Take your time."

Clare nodded and plunged into her lengthy account, describing her involvement with Malcolm Boerner and her vital reason for it, the devil's bargain she'd made with the shopkeeper to secure the amulet he wanted in exchange for the surveillance tape she needed to prove her sister's innocence and how and why Lieutenant Griggs had allied himself with her.

Mark watched Myers. At the onset of the interview, the guy hunched forward over the humming recorder, paying close attention, interrupting only occasionally to ask Clare for a clarification or to expand on a detail.

Gradually, though, the detective's mood changed. Mark could tell from the way he sat back, looking restless, that Myers regretted having invited Clare to take her time. Long before she finished her story with their visit to Professor Duval and the reason for it, Myers was nothing but impatient.

"In other words," he said curtly, "you have no factual information about the murder of Malcolm Boerner."

"Not exactly, no, but my sister and her husband's murder—"

The detective held up his hand. "That's for the police up in St. Boniface to handle. And as far as I can see, it has no connection with Boerner's death, other than your theory about it."

Which he considers verging on the crackpot, Mark thought. The man was a close-minded ass.

"All I want to know," Myers demanded, "is if either one or both of you were on the scene of Boerner's murder either before or after it happened? Or whether you actually witnessed anything that could help us solve this case?"

Mark could no longer contain his anger. "She told you earlier we didn't." That wasn't true, of course. They *had* been in Boerner's apartment, had discovered his body. But admitting that wouldn't help the police when they'd seen nothing useful. It could only get them in trouble, maybe even charged, and right now they needed to remain free.

"Look," Myers said, leaning forward again and looking like he could use a fresh toothpick in his mouth, "this business about a lot of wedges and a phantom killer who's after them…well, it's pretty fantastic stuff. In fact, if you ask me, it's downright farfetched. The reality is what we're working on now. That Boerner was in the business of selling guns, and a trade like that can be a motive for murder."

He switched off the recorder, a signal that the interview had been concluded. But Clare wasn't ready to let it rest there.

"All right, so you don't buy any of our solutions. But

the surveillance tapes *are* a reality. You can at least tell me whether you found any of them either in the Boerner apartment or his shop."

"Yeah, we found them," he admitted reluctantly.

"And the one that will prove my sister was in his shop at the time her husband was murdered?"

"The lab hasn't had time to examine all of them. But I can tell you this. They're not promising where results are concerned."

"Why?"

"Because the two tapes they did test had been erased. Now if something should turn up where your sister is concerned, we'll let the police in St. Boniface know."

Myers conducted them back to the elevator where, before parting from them, he issued a warning.

"You folks need to stop playing detective. That's strictly the business of the police. Understand? Oh, and thanks for coming in."

He might just as well have added: *Now buzz off.*

Mark could feel the hands down at his sides curling into fists. It would have been so tempting to pop him one, except that would have landed him in a cell leaving Clare unprotected.

She waited until they were outside the building before she expressed her own frustration with a disgusted, "He wasn't willing to seriously consider any of it! Not a single, damn word!"

"Yeah, it makes you wonder what the homicide division up there was thinking to put a guy like that in charge of the case. *Any* case."

"This was no better than the police in St. Boniface unwilling to be convinced that it might have been someone other than Terry who killed Joe."

Mark could see she was trembling with barely restrained outrage. She was in need of an antidote, and
he was ready to provide it.

"C'mere," he said, holding out his arms. She went
into them without hesitation.

Folding his arms around her, Mark rocked her gently,
murmuring some soothing sounds that didn't make
sense even to him. But they worked. After a moment
she was quiet.

Comfort, he knew, was rapidly morphing into something else. It would have been so easy to use this opportunity to kiss her. And so very satisfying, even out
here in the open like this. But there was a definite risk
in that. Not just because he needed to remain alert to
any external danger. There was the internal danger of
breaking his promise to himself not to get intimate with
her again. Of hurting her when the time came for them
to part.

Oh, hell, this was all such a complicated mess. Not
straightforward like the army, where he knew what was
right and what wasn't.

Maybe Clare felt that same risk, and that's why she
left his arms and moved back a safe step. She looked up
at him, discouragement written on her face.

"We're right back to where we started, aren't we?"

"Not true. We've collected a lot of information since
then. Information we trust, even if that fool upstairs
doesn't."

"But none of it proves Terry's innocence."

"Let's get you back home where we can work on it."

*Mark isn't ready to give up, whatever Detective My-
ers's caution to us,* Clare thought.

And neither should you.

Ashamed of her momentary weakness, she resolved she wasn't going to surrender. She just wished she had some idea where they could possibly go from here.

Nothing had occurred to her by the time they pulled up in front of her house. Mark had maintained a lookout all the way to the shotgun and now wanted to make certain the inside was still secure.

"You wait here while I check the rooms," he instructed her, leaving her just inside the front door.

He was gone before she could argue with him about it. In minutes he was back to report that everything was safe.

She didn't need to ask him why he suggested then they go out to the patio. She could already guess. He wanted to move her to a cheerful scene. It was scary how well she knew him after only a couple of days, she realized as she followed him to the back of the house. Even more scary was not just how much she had come to count on his being at her side but how much she relished his company.

They were on the patio, Clare gazing at her flowers without really seeing them when Mark said an encouraging, "You know, Clare, there's still the hope of that security tape turning up and not being erased like the others. Why would Boerner have erased it when he'd agreed to trade it for the pendant?"

"Yes, that is still our best chance."

She was far from counting on it, though. Even so, she loved Mark for doing his best to raise her spirits like this.

Loved?

No, that wasn't the right word. It wasn't at all what she meant. Not in the literal sense. What she intended was—

She got no further. The cell phone inside her purse began to chirp, announcing an incoming call.

Chapter 14

Maybe her school, Clare thought, digging the phone out of her purse. She had promised to let them know how much longer she would need to be gone. With everything that had been happening, it had completely slipped her mind.

But the call wasn't from her school.

"Clare, it's me."

Terry. It was Terry, and there was a tension in her sister's voice that immediately alarmed her.

"Terry, what's wrong? Are you all right?"

"I'm fine. I have something to tell you. It's important, so I need you to listen because I've only got a couple of minutes to explain it. There's just one line here prisoners are allowed to use, and there's someone else waiting her turn."

Clare was aware of an alert Mark watching her. Silently mouthing her sister's name, she beckoned him to her side. He joined her without hesitation. She transferred the phone to her other ear as a signal that she wanted him to listen in. Understanding, he lowered his head to her level, putting his ear close to the phone.

"Clare, are you still there?"

"Yes, I'm listening. Go ahead."

"Do you remember when you visited me yesterday," Terry went on hurriedly, "my telling you I had my lawyer bring in the stack of mail that had been piling up at home? That I needed to sort through it in order to learn what bills had to be paid?"

"I remember."

"Well, I went through the stack this morning. There was a letter addressed to Joe that had gotten caught inside a sale catalog. Or maybe he tucked it there after he read it. I would have missed it if it hadn't fallen out when the pile slipped off my lap. The police must have gone through that stack when they were at the house and overlooked the letter, because they certainly would have confiscated it otherwise."

"Terry, who was the letter from? What did it say?"

"It's too complicated to tell you over the phone. *And too private.*" Her voice had lowered to a whisper Clare strained to hear, making her guess the other prisoner was close by.

"You'll see for yourself. I gave the letter to my lawyer, and she promised to email the contents to you. It could be waiting on your laptop right now."

"But what—"

"I thought after all you and your lieutenant told me," Terry interrupted her, "you would know what to do with it. I suppose I rightly should have turned it over to the police here, but after the way they've been..."

"You did right in giving it to us," Clare assured her.

It was a reckless thing for her to say when she had yet to learn what this letter contained. All she knew was it had to be somehow connected with the murder charge leveled against her sister, and that was enough.

"Is he there with you?" Terry asked her.

"Yes, he's right here."

There was a pause at the other end. Clare sensed that Terry, worried about her relationship with Mark, would have liked to ask her more. In the end, all she said was a rapid "I have to go. I hope the letter helps. Take care of yourself."

She was gone before Clare could promise her anything.

In the silence that followed, Clare and Mark stared at each other with anticipation. It was a silence that lasted only a few seconds before both of them simultaneously expressed the same call for action.

"Your laptop."

"My laptop."

It was all they needed to send the two of them speeding toward the living room and Clare's computer. Excited with the hope that this mysterious letter *was* waiting for her and that whatever it contained would help them to clear Terry, she seated herself in front of her laptop and opened her email program.

"It's here!" she announced to Mark, who stood close behind her.

"I can't read the damn thing from this angle," he complained.

"I'll read it aloud for both of us." She could tell even before scrolling down that the letter was not a brief one. "There's a heading with a name and address. Someone called Hank Kolchek."

"You know the name?"

"I don't think so. No, I'm sure I don't. It's from Florida. A town called Muretta."

"Never heard of the place. It can't be very big."

"The street address is 130 Coral Drive. There's a phone number, too."

"Save that for later. Let's get on with the content," he urged.

"He has a greeting. *Dear Comrade*. Comrade? Mark, do you suppose this Kolchek is one of the mercenaries Joe and Malcolm Boerner served with in Afghanistan all those years ago? If it is, then he must be the one who has that fifth pendant we haven't accounted for—"

"We'll never know unless you move on."

"Right. This is what it says. 'I'm sending this same letter to the three of you here in the States. Don't know your email addresses or even if you have them. It's been too many years since we've been in any regular contact. But I was able to verify by internet that your mailing addresses are current ones, which explains my writing to you by snail mail. That and because I trust this method over email that in my opinion isn't always reliably safe or private.'"

Clare paused again with another realization. "*Three* letters, Mark. One to Joe, one to Malcolm Boerner and the third..."

"Yeah, had to be to our unknown stalker. Too bad Hank doesn't name him. When do we get to the good stuff?"

"Coming up next, I hope. Yes, here it is." Clare resumed reading. "'I don't know how closely you boys have been following what's been happening in Afghanistan, but in case you've missed it, the latest is that the Taliban have been cleared out of a certain mountain stronghold. I don't need to name it. You all know what I'm talking about.'"

"We don't," Mark said, "but I think it's safe for us to say this has something to do with the five pendants. A *lot* of something."

Clare had no reason to argue with that. She was more than ready to agree with Mark as she read on. "'None of us ever expected we would have to wait all these years to go back, but the waiting is over. We can safely return to that mountain. And because we chose our spot so well, there's no reason for all of it not to still be there waiting for us.'"

Clare broke off again. "The pendants, Mark! He's coming up to the pendants now! We were right!"

"Let's hear it."

"'There's one problem,'" she continued. "'Our man in Kabul is no longer with us. When I tried to reach him by phone to let him know we'd be coming over, I learned he had died. I don't need to tell you how vital his own pendant is to our recovery operation.'"

"*My* pendant now," Mark said.

"There's more. He goes on to say, 'But I was able to track it down. I found out he left the pendant to a cousin. Told him it was a valuable amulet and to keep it safe. The thing is, this illiterate cousin went and hung it around the neck of an army ranger, who was wounded protecting his son. I got his name. Lieutenant Mark Griggs.'"

"And that," Mark said, "is how Malcolm Boerner knew I had the phony amulet."

"Also that you'd been returned stateside. That comes—" she found her place on the screen "—here. 'The lieutenant was sent home to recover. With a little digging we should be able to locate him. Whether we can persuade him to give up the pendant…well, that's something else.'"

"Yeah," Mark said, "only Boerner went and beat him to it. The locating part, anyway."

"Along with his partner," Clare added. "Assuming our killer was his partner, that is."

"Right. The nameless whoever in this whole business. What else does Kolchek have to say?"

Clare went on with the rest of the letter. "'I think at this point the four of us need to get together and make some plans. Let me know where and when you'd like to meet, and I'll arrange something.'"

"Is that all?" Mark asked.

"No, there's one paragraph left, and I wish I knew what it meant."

"What is it?"

"Listen. 'I don't know about the rest of you, my friends, but I've moved on with my life since we last saw one another. I'm not the man I once was. Which is why, before I end this, I'd like to tell you that I'm going to propose something. I won't go into it here. It needs to wait until we meet. All I'll say is that I hope you'll agree to it. I think it's the right thing for us to do. If you feel otherwise, I'll understand. Either way, though, it's what I intend to do myself.'"

"And that's it? No other explanation?"

Clare shook her head. "It ends there with his…well, I suppose in the actual letter it would be his signature."

"That lack of an explanation has got to have confused the three of them on this end when they read it."

"Maybe not entirely, Mark. Maybe, with what they knew already, they were able to guess."

"Yeah, the information we lack ourselves, because he sure was as careful as hell not to go into specifics.

Could be he was afraid those letters might end up being read by the wrong people."

"But there's enough here for us to act on it. Something of real substance at last."

"You're thinking to go back to the cops with this."

Clare twisted around in her chair to look up at him. "Why not? This letter is proof the other pendants aren't just our imagination. That they're real and so valuable Joe and Boerner were murdered for them."

"It's not enough. Myers is too damn narrow-minded to listen again to what he considers a couple of cranks."

"Then we approach another detective in the homicide division."

"No good. With Myers in charge of the case, no other detective would risk it. And from what you've said about the cops up in St. Boniface, they won't touch it, either. You know what all of them will think, don't you? That this letter is a fiction, something we've concocted to clear your sister."

At this maddening moment, as much as Lieutenant Mark Griggs had come to mean to her, and that was more than was healthy for her, Clare could have smacked him. "Then what would be enough?" she challenged him.

"Hank Kolchek himself. He's all we've got left."

All we've got left. And the man was waiting down there in Florida for responses to his letter that would never come. It was a thought that saddened Clare.

It did, that is, until another thought suddenly occurred to her. A chilling one this time. "Oh, Mark, what if the killer got to Hank Kolchek first before he went after Joe and Boerner? He could be dead already."

"Yeah, that's a possibility. But not a certainty. If he is still alive, he should be told what's been happening here. Warned he's in danger. I'm going to try calling him. What's that number?"

"Wait. I'll print out a copy of the letter for you. We should have one anyway."

By the time she lifted the sheet from the printer, Mark had his own cell phone in hand. She held the copy for him while he read the number in the heading, watched as he punched in the digits and waited, knowing the result before he told her.

"No answer?"

"No answer. And no answering machine picking up, either."

"Not everyone has an answering machine. Maybe he's just not at home. I mean, if he has a job somewhere…"

"Could be that. Could be a lot of things. Or…"

He didn't say it, but Clare sensed they were both thinking the same thing. That Hank Kolchek was unable to answer his phone. Would never answer it again.

She went on looking at Mark. He had a frown on his face now. He kept passing his phone from hand to hand, as if he were playing with a baseball. It took him a moment or two before he made up his mind.

"I'm going to call the police in this—" he paused to consult the heading in the copy of the letter Clare was still holding "—Muretta. See if they can tell us anything. Do you think you can find the number for me?"

"If the town has an online phone directory," she said, swinging around to face her laptop again.

A brief search yielded both Muretta's directory and the number of the local police department. She read the number out to Mark. Although she listened attentively while he made the connection and spoke to whoever answered on the other end, she wasn't able to understand much of what, for her, was a one-sided conversation. It wasn't until Mark finally ended the call that he was able to satisfy her curiosity, which by now had deepened into a state of anxiety.

"The town must be a small one like I figured since it was Muretta's chief of police I spoke to. A friendly guy who's willing to do whatever he can to help us. Unlike the cops here and up in St. Boniface."

Clare didn't consider that a fair judgment of the New Orleans police force just because they'd had one bad experience with Detective Myers. "You're forgetting Officer Martinez last night and how he went out of his way for us," she reminded him.

"I stand corrected. As for St. Boniface—"

"Yes. Well, they would be biased when Joe Riconi was one of their own."

"Do you want to hear what I learned, or are you going to keep on interrupting?"

"Sorry."

Muttering something about her being overly sensitive where the subject of New Orleans was concerned, which she chose to ignore, Mark proceeded to give her the essentials.

"The chief didn't know about the murders of Boerner and your brother-in-law. The news wasn't major enough to reach that far, I guess. As for Hank Kolchek, he's heard the name but hasn't had any personal contact with him. He thinks Kolchek and his wife moved to Muretta from Orlando not long ago."

"What else?"

"He's promised to send his deputy out to the Kolchek house to check on the situation. As soon as the deputy reports in, he'll call me back."

"So we wait."

"We wait."

Clare put her laptop to sleep, looked at her watch and got to her feet. "It's almost noon. Would you like lunch? I think I can manage sandwiches."

Mark shook his head. "Maybe just some coffee."

That was totally unexpected. Since when did he not have an appetite? Probably, she decided, because he couldn't think of anything but getting that return call from Muretta. Which had to be why his hands were shoved into his pockets while he rocked back and forth on his heels. A restless reaction that by now was familiar to her.

He followed her into the kitchen where she started a fresh pot of coffee. She expected him to get out mugs and set them on the breakfast bar, as he'd done earlier, but he seemed unmindful of that necessity. She wished he would at least settle on one of the stools. He was making her nervous, wandering as he was around the kitchen.

He's still thinking about that call, she thought, and what might be happening down there in Florida.

Clare switched on the TV, hoping the twelve o'clock news would report some recent development on the Boerner murder. There was no mention of the case. The station seemed to be more interested in telling its viewers of a heat wave moving into the southeastern area of the country. Louisiana's residents could expect high temperatures for the next several days.

"Mark."

"Huh?"

"Mugs, please. The coffee is just about ready."

"Okay."

He obliged her this time by placing two mugs on

the breakfast bar. To her relief, he finally perched on a stool, his cell phone in front of him.

Clare poured the coffee, turned off the TV and joined him on the other side of the bar. They sipped their coffee in silence. The only sound in the kitchen was the soft tattoo of Mark's fingers tapping on his cell phone case, as if his action would hurry the call.

Were he and his fellow rangers like this before going into combat? she wondered. All taut and impatient for the signal to strike?

She was beginning to share that feeling when his phone finally rang. Scooping it up, he flipped it open and held it to his ear.

"Griggs here."

He listened without comment except for an occasional "Uh-huh." In the end, he thanked what she assumed was Muretta's chief of police and snapped the phone shut.

Clare leaned toward him, as eager now as he had been to hear the report. "What did he say?"

"Not a whole lot. His deputy called in to tell him there was no sign of foul play at the Kolchek house, recent or past. The place was locked up tight and the car gone from the port. The deputy talked to the neighbors on both sides, but they hadn't heard or seen anything suspicious and didn't seem to know much about the couple."

"Well, if they're new to the neighborhood, that's understandable."

"Either that, or they had a reason to keep to themselves. Whatever the explanation, I don't think we can expect anything more out of the police down there. Without something more to go on, the chief has gone as far as he can for us."

"You know, Mark, even if he didn't hear about the murders, it's possible that the Kolcheks did and cleared out. That wherever they are, they're safe."

"Could be."

But Clare didn't think he was ready to buy that easy explanation. Leaving his coffee to grow cold, he got up and began to pace again.

"What is it that's got you so wired now?" she wanted to know.

"I don't like it. Something is happening down there, or about to happen. Something bad. I can feel it in my gut." He was quiet for a few seconds, and when he spoke to her again there was a tone of sudden urgency in his voice. "I think we should go down there ourselves."

"You're serious."

"Yeah, I am."

"Why? What could we do?"

"Try to find Hank Kolchek."

It struck her as a rash proposal. On the other hand, if Hank Kolchek wasn't yet aware of the danger to him from a former comrade, a killer who seemed to want it all for himself, whatever that *all* was, then he should be warned. Also, she and Mark needed whatever information Kolchek could provide them in order to save Terry from a prison sentence. It was this in the end that convinced her.

"It's kind of extreme, but I can see the necessity of it."

"Good. You do whatever you have to do while I see if I can get us on a flight to Florida."

Clare left him in the kitchen with his cell phone and the travel section of *The Times-Picayune* that would provide him with the airline numbers. She went back to the living room where she had left her purse. Producing her own cell phone, she called her school. The office secretary who answered was able to put Clare's principal on the line.

She was a sympathetic woman who never failed to understand the family emergencies of her faculty. In this case, it was Clare's request to delay her return to the classroom. "You take whatever time you need. Your sub has got everything under control here," she assured her.

Clare missed her kids, but Terry was a priority.

"Any luck?" she asked Mark when she rejoined him in the kitchen.

"Afraid not. It turns out the nearest airport to Muretta is Orlando. There are two airlines from New Orleans that serve it. The first one I tried has a flight out later this afternoon, but it's already booked full. The second airline doesn't have an Orlando flight until tomorrow morning."

She knew that Mark would never be able to stand that kind of wait. It didn't surprise her he already had another plan.

"Look," he said, "we've got most of the day left."

"Well, a lot of it anyway."

"I say we drive to Muretta, travel through the night if we have to. We'd probably get there sooner than if we flew, especially when you figure we'd have the delay of hiring a rental car in Orlando. It must be interstate just about all the way, isn't it?"

"I think so." Maybe. Clare wasn't certain of that.

"There you go."

She knew that Mark wasn't going to be argued out of this one. She didn't try.

"I'm going out to the car and bringing up a map of the area we're headed on my GPS."

He started toward the front door. Clare trailed him as

far as her bedroom where she knew a change of clothing for the trip, which at this point was no longer questionable, was in order. With a heat wave threatening the whole southeast, she chose a pair of white shorts accompanied by a blue-and-white-striped T and tennies.

When Mark reappeared with the map in hand, he found her packing a bag with her toiletries and a few other practical garments.

"You all set?" he asked her.

"I'm good to go," she said, zipping the bag shut.

Since she knew he had never unpacked his own luggage, it was only a matter of carrying their things out to the SUV and making sure the house was securely locked behind them.

Clare directed him through the city traffic, across Lake Pontchartrain and east into Mississippi.

She hoped as they sped along the interstate that Hank Kolchek hadn't already suffered the same murderous end as Joe Riconi and Malcolm Boerner. That they would reach him in time to prevent that. Providing, that is, they could even find him.

Chapter 15

He's saving me for last.

There was no real evidence of that, but the indications were there. The bastard had been unable to steal his pendant from him last night. Unlike Riconi and Boerner, Mark had been ready for him. Nor had there been any sign of the blue sedan today, either in New Orleans or here on the interstate. Could be he'd replaced it with another car.

Where was he? Mark wondered. Already in Florida and hunting for Hank Kolchek? Would he get to Kolchek before he and Clare could reach him? Do whatever he was prepared to do to take Kolchek's pendant away from him? And then turn his attention back to Mark, where this time...

Yeah, he's saving me for last.

But he would find Mark no easier a target the next time than he had been last night.

What was on that mountain in Afghanistan, Mark wondered, worth so much this twisted SOB was willing to commit multiple murders to get it all for himself?

"I'm hungry," Clare announced. "We did miss lunch, you know."

"I guess I could eat something myself."

"Really? That famous appetite of yours has finally kicked in again, has it?"

"Seems like it."

They left the interstate at the next exit, stopping at the nearest fast food restaurant for a quick meal. Mark remained as watchful there as he did once they were back on the highway, still alert for any sign that they were being followed. Even though he'd convinced himself their stalker was far away now, he didn't want the risk of any surprises.

Paying attention to both that and the traffic wasn't easy. Not with Clare sitting there beside him in those shorts. He found himself stealing glances at her long, shapely bare legs. Visualizing them wrapped around... well, doing things he had no business imagining her doing with him.

It should have been safer for him to lift his gaze and keep it there. But that was no better. Now when he snatched those glances in her direction he kept thinking about her honey-blond hair, wishing she would take it down from that damn ponytail. That he could see it loose and sexy as she'd worn it that night in the Penguin Hotel bar. That he could sift his fingers through its silky waves.

Hell, Griggs, keep your mind on the road, will you?

He managed to do that, but it wasn't much of an improvement. How could it be when he was aware of her subtle, seductive scent assaulting his senses.

Face it, even when they were actively engaged in dealing with an enemy, this thing that was between them continued to simmer just below the surface. Longing for what they could experience on a bed or in a shower stall.

It wasn't until an innocent diversion captured his attention that Mark found relief. Clare was singing "Danny Boy" softly to herself.

"You're doing it."

She turned her head to stare at him. "Doing what?"

"That habit you told me about. Getting a song in your head and driving everyone around you nuts by singing it over and over. Everyone in this case being me."

"I'm sorry. Half the time I'm not even aware I'm doing it."

"Wouldn't be so bad if…"

"What?"

"Hate to tell you, sweetheart, but you don't have a singing voice."

"Well, thanks."

Mark chuckled. He couldn't help it. He loved teasing her like this. And so far, with everything they had been sharing being so intense, there hadn't been many opportunities for that.

"You know," she said, "the view outside this window isn't exactly stimulating. I had to do something to entertain myself. Besides helping you to look for a blue sedan that isn't there."

He could understand that. The flat terrain of the Gulf Coast was pretty monotonous. "I could put on a CD or play the radio," he suggested.

"Bad idea. I'd just get another song into my head."

He noticed she was the one now wearing a playful smile.

"Tell you what," she said. "Suppose you keep me occupied yourself by telling me about Amber and Valerie. I haven't forgotten how you talked about those hot babes in your sleep. And this time I want the truth."

"The truth, huh? Nothing omitted?"

"That's right."

"Okay," he drawled, "here it is. Valerie is my grandmother's age. They play canasta together back in Tennessee. That's about as hot as it gets."

"And Amber?"

"Valerie's eighteen-year-old granddaughter."

"Ah, more interesting."

"Not if it's someone too young for you wanting to play around every time you're home on leave. Why do you think I take off on fishing holidays?"

"Poor you."

Where entertainment was concerned, Mark would have preferred something far more intimate that wasn't situated in a car rolling along an interstate. But this light bantering had its own appeal.

There was something else that made him happy. They were making good time on a clear road. He shouldn't have congratulated himself about it, though. Mississippi was fine. Alabama wasn't. Getting around Mobile alone was a real headache. It involved a heavy rush hour traffic and long delays complicated by highway construction. The sun was setting behind them by the time they crossed the Florida state line. Mark managed to get them past Pensacola before he and the SUV finally reached their limit.

"The car needs a fill-up," he announced, "and I'm hungry."

They stopped at a gas station with an adjacent fast food restaurant. Mark fed the SUV at one of the pumps.

Then he and Clare fed themselves in the restaurant with another quick meal.

"Do you think you could take the wheel for a while?" he asked her when she emerged from the bathroom.

"Your leg is bothering you again, isn't it?"

"A little," he admitted. "It was all that stop-and-go in the construction areas."

"I'm a very good driver. You should have let me take my turn at the wheel back in Alabama."

They had stopped seriously searching for their pursuer long ago. Nor, now that night had closed in, was there any use in trying to look for signs of him. Still, once they were belted in, Mark felt the need to caution her.

"Keep a sharp watch behind you, huh? Let me know if any vehicle back there gets too close."

"Will do, Lieutenant."

They were only a few minutes on the road again when Clare realized it wasn't just his leg that had motivated him to surrender the SUV to her. He was clearly exhausted. Otherwise, he wouldn't have let himself doze off as he did.

The glow of the lights on the instrument panel was sufficient enough to allow her glimpses of him. He was slumped down in a corner of the passenger seat as low as his seat belt would permit, his legs stretched out in front of him.

Long and thick with muscles, they were legs to be admired. But that was true of his whole form from head to feet. All of him tantalizingly masculine, even the scent of him. So much so that she found herself aching to touch him.

This isn't good, Clare. Haven't we been through this

before? You're tormenting yourself with something you shouldn't want. Can't afford to repeat.

Her sharp self-warning was all she needed to rivet her attention back on the highway. She kept it there.

There were few cars now and, mercifully, no more construction zones. But there was no shortage of trucks, many of them massive eighteen-wheelers. She guessed they would travel through the night. Those in the other two lanes headed west probably had big city destinations like New Orleans and Houston.

Their oncoming lights in the darkness had a hypnotic effect. She had to be careful about that, make a concentrated effort to stay awake. Maybe the radio.

Keeping the volume low to avoid disturbing Mark, she found a station with easy listening music. It helped. At least it did until they were approaching the vicinity of Tallahassee.

Clare had no awareness of the drowsiness that crept up on her. The SUV must have started to drift to the right. The next thing she knew the wheels on that side were off the pavement and on the gravel of the shoulder.

Jerked suddenly, fearfully awake by the sensation, her foot instantly tapped the brake, slowing them to a crawl before she eased the SUV fully off the highway and came to a safe stop on the shoulder, sliding the gear into Park. She had just narrowly avoided what could have been a disaster, and the realization of that had her trembling.

Their halt had Mark sitting up on the passenger seat, alert and alarmed. "Why have we stopped out here along the road? What's happened?"

"*I* happened." She explained the situation to him, adding an embarrassed apology.

"You should have called me, had me take back the

wheel. We better change places now before someone plows into us. Where are we, anyway?"

"Coming up on Tallahassee. Mark, this driving straight through is no good. We're both tired, and Muretta is still a long way off. We don't want to risk what the next time could be a serious accident."

He thought about it for a moment. "Yeah, I guess you're right. We'll find a motel and check in."

They proceeded to the next exit, with Mark back at the wheel. There was a motel just off the ramp. Negotiating the frontage road, he swung into the parking lot and drew up before the lighted office.

Clare put a hand on his arm as he started to slide out from behind the wheel. "Mark, when we register, let's make sure we get a double, huh?"

He turned his head to look at her. "What are you saying? That you don't want us to share the same bed?"

This was awkward. But necessary she felt. "It makes sense, doesn't it? I mean, it's sleep we both need, not… well, you know."

"Sure, no sex. Agreed."

He was quick about that. But he must have seen it was for the best. That, whatever the temptation, and she couldn't deny it was there, not after the sexual tension that had thrummed between them all day, giving into it with both of them so tired would be a mistake.

There was an added reason for her resistance. Did Mark perceive it? Understand that she worried about making love with him again? Feared, as she had those other times, it would only lead to an eventual heartache?

She didn't know, but they didn't speak of it again. They went into the office, secured the accommodation they asked for and carried their bags toward the room they were assigned.

If she wasn't conscious of it before, she was now. The night was hot and humid. Not a breath of air stirred. It was the kind of sultry evening that made you think of forbidden things. Not a helpful analogy under the circumstances.

Mark unlocked the door, turned on one of the lights and stepped aside, allowing her to precede him into the room. She lowered her bag and stood there, welcoming the coolness of a droning air-conditioner. She heard Mark behind her relocking the door and fixing the chain. When she turned around, she found him leaning back against the door.

They hadn't exchanged a word since leaving the office. The silence between them remained uninterrupted. They simply stood there gazing at each other.

How long? Seconds, minutes? Whatever the length, in the end a kind of madness seized both of them at the same time. A recklessness ignoring all reason and which suddenly had them locked in a fierce embrace.

Clare didn't know who had crossed the room to reach the other, or whether it had been a simultaneous action. Nor had she a memory of any further restraint on her part.

Whatever their fatigue, it was gone now, as if it had never existed. There was nothing but this wild energy driving them. Nothing that mattered but his arms around her, his mouth on hers in an urgent kiss that she answered with a series of little moans from deep inside her.

His tongue plunging inside her mouth stopped those moans as he probed and searched, unwilling to be satisfied until his tongue was mating with her own. She tasted the male flavor of him with pleasure, inhaling it along with his distinctive scent.

How he managed not to break their connection as he backed her toward one of the beds she didn't bother to question. Only briefly did his mouth lift from hers when she fell across the bed. Fell across it with Mark on top of her, his weight pinning her down, his assertive mouth finding hers again in another deep, searing kiss.

It was at the same time too much and not enough. Because in the end what she wanted was something that demanded the complete removal of their clothes. Squirming underneath him, pushing at him, she finally won his release.

"Wait," she whispered, fighting for air.

Elevated above her now, his dark eyes smoldered with a desire that was in no mood for any control. "What?" he rasped. "If you want me to stop, I have to warn you you're going to have one frustrated mess of a guy on your—"

"Never. I don't want that. Our clothes—"

Understanding her then, he rolled away from her, sat up and began to tear at his shirt. On her own side of the bed, Clare clawed away her shoes, her shorts and T, following them with her bra and panties. Before they were done, the floor was littered with their discarded garments, the spread on the bed ripped off and flung on top of them in their frantic haste.

When they met again on the bed, it was as naked as they were, the sheets cool, their bodies hot. There was no lingering kiss this time, only Mark's mouth brushing quickly across hers before descending to her breasts.

She whimpered when his tongue found one of her rigid buds. A whimper that was all the instruction he needed. Complying, his wet tongue swirled around that peak before moving on to the other nipple. Not content, his mouth closed on each breast in turn, suckling them strongly until her whole body was writhing beneath his with a yearning she was too inflamed by then to comprehend on any clear level.

But Mark understood. Deserting her breasts, his mouth traveled downward, feathering kisses like light caresses over the quivering flesh of her belly. When he reached his destination, his attention centered on the mound between her legs, his fingers carefully parting the folds to the core of her womanhood.

His eager tongue was less gentle as it settled on the nub inside those petals. Clare knew then what she wanted. Experienced it with a silent, primal cry for release as, hands steadying her, that marauding tongue worked its magic. In the end her cry was not a silent one. It was torn from her, her hips lifting off the bed in a blinding orgasm.

Easing himself up alongside her, Mark held her until her spasms ceased. During the moment she rested in his arms, she realized they were not finished. He demonstrated that when he swung away from her, reaching for his wallet where he had deposited it on the bedside table.

When had he managed that? All she could recall was their feverish rush to get out of their clothes. She watched him extract a condom from somewhere in the depths of the wallet. "Pretty sure of yourself, weren't you?" she teased him.

"Hopeful. Only hopeful."

"Isn't that what teenage boys do? Carry condoms in their wallets with the hope of scoring?"

"Too far back for me to remember."

"Uh-huh."

He grinned and started to slit the foil wrapping. She put a hand on his arm to stop him.

"Not yet. When we're ready, I'd like to do the honors. In fact…"

"You have something in mind?"

"I do. I want to be on top."

"Hmm, seems like the last time you were in that position I ended up being handcuffed to a headboard."

"I promise you a much more satisfying performance this time," she purred.

He handed her the condom, his grin widening as he lay back down on the bed. "Looks like I'm a willing victim all over again. Perform away then."

Lifting herself above him on her knees, she straddled his legs. "Just look at you," she crooned.

And she did, admiring the length of him in his full nudity. Something she hadn't either enough leisure or enough light to properly enjoy until now. He was a superb sight, all sinewy, powerful male from his shoulders to his chest to his narrow hips.

"Take down your hair for me," he said, his voice gruff.

She accommodated him, lifting one hand to the back of her head, removing the hair tie there and shaking the strands loose.

He didn't have to tell her how much the sight of her hair tumbling to her shoulders turned him on. She could see it expressed in the gleam of ardor in his eyes. It was even more evident by the way that ridge of flesh above his thighs swelled to a greater hardness. An arousal that was in no condition to suffer a further delay.

Opening the packet and casting aside the wrapping, Clare leaned over him and began to roll the condom down his rigid shaft.

"If you go on being slow about it like that," he

warned her, "I'm not going to be responsible for any premature result."

She got the message. He couldn't wait. Nor did he have to. She quickened the act of sheathing him. Positioning herself over that now pulsing column, she introduced it into the opening of the vessel he was so eager to fill.

Clare took her time, adjusting to that hard length by slow degrees as she sank down onto him. He groaned with relief when he was finally, fully inside her. She rested for a moment, simply enjoying the sensation until Mark stirred with impatience.

"Now," he pleaded.

"Not yet. First I want to feel—" bending forward, she flattened her hands on his chest "—this."

There was already a sheen of perspiration there, making it easy for her to slide her palms over the slabs of gleaming muscle. He was hers now, and she liked having him in her possession. Liked this feminine power she'd never exercised before. At least not quite this way.

"Do you know what you're doing to me?" he growled.

"I know," she murmured.

Taking pity on him, she leaned back and began to rock on him. She was in control of the rhythms, measuring the strokes at her own pace toward the culmination of the journey they shared.

In the end, unable to bear the torture she was inflicting on him any longer, he heaved his hips off the mattress to permit himself one strong, upward thrust. It was all he needed to win climaxes for both of them, his immediately and hers swiftly following.

She didn't mind in the aftermath of their fulfillment, when she rolled away from him onto her back, letting Mark take back his authority. She had proved herself.

That was all that was necessary. And it was sweet having him tuck her close against his side, one of his arms curled around her protectively.

They were quiet then. Clare would have liked nothing better than to prolong that serene stillness. To have that and nothing more lull both of them into a peaceful, deep sleep. She hated it when, instead, the shadows crept into her thoughts.

They were the doubts that had visited her before. The realization that, no matter how much she wanted this man to belong to her in every way that mattered, he would never be hers. It was a foolish longing, because Mark could never be owned by anyone or anything but his revered army.

He had never tried to hide this from her. Had made it clear from the beginning that, when they had achieved the truth that would free Terry, when his leg was fully recovered, he would go back to his rangers. Nor, in all fairness, was Clare ready to risk the loss of another Alan Britten in battle.

The outcome should have been a simple one then. Something that, with resolve, they could both handle when the time came for them to go their separate ways. Except for one thing. No matter how determined she'd been not to recognize it, how much she had fought against it, she could no longer fail to admit the truth to herself.

Clare had made the terrible mistake of falling in love with Lieutenant Mark Griggs. She knew she would pay for that.

Damn it. Here she was beside him peacefully asleep, leaving him awake and dealing with emotions he'd like to evict from his head. And couldn't.

Why couldn't Clare be the kind of woman he was used to going to bed with? The kind who neither asked for, nor wanted, any personal commitment. Who understood he would be gone the morning after. Not only understood this but casually accepted it.

But Clare wasn't that type of woman. She was the forever sort who expected something more serious out of a relationship than a few nights of sex.

Come on, Griggs, be fair about it. Clare hasn't asked you for any commitment. Never even approached the subject.

True, but that didn't mean she wasn't thinking about it. Which left him with this guilt even worse than the guilt he'd experienced back in New Orleans. Because he was convinced when the time came for them to part, and ultimately that had to happen, he would hurt her.

He couldn't forget what she had suffered over the loss of her fiancé. Not that this was in any way the same thing. It wasn't like they were in love with each other. He couldn't be in love with her. Not after just three days. Nor could she possibly be in love with him.

So, what the hell are you worrying about?

Maybe because there was something else that haunted him. Something that he'd never been able to shake. Like his mother and the man who had fathered him, was he incapable of any permanent relationship? Could you inherit that kind of thing? Or was it simply a lesson he'd learned when they had deserted both him and each other? That you couldn't trust love. That in the end it would fail you.

Mark hated to think he was that kind of man, but there it was.

Chapter 16

"What are you doing?"

They were at a diner just down the road from the motel having an early breakfast. Or at least Clare was having breakfast. Mark seemed more interested in fiddling with his cell phone than in the plate of ham and eggs the waitress had just placed on the table in front of him. Given his appetite, she found this puzzling.

Instead of an answer to her question, she got a request.

"Give me the number to your cell phone."

"Why? Are you planning to call me from your side of the table?"

"Nope. Just want to program your number into my cell phone."

He was being mysterious again. She knew he wouldn't explain himself until he had what he wanted.

She gave him her number and watched him enter the ten digits.

"Now let me have your cell phone," he said.

There was no point in objecting. She took her phone from her purse and handed it to him.

"What are you doing with my phone?"

"Same thing I did with mine. Programming it so you have my own number on your list for quick connections. There, I've got it." He passed her phone back to her and began to eat his ham and eggs.

It was Clare's turn to ignore her own breakfast. "Why?" she asked him.

"I told you. I want us to have each other's numbers. Figured it was a good idea. You know, in case we should get separated and need to contact each other."

"No, I don't know. Why should we get separated?"

"It could happen. Can I have the salt, please?"

She slid the salt shaker over to his side of the table. "Mark, what's going on here? And no more evasions. You weren't interested in us exchanging numbers before this. Why now?"

He didn't answer her for a moment. He salted his eggs, tasted them and then, apparently realizing she was going to persist with her questions until she was satisfied, he put down his fork and leaned toward her with a brief "Because we're in Florida."

"And?"

"*He* could be somewhere down here. Probably is."

She knew the *he* Mark was referring to. The nameless enemy who needed his pendant.

"If he's already managed to get to Hank Kolchek, and let's hope we're not too late to prevent that, then I'm next."

"This isn't one of your combat zones, Mark."

"I'm a soldier, Clare," he said grimly, "and he used to be a soldier for hire. How do you suppose he's going to view it?"

"I think I'm beginning to understand. You want me out of the way when he comes after you again."

"I'm the target. The one who has what this lunatic wants."

"So you've said before."

"I'm saying it again."

"Yes, only this time you'd like to park me somewhere safe while you go into battle. That's it, isn't it? Very noble of you, Lieutenant. Only you can forget it. We're in this together, and there will be no arguments about that."

He considered her for another long minute, like the stubborn warrior he was. But in this instance her obstinacy was equal to his, and he must have understood this. That she wasn't going to relent.

"Let's eat up" was all he said. "We need to be on the road."

To Muretta, she thought, and whatever waited down there for them. Something that might be decidedly unpleasant, and she would have to be ready for it.

It was almost noon when they reached Muretta. As Mark had learned yesterday after speaking to its chief of police, it was not a large town.

"What's that address again?" he asked Clare.

She consulted the copy of Hank Kolchek's letter she had brought with her. "One-thirty Coral Drive."

Mark used his GPS to give him what he wanted. "Got it," he said after a minute.

Clare realized it was not likely they would have any better luck than the deputy who had paid a visit to the

Kolchek home yesterday. But she and Mark had agreed beforehand they would have to start somewhere, and it might as well be the Kolchek address.

Coral Drive turned out to be one of the winding lanes inside a gated community that had the look of a new development. Maybe because there were no large shrubs or trees in any of the yards, Clare decided.

With minor variations meant to individualize them, the houses were all the same. Single-story, Mediterranean-style villas with stucco walls and red, tiled roofs.

"There it is, 130," Clare said, pointing out a residence with bougainvillea flaming around the front door.

Mark turned into the driveway. "Still no vehicle in the port," he observed, referring to the deputy's report. "Maybe you should wait here in the car."

He's still trying to protect me, she thought. "If our bad guy did manage to pay a visit here himself, I don't think he'd still be hanging around."

Mark offered no further objection when she followed him out of the SUV and up the walk to the front door, where he rang the bell. She could hear the sound of chimes inside. They waited, but there was no answer.

Clare hadn't expected one. There was a feel of desertion about the place. She tried not to compare it to that sinister quality of desertion that had chilled her in Malcolm Boerner's courtyard just before they had discovered his body on the floor of his apartment.

No reason for her to be chilled today. Not in this sweltering heat.

Mark tried the door. It was locked. "Let's check around the back," he said.

Something else the deputy must have done, she thought, trailing Mark around the side of the house.

Had the deputy also peered into the windows? If so, he couldn't have discovered any bodies on the floor. The chief of police would have told them that.

Wherever the Kolcheks were, Clare prayed they were safe. That Joe Riconi's and Malcolm Boerner's killer hadn't found them.

She stood behind Mark when they reached the back door. There was no bell to ring here. He knocked, and they waited again. Clare had the uneasy feeling of being watched. When she looked over her shoulder, she was startled to discover a face poking out from the glossy leaves of a young orange tree in the backyard of the house behind the Kolchek property. It was a brown and very wrinkled face, as if it had been out in the Florida sun too long and too often.

"We have company," Clare murmured, nudging Mark.

He swung around as an elderly woman emerged from the cover of the orange tree and approached the low fence that divided the two properties.

"They're not at home," she announced, leaning over the fence.

Clare joined her at the fence. "Would you happen to know where they are?"

"At work, I imagine. They are every day, including weekends, which is why the neighborhood hasn't had a chance to see much of them. That, plus they're new in town."

She seemed to know all about the Kolcheks and was willing to talk about them. It made Clare wonder why the woman hadn't shared this information yesterday with the deputy.

Mark had to be thinking the same thing. It was why, when he appeared now at Clare's side, he addressed the woman with an amiable "There was a police officer here yesterday wanting, like us, to find the Kolcheks. He called on the neighbors. Did you speak to him?"

"Wasn't at home to speak to anybody. I was out playing golf yesterday. Why did the cop want the Kolcheks? They do something wrong?"

"Nothing like that." Before she could question Mark any further, he went on with a quick "Could you tell us where they work?"

"Sure. They're both Realtors. Have their own office down in Orlando. That's an easy commuting distance from here, you know."

"You must have struck up a nice friendship with them," Clare said.

"Me? I never had so much as a single conversation with either one of them."

"Then how do you know…"

"Saw it lettered on the side of their van. *Kolchek Real Estate. Representing the Best Orlando Has to Offer. Agents Wendy and Hank Kolchek.* I could never make out the street address or phone number, though. Too small from my kitchen window."

"That should be enough for us to locate them," Mark said. "Guess we'd better be on our way."

The woman is inquisitive, Clare thought. She would want to know how they were connected with the Kolcheks and why they were looking for them. It explained why Mark, expressing a fast thank-you, hurried Clare off to the SUV.

"Chatty old dame, isn't she?" he said when he'd settled himself back behind the wheel.

"For which we have to be supremely grateful."

"You get no argument from me." He started the engine and backed out of the driveway. "I guess we know where our next destination is."

Clare had wondered why the Kolcheks had moved their residence from Orlando to Muretta. If it was because they wanted to live in a much smaller, quieter community, she could understand their rationale when she and Mark reached Orlando.

Orlando was neither small nor quiet. Its giant theme parks had been largely responsible for the sprawling city it now was. A place heavy with traffic and tourists.

Mark pulled over to the side. This time he used his smartphone to learn that Kolchek Real Estate was located at 1040 Blue Springs Road.

Their objective turned out to be on the other side of Orlando. Stores and offices lined the busy street on both sides. Mark cruised down its length while Clare looked for the number they wanted.

"Up there on the right," she announced after spotting it. "One thousand and forty."

Mark found a parking lot several doors away. They walked back to Kolchek Real Estate, a small operation tucked between a sandwich shop and a clothing boutique. Both the boutique and the sandwich shop were active with customers. Kolchek Real Estate was not.

They stood there on the hot pavement and gazed in disappointment at the locked door with a Closed sign behind its glass. The large front window revealed an unlighted interior and a trio of unoccupied desks.

"Let's face it, Mark. Both their home and their business deserted. There's a reason for that. They've cleared out. They must have somehow learned of the murders, even if Muretta's chief of police hadn't, and now they're on the run."

"Possible, but not a certainty."

He was right, although she could see no other explanation for it. "So where do we go from here?"

"How about the sandwich shop next door?"

"Only you would be hungry at a time like this."

"Hey, it's not just my stomach I'm thinking about. Could be they could tell us something in there. Neighbors, remember? We got lucky back in Muretta. Maybe we'll get lucky here."

Since it was past midday and the usual lunch hour, they were able to get one of the few vacant tables at the rear of the shop. The tall server who arrived at their table to take their orders couldn't have eaten much of what the place offered, Clare thought. He was as thin as a reed, with a long, narrow face. It was a face, however, that wore a welcoming smile.

Mark spoke to him. "We were hoping to discuss something with the real estate agents next door, only there's no one there."

"Yeah, that Closed sign has been on their door for the past couple of days or so. Too bad, because they could be missing sales now that the market is looking up again."

"I don't suppose you could tell us how we could reach them. It's kind of important."

"Sorry, can't help you there. What will you folks have?"

"Another disappointment," Mark muttered after the waiter had departed with their orders.

Clare shared his frustration. Were they at a complete dead end this time, with nowhere else for them to go? It seemed so. The Kolcheks could be anywhere. Neither she nor Mark had a suggestion to offer as they waited for their orders.

Their glum moods lifted immediately when the waiter returned moments later with their sandwiches, sodas and a hopeful solution.

"You know," he said brightly, "I got to thinking about your problem, and that's when I remembered there is someone who might be able to tell you how you can get in contact with the Kolcheks."

"Who?" Clare asked him.

"Jennifer Lu. She was a third agent in their office. They hated letting her go, but when the housing market tanked they couldn't afford her any longer. She and the Kolcheks had a close relationship, and from what I could see whenever the three of them stopped in here for lunch they were still on friendly terms."

"I don't suppose…"

"I could tell you how to find Jennifer? Easy. She managed to get a position at a much larger agency. Star Real Estate. That's just down in the next block. Same side of the street."

They thanked him, ate their sandwiches, drank their sodas, left a generous tip on the table and headed on foot for Star Real Estate.

Both of them were perspiring freely and grateful for the cool air that delivered them from the heat when they entered the office of Star Real Estate. A receptionist directed them to a nearby desk carrying a nameplate that identified the woman seated there as Jennifer Lu.

Young, attractive and noticeably of Asian descent, she rose from her chair to greet them. Introductions exchanged, she saw them settled in side-by-side chairs. Seating herself back behind her desk, she asked them, "So, how can I help you?"

"One of the waiters back at the sandwich shop told us you're a friend of the Kolcheks," Mark said.

"Wendy and Hank? Yes, that's right. If this is in connection with a property they represent, their agency is just next door to the sandwich shop."

"Yeah, we know that. Thing is, the agency isn't open. There's a Closed sign on the door and no sign of the Kolcheks. We're anxious to locate them."

"And you thought I could help you with that?"

Clare realized the woman was no longer smiling at them. That she looked puzzled, even a bit suspicious.

"Mark, I think before we go on we need to show Ms. Lu some ID."

He nodded, produced his wallet and displayed his army identification that indicated he was currently based at Ft. Bragg. The agent glanced at it without comment and then at Clare's driver's license. Only then did she speak.

"What's this all about?"

Clare was apologetic. "I'm afraid we're being a bit mysterious here." She went on to explain as briefly as possible their need to find the Kolcheks, taking care not to alarm the agent by telling her that her friends could be in serious danger.

She'd omitted so many details she wasn't sure Jennifer Lu was satisfied when she was finished.

"Tell you what," the young woman said, reaching for her phone. "I'll try to contact the Kolcheks for you. If they're willing, you can speak to them yourself."

Clare and Mark watched her as she dialed a number, waited, apparently had no answer and then tried what Clare guessed was another number. Again there was no result.

The agent frowned. "That's funny. Neither of them is answering their cells."

Clare understood what she meant without being told.

It was essential to Realtors that they always make themselves available to any prospective buyers. That neither Wendy nor Hank Kolchek was picking up had her fearing they were unable to do so.

Mark caught her attention with an expression on his face that told her without spoken words: *Let's not start imagining the worst. Not when we're not sure of anything yet.*

Jennifer Lu's own expression was a thoughtful one. "It's just occurred to me there could be a reason why they're not answering. It's possible they're not hearing their cells over the noise of that rental equipment they might be using."

Mark's reaction was a perplexed "Uh…"

"That needs an explanation, doesn't it?" The agent went on to give them one. "Wendy's grandmother died some months back and left her with this house she and Hank are trying to sell. From what they told me, it's kind of rundown. No curb appeal and the interior in poor shape, especially the floors. It's a long way off, but they've been going down there whenever they could to give it a facelift. I bet that's where they are now and busy with electric sanders and the like."

Or using the house to hide out, Clare thought, daring to hope this was the case and that the Kolcheks were still safe.

"Could you tell us where this place is?" Mark asked the agent.

"I'm not sure that I…" She left the rest unsaid, the implication being that her friends might not appreciate being located by two people they didn't know.

"Please," Mark appealed, "it really is vital we see them."

The woman hesitated before making up her mind.

"Well, if it's as important as you've both said…the house is in a town called Conch Beach. That's on the Gulf Coast just south of Fort Myers. Here, let me give you the address. It's on multiple listings, so I have it available."

Tapping a few keys on her computer, she brought up the multiple listings, scanned the screen and found the address. "Twenty-eight Canal Lane. I'll jot it down for you."

Reaching for a card and a pen, she printed the address and handed the card to Clare. Both Mark and Clare thanked the agent for her help. She wished them luck as they rose to their feet.

They left Jennifer Lu with a pleasant smile on her face, but Clare had the feeling it wasn't altogether genuine. That perhaps the young woman was already wondering if she'd made a mistake in not being more cautious with her information.

A mistake for which Clare couldn't help being anything but grateful.

They didn't talk as they found their way out of Orlando and headed toward Conch Beach. Each of them was occupied with their thoughts. Clare wondered if Mark's were similar to her own.

Hank Kolchek. Were they at last able to reach him? Would they find him alive and unharmed? Or had a vicious killer managed to find him first?

Clare prayed that wasn't the case. Not just because, if they could enlist his support, he had the knowledge to prove Terry had no motive to murder her husband but that one of his former comrades did.

There was that, of course. There was also Clare's

earnest hope that Hank Kolchek wouldn't have to pay with his life for the sake of his pendant.

The highways she and Mark traveled were all four-lane expressways. Those highways should have made their journey a swift one. And didn't. Not only was the distance to Conch Beach a lengthy one, it was complicated by some of Florida's heaviest traffic as the route took them through Gulf Coast cities like Tampa, Bradenton, Sarasota and Port Charlotte.

It seemed to Clare like one unending urban corridor. All that did change, now that they were much farther south, was the vegetation. It became almost tropical in character, dominated by ranks of tall palm trees.

Night overtook them as they reached the vicinity of Conch Beach.

"Look," Mark said, "let's be sensible and find another motel. We can locate this Canal Lane with the GPS, but if we show up there after dark, a pair of strangers, we risk seriously alarming these people."

Much as she hated the idea of another delay, she knew he was right. Also, though he wouldn't admit it, Mark was clearly exhausted. They both were. It would be much better if they met the Kolcheks in the morning, rested and clearheaded.

They registered at a motel on the northern edge of Conch Beach. There was only a scattering of cars in the parking lot, an indication that the place had few guests. Clare understood why. This was not the high season for southern Florida.

"I'm going out again for a minute," Mark said after they'd deposited their bags in the room. "There's a newspaper vending machine outside the office. I think I'll pick up a local paper. See what the weather is going to bring us tomorrow."

"Not as hot as today, I hope." Even long after dark like this, the heat and humidity outside were oppressive. "While you get your paper, I'm going to hit the shower."

"I'll take the key and lock the door behind me."

Security is still a priority for him, Clare thought, picking up her bag and heading for the bathroom.

The shower, just as she'd intended, refreshed her. It also had her in a better mood when she emerged from the bathroom, belting her cotton robe at the waist.

That mood vanished when she found Mark seated on one of the two beds. He had the newspaper in front of him and the darkest of expressions on his face. Something was wrong.

"What is it?" she asked him. "What are you reading?"

He flipped the newspaper onto the spread, the forefinger of his left hand stabbing an article on the front page. Clare leaned over the bed, scanning the piece. Her heart felt in that moment as if a fist was squeezing it.

They were too late.

Chapter 17

It was a brief report, but the essentials were all there:

MAN ATTACKED AND LEFT FOR DEAD
Orlando Realtor Hank Kolchek was brutally attacked late last night outside the home he and his wife were occupying on Canal Lane. The assailant, who fled the scene, was not identified. There was no motive provided and no witness to the assault. Mrs. Kolchek was inside the house at the time and only discovered her husband in the street when the couple's dog he was walking barked at the door. Kolchek was taken by ambulance to St. Andrew's Hospital where he remains unconscious and in critical condition. The Conch Beach Police are asking anyone who might have further information to contact them.

Mark got to his feet, raking his fingers through his hair. "We don't have to guess who that assailant was, do we?" he said, his voice as sour as the expression on his face.

Clare shook her head, sick at the thought of the vicious attack on Hank Kolchek. Wondering if the poor man would survive it.

"Or," Mark added, "whether the bastard managed to get his hands on another pendant."

"Providing Kolchek was wearing it."

Mark nodded with certainty. "He was. Otherwise, this lunatic wouldn't have left the scene. He would have invaded the house itself and not hesitated to take down Kolchek's wife before tearing through the place in search of the pendant."

He looked thoughtful as Clare gazed at him, hoping he wasn't going to resurrect his familiar habit and start pacing restlessly around the room. Her nerves were already too strained by the situation to bear that.

To her relief all he did was stand there quietly for a moment before expressing an angry "What gets me is how he managed to find the Kolcheks."

"We might never learn the answer to that. There's only one thing we do know for certain. A lunatic he might be, but he's a cunning one."

"Yeah, he'd have to be to hunt down a couple who thought they'd reached a haven that was safe. Looks like we were right in thinking he'd stopped following us back in New Orleans because he'd switched his attention to Florida."

"But he hasn't given up on you, Mark. Now that he has Hank Kolchek's pendant, he'll come after you again."

"He can try it," he said, steel in his words.

The valor of warriors. You had to love them for it. And fear for them. Because as able as she knew Mark was, the prospect of another deadly encounter terrified her. "So what do we do now?" What, after all, was left for them to do? she asked herself sorrowfully.

Mark, however, was at no loss for a decision. "We get us a good night's sleep. If that's at all likely. Then first thing in the morning we go to this St. Andrew's Hospital. Wendy Kolchek is sure to be there with her husband. If she's available and willing, it's possible she can tell us what he can't. At least we can find out if the guy is still alive and has any chance of making it."

Yes, Clare silently agreed, that much anyway was the decent, caring thing for them to do. Getting a night of solid sleep was another matter.

Just as they had the night before, she and Mark ended up sharing the same bed. But not for the same reason. There was no question of sex tonight. Not just because, with their minds on the Kolcheks, they couldn't be interested in that kind of intimacy. Nor in permitting themselves to violate self-promises that involved guilt and an eventual heartache.

This was an intimacy that was strictly for the sake of comfort. A comfort Clare realized Mark understood she needed. It was why, when they climbed into bed, he held her snugly against his side.

They didn't talk. There was nothing left to say. It was enough for them to be close together like this.

The unrelenting heat hung heavy in the air the next morning when they emerged from the motel after, fatigue finally overcoming them, they'd managed to get an adequate night's sleep. Following a quick breakfast at a fast food restaurant, they went in search of St. Andrew's Hospital.

There was no need to ask for directions. Blue road signs posted at intervals marked a clear route to the hospital. There was another blue that would not have been welcome. Both she and Mark were careful to watch for it, but to Clare's relief there was no sign of the hated blue sedan. It could be, though, he was using another car now.

The hospital when they reached it was a large building, an indication it served an area much wider than Conch Beach. Parking the SUV in the expansive lot that adjoined it, they found their way into the entrance lobby where one of the two attendants behind the counter stepped forward to help them.

"We've come to ask about a patient," Mark said. "Hank Kolchek."

The woman didn't need to consult her computer to answer him. Hank Kolchek was news, after all, Clare thought.

"Mr. Kolchek is in intensive care. You'll have to make your inquiries at the nurse's station outside the IC unit. Take the elevator over there to the third floor, turn right, cross the sky bridge to the next wing and proceed along the corridor."

Thanking her, they caught the elevator, crossed the windowed sky bridge as she'd directed and found the nurse's station midway along the broad corridor.

A male nurse behind the desk, redheaded and freckled, looked up from the chart he was checking. "Help you?"

"Any chance of our learning how Hank Kolchek is doing?" Mark asked him.

"Are you family or friends?"

"Not exactly, no. Just two people who care."

"Then I'm afraid I can't tell you anything other than he's in ICU. Not without permission from his doctor."

"What about his wife?" Clare said. "Is she here?"

"She's with her husband in his cubicle. But you can't go in there. Only close family members are permitted inside the IC unit."

"Could you ask her to join us out here? Please, it's very important we speak to her."

The young nurse hesitated, then picked up a phone at his elbow and pressed one of its buttons. From the conversation that followed, Clare assumed he was speaking to another nurse at a desk inside the unit. A long pause followed, then another brief exchange of dialogue before the nurse at their end replaced the receiver.

"Mrs. Kolchek has agreed to see you," he reported. "She'll be coming out those double doors down there."

Clare and Mark drifted in the direction he nodded. A moment later one of those two doors whisked open. Wendy Kolchek emerged and started toward them down the long corridor. She was a petite woman with neat, chestnut hair liberally sprinkled with gray.

Delicate features, Clare observed as she approached them.

And shadows under her eyes. Understandable, if she'd spent a sleepless night at her husband's bedside, which she most likely had.

She might look fragile, Clare thought, but there was a strength there. That much was evident when she confronted them with a sharp "You're asking about my husband, but I don't know you. Who are you, and what is this all about?"

Clare waited for Mark to tell her. When he said nothing, she turned her head to gaze at him, expecting him to signal her to do the explaining. To her surprise, she found him raising the pendant from beneath the front of his shirt, lifting it by the cord over his head and silently extending it toward Wendy Kolchek.

The woman stared down at the pendant where it rested in the palm of Mark's hand, then looked up into his face. There was no question when she spoke, just a soft statement of fact.

"You're Lieutenant Mark Griggs."

"Yes, ma'am," he said, stringing the pendant back over his head.

"And you?" she asked, turning her attention to Clare.

"Clare Fuller. My brother-in-law was Joe Riconi."

Mrs. Kolchek nodded, as if satisfied by that alone. Her husband had apparently shared everything with her, which should make their visit easier. That and because, after seeing the pendant, she seemed to accept and trust them without any further suspicion.

But Clare felt she deserved a better explanation. "I'm guessing you know that Joe was murdered."

"Yes, we heard."

"The thing is, my sister was arrested and charged with his murder. The police aren't listening to any of us."

"Which is why you're here. You're trying to prove her innocence. Is that right?"

"Exactly."

"I'm sorry about your sister. Look, I need to stretch my legs after doing nothing but sitting for hours. Would you mind if while we talk we walk along the hall here?"

Clare and Mark fell into step with her as they strolled toward the far end of the corridor.

"I have a sister, too," she told them. "That's how Hank and I learned about the murders of your brother-in-law and Malcolm Boerner. I suppose it was on the internet, too, but Hank was so busy with listings we never looked at the news there. Anyway, my sister Angela lives in Baton Rouge. One of the papers there reported the murders. She called to let us know but didn't mention anything about Joe's wife being arrested. Maybe because the newspaper didn't cover that part. Otherwise, Hank would have called the police in St. Boniface."

"Because he knew who killed both men? Is that what you're saying, Mrs. Kolchek?"

"Wendy will do. No, he didn't have the proof you want. How could he? But he *knew* all right. 'Two of them,' he kept saying to me after Angela phoned. 'He went and murdered two of them, just to get his hands on their pendants.' That disbelief was still on Hank's mind when I found him in the street. They were his last words to me before he slid into unconsciousness. 'Two of them.'"

"Guess your husband must have figured he'd end up being the third if you stayed in Muretta," Mark said.

"We thought we'd be safe here. We weren't. He managed somehow to find us anyway." The thought must have occurred to her that Clare and Mark had also located them in Conch Beach. "And you? How did—"

"Jennifer Lu," Mark said, and went on to explain how the agent had tried to phone them and got no answer.

"I must have been in the ICU with my phone turned off. Cell phones aren't allowed to be active in there. They can affect the equipment, I suppose."

Her words triggered a sudden guilt for Clare. Asking the woman about Hank's condition should have come before anything else. "Your husband, Wendy. How is he doing?"

"He's on life support, still unconscious and hanging on, but there's no certainty he'll make it. He took a pretty bad battering, a couple of serious cuts with a knife and blows from some kind of blunt instrument."

No gun, Clare thought. Either Hank's attacker hadn't acquired another one since leaving New Orleans, or else he hadn't wanted to alert the neighbors with the sound of gunfire.

They had reached the end of the corridor where the three of them turned and started back.

"Hank would be dead, if hadn't been for Pepper barking at the door and my finding him in the street in time to get an ambulance."

"Your dog," Mark said. "Yeah, we read about that in the local paper along with the attack."

"Pepper saved Hank. I hate having to board her in a kennel, only the situation being what it is…" She waved her hand, as if pushing the subject aside. "But this isn't what you want to hear."

There was a lounge area furnished with chairs and a sofa opposite the doors to the ICU. Wendy stopped here.

"I should stay close by in case they want to call me back to Hank's side. Why don't we get comfortable in there," she suggested, "and I'll tell you the whole story? I'm not sure it will be enough to clear your sister, but it should certainly help."

Wendy Kolchek didn't need to be this understanding, this willing to lend her support, particularly when her husband was at this moment fighting for his life. Clare was deeply grateful for that and expressed as much to the woman.

"It's what I want to do," she said. "For Hank's sake as well as your own. I want his attacker caught and brought to trial for those two murders and his savage assault on my husband."

The lounge was unoccupied. Clare and Mark settled side by side on the leather sofa, Wendy in a chair she drew up close to them. They watched her as she removed a wallet from her purse.

"This is Hank's wallet," she said. "I needed to keep it with me for the health insurance cards." Opening the wallet, she withdrew a photograph from a protective plastic sleeve. "He always carried this picture inside. A memento of his younger days. He couldn't have guessed how useful it would be now."

She passed the photo to Clare, who held it close enough to Mark for him to share its subject. What it revealed was four men in fatigues posed against a barren background.

A bleak landscape that was familiar to Mark. "Afghanistan," he murmured.

"Yes, Afghanistan," Wendy said. "It was taken when the four of them were there all those years ago." She leaned forward, her long nailed finger singling out a grinning figure with a broad, Slavic face, his arms draped across the shoulders of the two men who stood on either side of him. "This is Hank."

Even though they had changed with the passing of the years, Clare needed no help in recognizing the other two men. "Joe Riconi," she said for Mark's benefit, pointing to the good-looking, distinctly Italian face of her late brother-in-law. "And the one on this side is Malcolm Boerner."

That left the fourth one of the group. As if deliberately choosing to be apart, he knelt on the ground in front of the other three, a rifle under his arm. His was a thin, unsmiling face. A predatory face. Nameless as he still was for Clare and Mark, she knew who he was. Who he had to be.

It was Wendy who gave them his name. "Roy Innes," she said softly, bitterly.

Roy Innes. It was a relief for Clare to finally be able to attach an identity to this merciless killer. "He looks…"

"Yes, I know what you mean," Wendy said. "Hank used to say that even back then, it was never about the adventure of being a soldier of fortune for Roy but always about the money."

"I think we're ready for that story now," Mark prompted her.

Without any further urging, Wendy related the tale of the four comrades. A tale that Clare found riveting as it unfolded.

"They were working security at the time for an American construction company whose tools and materials had been disappearing from its site. That job ended, leaving the four of them stranded when the company abruptly pulled out of an Afghanistan that had become too dangerous."

"The Taliban?" Mark asked.

"That's right. It was back in the nineties, and the Taliban was gaining strength, getting ready to topple the existing government and take control of the country. That's when Hank and his fellow soldiers-for-hire were approached by an Afghan named Hamid Zahir."

"Think I heard that name mentioned," Mark said. "Had to be the cousin of the man who strung this pendant of mine around my neck."

"It was, but how did you—"

Clare interrupted her. "I think we're going to confuse you if we don't tell you we read the letter your husband sent to Joe, Malcolm Boerner and Roy Innes." She went on to explain how her sister had discovered Joe's letter and passed on its content to Mark and her.

"I see. But Hank didn't name Hamid Zahir in his letter."

"Then it must have been his cousin who mentioned the name," Mark said, "and that Zahir had been an important man in Kabul."

"He was a ceramics restorer in the National Museum there," Wendy continued. "He told Hank and the others how the government was so weak it was unable to protect the thousands of ancient artifacts in the museum. How so many of the pieces in its valuable collections had already been looted and sold to collectors in other countries."

Wendy paused, as if searching now for the right words. Words that wouldn't make her husband sound anything but humanly vulnerable to a temptation that few men could have resisted.

"I want to make it clear," she went on, "that Hank is ashamed now of what he did."

"Which was?" Clare said.

"Hamid Zahir proposed, with the support of the four of them, because he needed men of their experience for his scheme to work, that they break into the museum and help themselves to its treasures. The kind of small things, a lot of them in gold and silver, that would have eventually vanished anyway. Not that it made what they did right."

"So they carried off this stuff on some dark night," Mark conjectured. "And then what?"

"The plan was for the five of them to share equally in the profits. Only at that point the situation in Afghanistan had deteriorated so badly it would have been impossible to get their treasures out of the country. Not with the Taliban at the borders making certain nothing and no one got in or out without their wanting it to get in or out."

"But one of the five men had a solution," Mark said.

He would know that from Hank Kolchek's letter, Clare thought. Just as she knew it.

"Hamid Zahir, yes," Wendy said. "What he asked was that the five of them agree to hide their treasures until they could be safely recovered and removed from the country."

"A temporary measure," Clare said. "Except what none of them imagined was that it would be years before they could go back for those treasures."

"Exactly."

"I'm sorry," Clare apologized. "We keep interrupting you."

"It doesn't matter. Not if it clarifies the whole thing for you."

"This hiding place," Mark said. "Did Zahir suggest that, too?"

"He did. A remote mountain region well away from Kabul. They drove there in his car as far as the road would take them, divided the valuables into five backpacks and set off on foot. It was necessary by then to hire a local guide who led them into an isolated valley. The route was so complicated Hamid drew a map and kept adding to it along the way."

Because without such a map, Clare realized, they would never find their way back to that valley.

"The guide left them at the foot of what he called a sacred mountain, refusing to go any farther. He told them there were caves everywhere on the mountain. That his people were forbidden to visit them, fearing they would anger the spirits who lived in them. Hamid had heard about the mountain and its caves. He'd counted on the guide not hiking up there with them.

"I remember Hank telling me the cave they finally chose had a mouth so small, and then a ceiling so low once they squeezed inside, they had to crawl all the way through this long, narrow passage on their stomachs."

Clare could picture those five men wriggling into what must have been no better than a damp, dark hole while dragging their heavy backpacks behind them. Until they reached what?

Wendy answered that question for her. "In the end, they found this deep, black cavity. And that's where they shoved the backpacks just as far as they would go."

"The story doesn't end there, does it?" Mark said.

Wendy shook her head. "By the time they got back to Kabul, they no longer trusted one another. At least that was true of Roy Innes. Hank said he was always something of a loose cannon with an unpredictable temperament. Malcolm Boerner was suspicious, too. With only the one map in Hamid's possession, what was to prevent him from going back to the cave alone and taking the treasures for himself? His offer to draw four identical maps was no guarantee either that any one of them wouldn't empty the cave on his own."

"And that's where the pendants came in," Mark said.

"I see you've figured that out."

"It seemed to make sense once we started to put things together."

"It made sense to the others, too, when Hamid thought of it. They went with him to his home studio to make sure he didn't trick them. Being as experienced as he was with ceramics, he created a clay disk, etched a picture map into both of its surfaces and divided it into five equal wedges before firing and glazing them."

Just as Professor Duval surmised, Clare thought.

"Each man received one of those wedges strung on a lanyard for safekeeping," Wendy said. "Only when the five pieces were fitted together would the map have meaning. After Hamid burned the paper map in the presence of all of them, the five men went their separate ways."

With the four Americans eventually finding their way home to make other lives for themselves, Clare realized.

Wendy finished her story by telling them, "Hank was essentially always a good man, which is why he came to regret the role he played in the robbery. In the end he wanted to see those stolen treasures returned to Afghanistan's National Museum, where he felt they belonged. He hoped to persuade the others to agree to that."

Mark made a sound of disgust. "Obviously, Innes had a much different intention. Probably Boerner, as well. We think they might have been partners before they had a falling out and Innes ended up killing him."

After he murdered Joe, Clare thought. Was it possible that Joe eventually felt the same guilt as Hank Kolchek? If so, it could account for his drinking all these years. Something her sister had never understood. Terry would be glad to hear an explanation for the husband she had always thought much better than Clare had ever given him credit for.

She had been holding the snapshot all this while. She gave it back to Wendy, who replaced the photo inside her husband's wallet before returning the wallet to her purse.

"Did the Conch Beach police see that picture?" Clare wanted to know.

"They did, and made a copy of it. I'm not sure, though, they felt it would be of much use to them. It would have been different if I'd witnessed the attack myself. Only Hank can put a name to his attacker."

If he ever regains consciousness, Clare thought.

"There is one thing I can and will do," Wendy assured them. "I can tell both the New Orleans and St. Boniface police all I know, which is a good deal. It should help to clear your sister. And, of course, Hank would be ready to give evidence providing…"

She didn't finish. Clare sadly and silently finished the sentence for her. *Providing he survives.*

She was about to thank Wendy for her offer when one of the IC unit doors across the hall flashed open. A nurse emerged, spotted Wendy in the lounge and came to the open doorway.

"Encouraging news, Mrs. Kolchek. Your husband is awake and asking for you."

The announcement couldn't have been more timely than if it had been staged. Or more welcome.

Wendy surged to her feet and hurried out of the lounge. She was halfway across the hall when she paused and looked over her shoulder, a concerned expression on her face.

"Be careful, won't you?" she called back to them. "Roy Innes needs that last pendant, and there isn't anything he won't do to get it."

Chapter 18

"She was gone before we got to tell her how glad we were for her that Hank is awake," Clare said.

"Or that I wasn't planning to let that greedy bastard get anywhere near us," Mark said.

"I suppose she knew that but felt she had to say it anyway."

Just as Wendy must realize as we do, Clare thought, *that her husband's state of consciousness is a hopeful sign but no guarantee he'll recover. Or that he'll be strong enough to talk to the police before Roy Innes comes after Mark again.*

She and Mark went on sitting there in the lounge, both of them quiet now.

"I have a suggestion," he finally said. "I say we go to the cops here and fill them in on all we learned back in Louisiana. Added to what Wendy must have already told them, it should give them a better handle on hunting down Innes."

"I say you're right."

Getting to their feet, they left the lounge and started down the corridor, both of them lost in thought again.

There was more than just the police on Clare's mind. There was Terry to contact with the positive news which could soon bring her sister's release, her car to be recovered from that service garage, her classroom waiting for her return back home.

All of these involved some degree of emotion for her. But none of those emotions were as deep or as conflicted as the one concerning Mark and her. Because if what they had shared was winding down, about to reach a conclusion, as Clare felt it was, then it meant what she couldn't bear to address. A parting of the ways. Unless—

What? The something she so ardently wished for but, given all the complications, all the problems and barriers, she didn't dare to consider as a realistic possibility?

Not now. Don't let yourself think about it now. There's time for that later.

They had crossed the sky bridge and were on their way to the elevator when, rounding a corner, Clare stopped at the door to a women's restroom.

"I'm going to stop in here for a minute."

"I'll wait outside for you right here," Mark assured her.

Clare was not the exception. He had never known a woman yet who, just before ducking into a restroom, hadn't said something like, "Be with you in a jiffy." And then, of course, she had managed to be forever.

Mark was prepared to wait. There was a window

just a few paces away from the restroom door. He went and stood there at the glass, occupying himself with the view of the hospital grounds spread below him.

There was little to capture his attention, unless he was willing to count the figure of a man who swung into view. He wasn't, but he did idly watch the guy as he stopped on the sidewalk to light a cigarette.

Mark was about to turn his gaze elsewhere when the fellow lifted his head to exhale a stream of smoke. That's when he saw his face, and even from this height there was something about those gaunt features and that narrow head that seemed weirdly familiar.

Where had he seen that face? Seen it recently. And then it struck him. The photo Wendy Kolchek had shown them!

No, that was crazy. It couldn't be Roy Innes down there. What would Innes be doing here outside the hospital, of all places, strolling innocently along a sidewalk with a cigarette in his hand as though it wasn't against the rules? He was imagining it might be him.

The figure moved. Mark moved with him in the same direction, which took him around the corner and out on the windowed sky bridge where he picked up the figure again headed toward the parking lot.

Mark went from window to window, striving to keep him within range. Not easy with shrubs and trees in the way. But he had to know, had to be sure he *was* imagining it was Innes.

He was on the far end of the sky bridge when the figure disappeared altogether. Not willing to give up, he stood there at the glass in a state of tense frustration. Waiting, searching.

There! The guy was in view again. Crossing the parking lot now. No chance of another glimpse of his face, was there? Damn, he'd gone and vanished altogether somewhere in that sea of vehicles.

Clare, Mark remembered. He had to get back to Clare.

He was returning to his post outside the restroom when, midway along the bridge, his gaze caught a movement through one of the windows. Not the figure of a man this time. A car rolling along one of the parking lot lanes in the direction of the exit to the street. A blue sedan. Maybe not the same blue sedan that had followed them in Louisiana, but it could be.

Clare had emerged from one of the two bathroom stalls and was at the sink washing her hands when the restroom door swished open and shut again.

A slender figure approached the sink. Clare could see the woman behind her in the mirror above the sink. A striking brunette in a pale yellow sundress similar in style to her own lime-green sundress. She started to move aside to give her room.

"Stay right where you are," the woman ordered her in what sounded like a faint Hispanic accent.

Clare was aware of something hard suddenly pressed into her back. Something that, to her disbelief, actually felt like a gun.

"No, don't try to turn around. That would be a big mistake. Just hand your purse back to me."

Dear God, was she about to be mugged in a hospital restroom? She did the wise thing and passed the purse to the brunette, watching her fearfully in the mirror as she skillfully continued to hold the gun on her with one hand while managing with the other to burrow into her purse that she'd hooked by its strap over her wrist. It was the wallet she wanted, of course.

"Look," Clare said, "just take the money in my wallet and leave me with the rest, please. I promise you I don't have any other valuables in there."

"I don't want your damn money. I just want to be sure—" there was a pause while the hand still buried inside the purse searched for something "—you have this."

"What? What do I have?"

"A valid driver's license."

What on earth—

"I will take this, though."

She removed Clare's cell phone before reaching around her and depositing her purse on the counter.

No money. Just a cell phone. This didn't make sense. "What's this all about? Why are you—"

"No more questions. Pick up your bag and turn around. *Slowly.*" Clare was aware of that gun still directed at her, even though its owner had backed away a few feet. When she hesitated, she was issued a sharp, "Do it."

By the time she obeyed and was facing the brunette, the woman's own purse, which had been hanging from her shoulder, was now in her hand. Presumably, the cell phone was now inside it.

"This is what's going to happen," she instructed Clare. "We're leaving here together. You will walk close beside me to the elevator, across the lobby when we get there and out of the building to my car. When we reach my car, you'll take the wheel and drive where I tell you to. And all the way, *all the way,* I'll be holding my gun here out of sight under my purse. If you speak to anyone, try to signal them, I won't hesitate to use it. Understand?"

Clare, given no other choice, nodded mutely.

"Now move."

Mark, she thought. Mark was there outside the door. He wouldn't just let her walk off with a strange woman. He would try to prevent that, not knowing about the gun. He was at risk of being shot if she didn't find some way of warning him.

But, to her dismay, Mark wasn't waiting there outside. He had disappeared somewhere. She was both relieved and, at the same time, deeply worried by his absence.

Not a robbery, she thought as, trembling, she accompanied the brunette toward the elevator. This was a kidnapping. But why?

No Clare. She was still inside the blasted restroom.

Mark was on fire with impatience as he took up his post again outside the door. They had to get to the police station. Not just to inform the cops of all they had learned back in Louisiana. He needed to report his sighting from the windows on the sky bridge.

All right, so it probably hadn't been Roy Innes. A resemblance didn't mean anything, not when Innes had been on his mind. As for the blue sedan...well, blue sedans were common enough, weren't they? Anyway, Innes could have switched cars before leaving New Orleans. Just the same...

Where the devil was she?

No longer willing to keep his vigil, Mark cracked open the restroom door just far enough to call out a loud, "Clare, what's keeping you?"

No answer. Silence.

He didn't care what females were in there or what objections they might make. He was going in. Smacking the door wide with the flat of his hand, he strode into the restroom. And found it empty, stalls and all.

He walked out of the place concerned but not alarmed. All the while he'd been waiting for her, and here she was gone. But where and why?

It occurred to him then that she had to have come away from the restroom only to find him not there. She'd probably wondered the same thing he was wondering. Where had he gone and why? She must have taken off in search of him.

Cell phone. He could reach her on her cell phone, ask her where she was. Tell her to stay there until he joined her.

But when he slid his cell out of his back pocket, opened it, scrolled down the list to her number and hit the send button with his thumb, he got nothing.

It rang on her end, yes, rang repeatedly, but Clare wasn't picking up. Now he was getting closer to being alarmed. Something wasn't right.

The image of that figure below the sky bridge windows flashed through his mind. What if it *had* been Innes? What if he had grabbed Clare? No, that wasn't possible. For one thing, the timing for such an action had been all wrong. Besides, whoever it was, had been alone down there. Alone, too, when Mark had seen him drive off.

She has to be somewhere in the building. Unless—

The car. She could have gone out to the car, thinking she'd catch up to him there.

He wanted to convince himself that was the explanation. Except for one thing. Why wasn't she answering her cell?

Are you going to go on standing here, or are you going to hunt her down?

Yeah, he was wasting time with these speculations. The certainty was barely out of his head before he was racing toward the elevator. He looked for her when he reached the lobby. There were people there, but Clare wasn't among them.

Approaching the reception desk, he got the attention of one of the attendants. "There was a young woman with me when we arrived earlier. We got separated. Have you seen her, maybe passing through the lobby? Blonde, in her twenties, wearing—" What the hell had she been wearing when they'd left the motel? He tried to remember. "A kind of sundress affair, I think. Green maybe. Yeah, green."

The woman shook her head. "We've been busy all morning. If she was here, I didn't notice her. Sorry."

He didn't bother asking the other attendant. Time. He was wasting time again. He needed to try the car.

A heavy heat blasted him when he exited the air-conditioned building. Ignoring it, he sped toward the parking lot. Reached the SUV. She wasn't there. No sign of her. This time he wasn't just alarmed. He was borderline desperate.

Now what? The hospital security. He'd have to go back and alert the hospital security, report a missing woman, demand that they search both the building and the grounds for her.

He was trotting away from his SUV when the cell phone, still in his hand, buzzed an incoming call. Clare. The display showed him it was Clare. Thank God.

Punching the talk button, he answered her with a fast "Clare! Where are you?"

"She's right here beside me, Lieutenant."

Not Clare. This was a woman, but with a deeper voice and a slight accent. What in the name of all that was holy was going on? "Who are you? What are you doing with her cell phone? Let me speak to her."

"That won't be necessary. The fact that I'm calling on her cell phone is proof enough that we have her."

We?

But Mark didn't need that *we* explained to him. It took him only an instant to realize that it *had* been Roy Innes he had spotted here in the parking lot earlier. And that Innes had an accomplice. A woman they had known nothing about, who had snatched Clare while Mark had been kept busy elsewhere.

He knew why. His pendant, of course.

"If you hurt her," Mark raged, "if either you or Innes so much as touch her, I swear that I'll—"

The woman cut him off with a threatening "Providing you do what you're told, she won't be harmed."

"You want the pendant in exchange for Clare. How do I know you'll let her go once you have it?"

"You don't have a choice, Lieutenant, but to accept my word for that. I'll be calling you again with instructions on exactly what we want you to do. Do I need to warn you that in the meantime you will not go anywhere near the police or make any effort to contact them? Because if you do, you'll never see your Clare again. That's all for now."

"Wait! Don't hang up!"

Too late. There was silence on the other end.

Mark stood there, shaking with anger and cursing himself for not having remained on guard outside the restroom door. Fool that he was, he had gone and let himself be lured away.

Innes and his female accomplice. How had they learned he and Clare were here in Florida, never mind at the hospital?

This was no good. He was losing time, when what he needed to be doing was finding Clare and getting her back. Because he sure as hell didn't trust Innes or the woman to release her once they had what they wanted.

He couldn't risk the cops, not after that warning. He had to do this alone. He was a ranger, after all. And rangers didn't just stand by and wait. They were resourceful, and they acted on that.

Now that he had armed himself with his resolve and was steady again, Mark remembered something. There had been background noises during that phone call. The chug of an engine, the throb of a motor, the honking of a horn. Not the sounds connected with vehicles, either.

Boats. That's what he'd heard, boats. The traffic of a busy harbor. The call had originated from somewhere close by a harbor. Conch Beach was located on the Gulf. It figured the place would have a harbor, a marina at least.

He would start there. It was all he had.

Just as she had been ordered, Clare had parked the small van between two rotting, abandoned boat sheds. Also as ordered, she'd lowered the windows on both sides, turned off the engine and handed the keys to the woman beside her in the passenger seat. She hadn't dared to disobey the brunette, not with that gun still pointed at her.

A good fifteen minutes must have passed since the phone call to Mark. Silent, unnerving minutes without a single exchange of dialogue. Clare didn't have to wonder what they were waiting for. The conversation between Mark and her captor had been enough for her to guess why they were waiting here.

The arrival of Roy Innes.

Without air-conditioning, the van, even with its windows down, was like a furnace. Stifling. Clare could feel the perspiration collecting under her breasts. But her state of fear could be as much to blame for that as the heat. She tried not to think what was going to happen to her. Or to imagine what Mark might be feeling in this moment.

Unable to bear the sight of the gun, she focused her attention on the view in front of her. It wasn't much of a view. The boat sheds close on either side narrowed it to a strip of water with a crumbling pier somewhere on the far side of the harbor they had passed to reach this deserted spot.

The muted sounds in the nearby harbor were suddenly joined by the louder sound of a car engine. Startled, Clare turned her head to see a blue sedan pulling in beside them. There was just enough room to accommodate the sedan between the sheds that concealed the two vehicles.

Within seconds, the single occupant of the sedan had popped out of his car and installed himself in the rear seat of the van. Clare gazed at him in the rearview mirror. And shuddered at the sight of his grinning, brutal face.

"Missed me, did you, Ava?"

"You've been gone long enough," she complained.

"Couldn't be helped. Preparations for our guest, remember? She give you any trouble?"

The woman called Ava shook her head. "But I don't like this elaborate plan of yours. It's risky."

"But necessary after tangling with the teacher's solider boy back in New Orleans and learning he's no pushover like the others. It's working, isn't it?"

"As long as we don't make any mistakes."

"You take care of your end of it, and we'll be fine. Give me the gun."

Ava passed the gun back to him.

Innes, who had ignored Clare until now, trained his attention on her. "Get out of the car," he commanded her. "You and I are going to take a little voyage together."

When she hesitated, he held the barrel of the pistol under her nose.

"Be smart, Clare. You won't like it if I have to use force."

Trying not to let him see how frightened she was, she climbed out of the van. He exited it at the same time. Clare had wondered why, with a temperature that had to be high in the nineties, he should choose to wear a jacket, even though it was lightweight. She learned the answer to that when he shoved the gun into one of its deep pockets.

"Yeah, it's out of sight," he said. "Doesn't mean I can't fire it. Don't give me any reason to do that. All right, we're going down to the pier there. You walk close beside me, just like we're a happy couple."

She looked back at Ava, who remained in the van.

"No, she's not joining us," he said. "Our Ava isn't fond of being on the water. Not to mention she has business to take care of here on shore."

Another phone call to Mark, Clare realized, to arrange a rendezvous.

Innes called back to the brunette. "Give me plenty of time to get where we're going and to make sure everything is secure at that end before you call soldier boy."

Clare wouldn't miss the woman's company, but she didn't like the idea of going off alone with Roy Innes.

The man was capable of anything. No choice about it, however, but to fall into step beside him.

Not until they reached the pier did she see what had remained out of sight until now. Waiting for them was a sleek, inboard cruiser.

"Down the ladder, teacher."

Descending the ladder into the open cruiser, she started to settle on one of its back seats. "Not there. Up in the bow. I want you next to me where I can keep an eye on you."

The cruiser was obviously a powerful one, which had Clare wondering why he kept the craft at a crawl as they left the pier and moved out into the open water. Leaving the engine idling, Innes produced a roll of duct tape. "Turn around, arms behind you." He wanted her helpless, and she didn't want to be helpless. "Stop stalling," he growled. "It isn't going to do you any good."

Clare knew that, which was why she submitted, turning her back to him. He began to bind her wrists together with the tape.

"I don't want you jumping overboard and trying to swim for shore. You're too important to me, teacher, for me to risk losing you. You're going to win me that fifth pendant.

"Know what it'll get for me when I have it?" he gloated. "Treasures worth more than a man can imagine. Ancient coins and jewelry, objects of gold and ivory, even Alexander the Great's drinking cup..."

He isn't going to let you live when all this is over. He wouldn't be telling you this otherwise.

It was a realization that should have terrified her. But all she could think about was Mark. The possibility of never again seeing the man she loved so deeply.

The prayer that, even if she didn't survive, Mark would remain safe.

"There," Innes said with satisfaction, using a sharp knife to separate the tape wound around her wrists from the roll that had supplied it. "All snug and tidy. Now we can go."

This time he opened the throttle wide. The cruiser leaped forward, roaring toward the horizon and an outcome she didn't permit herself to think about. The only thought in her mind now was hope. Because if there was an opportunity for her to escape, she would seize it. She might go down, but she would go down fighting.

Chapter 19

Mark stood on Conch Beach's public dock and gazed out beyond the harbor to the open waters of the Gulf. He had already dismissed the buildings on both sides, as well as the boats moored in the harbor, as unlikely targets for his search. Too much activity here, too many people about.

Innes and his accomplice wouldn't have hidden Clare in an area where there was the risk of her being discovered. Of course, there was the possibility that she'd been driven away from the harbor to somewhere inland. But he didn't think so. Because if that were the case, then why would she have been taken first to the harbor?

And Clare *had* been here nearby. Otherwise, he wouldn't have heard those unmistakable nautical sounds in the background when the woman had phoned him. He just had to determine where she was being held. It was why he continued to stare at the horizon.

There was a haze out there over the waters, but nothing so thick that it prevented him from seeing a cluster of small islands separated from each other by narrow bands of water. He judged them to be a mile or two away from shore. The more he looked at those islands, the more they interested him.

An elderly man, seated on a camp stool, was fishing off the end of the dock. Mark approached him.

"Mind if I ask you about the islands out there?"

"What d'ya want to know? Those are the Sister Islands. Though calling them islands at all don't make sense. None o' them is bigger than an islet."

"Looks like there are four of them," Mark observed.

"Yeah, four o' them, it is."

"Any of them inhabited?"

"Naw, like I say, too small."

"I was just wondering, because I think I can see the corner of some structure peeking out from the side of the third one from the right."

"Wouldn't be anything permanent. There's no building over there. More likely to be a rental houseboat. Them houseboats is meant for the canals, but sometimes one o' 'em gets parked out there in a sheltered spot. Fishing is good there."

A houseboat. The more Mark thought about it, the more convinced he was this was where Clare was being held. And why not? It made a perfect hideaway, isolated, not easily reached.

He prayed he wasn't deceiving himself. He couldn't afford to make a wrong choice. Not when he could be receiving that second phone call at any time, and to try to stall the caller would be a mistake. It was imperative that he rescue Clare as soon as possible.

"Think I'll try my own luck fishing out there in the

vicinity," he told the old man. "Know where I could rent an outboard?"

"Sure thing. The fishing store down there off the foot of the dock has it all."

The guy knew what he was talking about. The store was not only able to provide Mark with a small, fiberglass boat whose transom featured both a gasoline motor and a battery powered trolling motor, but all the other gear he needed. Securing his swimsuit from the SUV, he found a public restroom where he changed.

When Mark chugged away from the harbor, seated at the tiller of the boat, he looked like nothing more than some yokel in a hokey cap and T. Those, together with his sunglasses, should make him unrecognizable to any suspicious observer on that houseboat, as long as he didn't get too close. Which was why he was headed, not directly to the islands, but well off to the right.

The snorkel mask was out of sight at his feet, the knife, the pendant, his car key and cell phone squeezed into the waterproof pocket inside the waistband of his swimsuit. His wallet and watch he'd left behind locked away in the SUV.

Even out here on the open waters, the air was sultry, almost suffocating. Mark didn't let it bother him. He was too busy concentrating on his mission, one that was every bit as vital as any he'd been assigned as a ranger.

Clare. Rescuing Clare was all that mattered. And if Innes had harmed her, or worse, he would make it his business to send the bastard to hell. But he didn't want to think about that something worse. He was as afraid of it as he was of his feelings for Clare. Feelings he didn't permit himself to examine, that would have to wait for later when she was safe again back at his side.

All he knew in this moment, and was unable to deny,

was that he couldn't lose her. If that happened, it would kill him.

But you're not going to allow it to happen, Mark promised himself fiercely.

He waited until the first two islands off to his left were between him and the outboard, when there was no longer a possibility of being sighted from the houseboat, before cutting the engine. Tilting it out of the water, he moved on to the trolling motor that shared the transom, easing it down into the flat waters.

The battery powered trolling motor, unlike the gasoline engine, was quiet, no more than a soft hum whose sound couldn't be detected from the houseboat. Stationing himself back at the tiller, he aimed the bow toward the first island. Slowly, steadily, the boat glided smoothly to the shore.

Just before the prop scraped bottom, Mark switched off the power and swung the motor out of the water. Barefoot now, he hopped out of the boat and waded to the narrow beach where he dragged the boat up on the sand.

His first order of business was the cell phone. Removing it from the pouch, he muted it before returning it to the zippered, waterproof pocket. Even though silenced, he would know if it rang, would feel it vibrating against his hip. He knew if he didn't or couldn't answer the call, Innes would be alerted. Stripping off the T-shirt and tossing both it and the cap into the boat, Mark scooped up the snorkel mask and took off into the interior of the island. The tropiclike growth was so thick and the insects so bad it was like a jungle. He was relieved he had only to go a couple of hundred feet before he was able to break through to the beach on the other side.

Swimming from there across a channel to the second island, he struggled through another heavy vegetation and swam another channel to the third island. It was here when he waded ashore that he heard it. The sound of country music carried from what was probably a radio on the houseboat.

It can't keep you from being seen, but it can help you from being easily heard.

Remembering the houseboat was positioned between the third and fourth islands, Mark felt his safest approach was to edge around the beach that faced the wide open sea. When he judged he could go no farther without being seen from the houseboat, he pulled the snorkel mask over his face, moved quietly into the Gulf and sank beneath the water, breathing through the tube that poked above the surface.

A moment later, after rounding the curve of the island, he worked his way underwater into a lagoon between the third and fourth islands to the hull of the houseboat anchored there. Feeling his way along its side, pinning himself against the hull to prevent the discovery of his arrival from onboard, he risked surfacing.

His glimpse was both silent enough and brief enough to provide him with all he needed to know. Roy Innes was seated on the open front deck of the houseboat, listening to the radio at his feet and looking out toward the coast. There was no sign of Clare. She was somewhere inside.

Mark felt it was best, if it was at all possible, to avoid a confrontation with Innes, who might have a gun by now. Hoping he could reach Clare from the back of the houseboat, he worked his way to the rear. There was a second deck here, a shorter one.

Lifting himself over its edge with all the stealth of a

ranger prepared to sneak up on the enemy, he got to his feet. An open door faced him, looking straight through the interior to an opposite door wide open to the front deck. Not good. If Innes happened to swing around, he couldn't fail to see him.

Taking care this didn't happen, Mark padded cautiously into the houseboat. Something swelled inside him at the sight of Clare lying in a lower bunk, relief that she was still alive mingled with an emotion he wasn't ready to call anything but tenderness.

Anger was in there, too, at finding her wrists and ankles bound with duct tape, although he should have expected this. She seemed unharmed otherwise.

His sudden appearance in the cabin, streaming with water like some strange sea god risen from the depths, had her staring at him with wide, startled eyes. At least she had the presence not to call out, which she could have done because her mouth hadn't been taped. Probably because Innes had felt it unnecessary out here where she couldn't be heard.

Understanding Mark's silent signal, Clare turned on her side to give him access to her wrists with the folding knife he extracted from the pocket. As quickly and quietly as possible, he sawed through the tape with the sharp blade, pausing to check on Innes before he attacked the tape around her ankles.

Innes hadn't stirred, hadn't bothered to so much as look around. Why should he when he had no reason to assume she was anything but helpless?

Once she was freed, and the knife restored to the pocket, Mark helped her to rise from the bunk and through the back door on legs that were unsteady after her long confinement.

Drawing her around the corner where they were no

longer in view of the open doorway at the other end of the cabin, he put his mouth to her ear and whispered a rapid "You know how to swim?"

"Like a fish," she mouthed back.

He was grateful for that, but the sight of her sundress with its full skirt could be a problem in the water. Understanding the meaning of his gaze directed at the skirt, she held up one finger, then surprised him by detaching the skirt from the top and stepping out of it. Underneath was a pair of shorts whose green pattern matched the rest of the three-piece outfit.

Sonofagun.

Tossing the skirt to the floor of the deck and kicking off her sandals, Clare preceded him to the rail, slid beneath it and lowered herself into the water below.

Mark followed her immediately. There was no need for the snorkel this time, not as long as they kept the back of the houseboat between them and its front deck. Nor were the sounds of their strokes through the water a problem when the country music continued to wail as they put distance between them and the boat.

Not until they were out of sight around the curve of the island did they wade ashore. It might have been safe for them to talk here, but both of them realized the wisdom of saving their wind.

Retracing his route, Mark led the way along the beach, across the first channel, through the tangled growth of the second island to the other channel and on to the last island. The houseboat was well behind them now and the outboard just ahead when he felt the untimely vibration of his cell phone.

Damn, he'd hoped for them to be in the clear when this happened. Clare had halted with him and was gazing at him now in puzzlement.

"My cell is buzzing. Innes's girlfriend is calling me with those instructions."

"Ava," she said. "Her name is Ava. Are you going to answer her?"

"No," he decided. "Listening to her could waste too many minutes. And we need those minutes to get out of here before we're caught. What kind of craft did Innes use to take you out to the islands?"

"An inboard cruiser."

That could be bad if it was powerful enough, Mark thought. It must have been tied off on the other side of the houseboat, because he hadn't seen it.

He hurried them through the rest of the vegetation, gaining the beach where he'd left the outboard. Another problem faced them here. The air was no longer still. A wind had sprung up off the Gulf, kicking up the waters.

Clare helped him to shove the little boat down the sandy incline. When it was afloat, and they were both aboard, she settled in the bow and Mark at the tiller. One pull of the cord, and he had the gasoline engine throbbing.

They headed toward the coast through a choppy sea. Had the dock been this far away? The distance between the harbor and the islands seemed to have increased noticeably, maybe because he was having difficulty keeping them on course. The little boat was bouncing erratically in the swells.

Nor did Mark like the sound of the engine struggling to keep them moving. An outboard like this was meant to operate in smooth waters, not rough seas. There was no question of that when, sputtering and coughing, the engine stalled.

His repeated tugs on the starting cord were useless. The engine was gone.

* * *

Clare, facing Mark from her seat in the bow, was the first to be aware of their pursuer. Her heart dropped at the sight of the cruiser sweeping around the back of the islands. Innes, at the wheel, must have either been alerted by Ava or had checked and found her gone from the houseboat.

Clare shouted a warning to Mark, who twisted around in his seat. They watched together, helpless, as the cruiser roared straight toward them. Unlike their own boat, the inboard had no trouble plowing through the waves, effortlessly slapping aside a path with its pointed bow.

Within seconds, the cruiser, speed reduced to an idle, coasted alongside them, bumping into their craft. Innes cut the engine and got to his feet, a pleased grin on his bony face, a pistol in his hand.

"You know what I want, soldier boy. Hand it over, and maybe I'll let you live."

Clare watched Mark get to his feet, his legs braced apart to steady himself in the rocking boat. She didn't like the rigid line of his jaw. It was clear evidence of his barely restrained anger.

"I don't have the pendant with me."

"No? I think you do. I think you wouldn't have left it behind. You would have wanted it handy in case you had to do some bargaining."

"I don't bargain with murdering lunatics, Innes."

"Mark," she pleaded, "don't challenge him. He won't hesitate to shoot you."

"That's right, soldier boy. I won't hesitate to shoot you. Or better still—" the pistol swung slowly in Clare's direction "—maybe it would be more effective if I were to shoot your little sweetheart here."

The threat was all Mark needed. With a howl of rage, he hurled himself with all the force of a missile over the sides of both boats. The impact of his body slamming into Innes's was so powerful it sent the gun flying and both men over the far side of the cruiser and into the water.

Clare came to her feet with a cry. Her wild movement almost pitched her into the sea herself. Kneeling on the bottom of the boat, she gripped the gunwale to keep herself in place. Without anything to hold them together, the cruiser and the outboard had separated.

The cruiser had drifted off, exposing the area where the two men had disappeared. The area which she frantically searched. There was no sign of them.

They were down there beneath the rolling surface locked in some terrible struggle. And if Mark lost the battle—

Dear God, he could die. Don't let him die. He can't die.

How long could they stay under without air? This was too long. Much too long. It seemed more than just seconds. It seemed minutes before her silent plea was answered. A head finally rose to the surface, breaking water.

Mark or Innes? She couldn't tell. Not until he twisted around, gulping air and searching for one of the boats was she able to identify him. It was Mark. Thank God, it was Mark.

She watched him as he paddled toward the outboard, fighting the turbulent waters as he strove to reach her extended hand. Only when his fingers finally made contact with hers did she ask him, "Innes?"

He shook his head, managing to gasp, "Lost him somewhere down there."

And then his strength gave out. He was barely able to cling to the side of the boat with his other hand, but unable to lift himself aboard. It was Clare who somehow found the strength, aided by whatever little energy Mark had left, to haul him into the boat.

Her treatment was anything but gentle. She feared she had hurt him, maybe seriously, when his leg—it would be the wounded one—connected so hard with the gunwale he sucked in a mouthful of air. That evidence of pain was the last sound he made before collapsing on the floor of the boat and passing out.

There was still no sign of Innes. Had he drowned? He must have drowned. But Innes didn't matter. Only her concern for Mark mattered. He could be more than just unconscious. He could be injured, in need of medical treatment.

The outboard was without power, the trolling motor useless in waters like these while the empty cruiser was far out of reach now, headed seaward.

You're not helpless. You can't permit yourself to be helpless. Think.

Mark's cell phone. She could see the outline of it in the pocket of his wet suit. Had it remained dry? Would it still work?

Leaning over him, she unzipped the waterproof pocket, closed her hand over the phone inside, drew it out and examined it for both power and a signal. Yes! She had both.

Within seconds, she was reporting their plight to the emergency service on shore. "I need help. I'm out here between the harbor and the islands in a small boat with a failed engine. I have an unconscious man who could need treatment."

The Coast Guard was on its way. Clare ended the call with a relieved sigh. Now all she had to do was wait.

But that wasn't all. The wind had strengthened in force, and the waves with it. They weren't just being tossed about. They had been turned sideways and were wallowing in the troughs between the swells. In this position the small boat was in danger of capsizing.

Clare knew just enough about such a situation to realize that she had to swing the outboard around so that its prow was headed into the oncoming rollers, and to keep it that way.

There was an emergency paddle in the bottom of the boat. Seizing it, she got to work, dipping and stroking until she'd managed to move the bow into the wind. They were riding the whitecaps now. But in order to maintain that attitude, it was necessary for her to move with the paddle from one side of the boat to the other, correcting the direction whenever they started to turn again.

Back and forth she went, the boat bouncing over the crests, hair whipping in her face. Her arms grew tired with the repeated effort.

Don't give up. You can't give up.

She didn't, and was rewarded for her endurance a few minutes later by the appearance of the Coast Guard rescue vessel slashing through the waves, sending up spray as it charged toward them.

Clare had never seen a more beautiful sight.

Chapter 20

Mark was awake and complaining when they were delivered to the dock where an ambulance was waiting.

"No hospital," he grumbled. "I'm not going to any hospital. There's nothing wrong with me."

He did agree, however, to having the two medics standing by check him over. They pronounced him fit, although he did admit the leg that had been wounded in Afghanistan was aching a bit. But that wasn't unusual, considering what stress it had been subjected to out there in the Gulf. All he would accept, and got, were a couple of aspirin and a bottle of water.

Once released, he and Clare made their way to the SUV, selected dry clothing from their luggage and changed in a pair of public restrooms. They drove afterward to the police station, which had been told by the Coast Guard to expect them.

Clare soon learned that, though the Conch Beach police force was not a large one, it was an efficient one. They were assigned to the same officer who was handling the Hank Kolchek case. Sergeant Will O'Hara was built more like a Miami Dolphins linebacker than a good-natured cop.

The sergeant listened patiently to the story she and Mark alternately related, taking down the pertinent details of all that had happened beginning in New Orleans and ending here.

"I'm going to phone the New Orleans and St. Boniface departments," O'Hara told them, "and if everything checks out both there and with the Kolchek situation, I see no reason why your sister shouldn't be released in the near future. Meanwhile, Ms. Fuller, I'm going to have you look at some mug shots. If this woman called Ava has a record, I want to know what it is."

Moments later, Clare found herself seated in front of a computer scanning photos of women who had served time. She was growing weary of the search, thinking it was hopeless, when she finally spotted the brunette.

Her full name was Ava Santana, and she had a history of extortion. It was all the Conch Beach police needed to issue an APB and an order for her to be picked up.

Sergeant O'Hara had good news for Clare when he finished making his calls. New Orleans had informed him they'd located the security tape time stamped with Terry's visit to Malcolm Boerner's shop on the afternoon of her husband's murder. The tape was in Boerner's safety deposit box.

"Your sister's release is just a formality now. As for the rest, I'm going to ask you and the lieutenant here to come back tomorrow. I should have further results for you by then."

Mark had remained at Clare's side throughout the proceedings. He stayed close when they came away from the police station, ate an early dinner at the harbor front and registered for the night in another motel. Physically, that is. Emotionally, now that everything was ending, she felt a widening gulf between them.

Once settled in the motel, and with her cell phone still in Ava Santana's possession, Clare asked to borrow Mark's cell. He obliged and proposed taking a walk while she made her call. His leg was no longer aching but needed exercising.

A genuine motive, she wondered, or an excuse to get away from her? Terry was ecstatic when she managed to get her on the phone. Clare wanted to be more excited for her sister. But sadness, bordering on despair, pervaded her both then and throughout the evening. Were she and Mark nothing now but polite strangers?

They saw Sergeant O'Hara again late the following morning. He had a good deal to tell them about the developments since yesterday.

Roy Innes's drowned body had washed ashore a half mile down the coast. Both boats had been recovered and returned to the owners who had rented them, while the houseboat had motored back to the canal from which it had originated where the police had visited it. The two officers found Clare's purse and discarded skirt, which were turned over to her.

They had also discovered the four pendants Innes had hidden in the houseboat. Mark gave the sergeant his own pendant, asking that when the police were finished with the collection that it be given to Hank Kolchek, who intended to use it to restore the treasures to Afghanistan's National Museum.

"And this I've been saving for last," O'Hara said. "Ava Santana was apprehended last night at the Miami-Dade Airport where she was waiting to board a plane to Texas, which was apparently where she and Innes first met and hooked up. She's here now in a holding cell."

He went on to tell them Ava cooperated for the promise of a reduced sentence. Innes had left her behind in New Orleans to keep track of Clare and Mark while he went after Hank Kolchek in Florida. Because they had been watching for a man at the wheel of a blue sedan, they'd had no reason to be suspicious of a woman in a green van.

Ava had followed them to Florida and afterward to the Conch Beach hospital. She'd been looking for a chance to rob Mark of his pendant while Innes waited outside in his car.

It was Ava, seeing Clare enter the restroom, who'd devised the plan to take Clare hostage and hold her in exchange for the pendant. She'd called Innes in his car, asking him to lure Mark away from his post, which enabled her to snatch Clare.

"I think that about covers it," Sergeant O'Hara said. "It won't be necessary for you to appear as witnesses. The statements you made and signed yesterday are all we need. Before you leave, though you might like to know Hank Kolchek is off the critical list and has been moved out of the ICU into a recovery room."

"He able to have visitors?" Mark asked.

The sergeant thought he could, since one of their officers had been permitted to take a statement from him earlier.

"Let's go see Kolchek," Mark proposed when he and Clare came away from the police station. "I'd like him to know the five pendants will be turned over to him."

Clare agreed.

* * *

"Well, it's finished," Mark said, satisfied by their visit and Hank's gratitude when they left the hospital a half hour later. "We can go home now."

Clare knew it wasn't finished, that what remained to be resolved could either be a beginning or an ending. And that dealing with it could break her heart. But delaying it, whatever the outcome, was something she couldn't bear.

It was why, as they started for the parking lot, she urged, "Look, there's a bench there in the shade of those palms. Let's sit for a little. There's something we need to settle."

She saw at once her suggestion made him uneasy. Not a good sign.

"Can't it wait until we're on the road?"

"No, Mark," she insisted, "I want it settled now."

He was more than uneasy now, he was unwilling. But she left him no choice. He followed her to the bench, where they seated themselves side by side.

"Okay, what is it?" he asked, turning to her.

He knows what it is, she thought. He just hates having to face it. Well, so did she.

Fortifying herself with a deep breath, she said as evenly as possible, "I think you know I'm in love with you, Mark. And if you imagine that was easy for me to say, it wasn't." He opened his mouth to react to that, but she held up her hand to let him know she wasn't finished. "What's more, I think—and this isn't easy for me, either—that, much as you resisted it, you couldn't help falling in love with me. Or am I wrong about that?"

He wasn't so ready to answer her this time.

"Mark?" she prompted him.

"Okay, so maybe it's true."

"Then what are we going to do about it?"

"Nothing."

She'd known the risk in loving him, knew it all along, and now she was about to pay for it. It was going to end as badly as she'd feared it would.

"I didn't want to hurt you, Clare. It's killing me to hurt you, but there can't be anything permanent for us. Your life is in New Orleans, and mine is with the rangers."

She should have left it there, accepted the inevitable, but she couldn't do that. Not without a struggle. "Why does that have to be an obstacle? Other couples have partners with opposing careers, live in different locations even and manage to work out successful relationships."

"Maybe, but it's different if your career is the service. I've seen too many marriages fail when the partner, man or woman, is repeatedly deployed overseas in dangerous zones for months at a time. Not to mention the possibility of being permanently disabled in battle and sent home for a wife or husband to care for them the rest of their lives. Or, worse, being killed. I won't do that to you, Clare. I won't risk having you suffer the grief of another Alan Britten."

"And you're giving me nothing to say about it?"

"It wouldn't matter. I'm not going to change my mind. I *can't.*"

She could see how miserable his decision was making him, as miserable as she was, and all because he was stubbornly convinced he was doing the right thing letting her go. There was no point in going any further with this.

She got to her feet. "Would you get my bag from the car?"

"Why?"

"Because I'm going home."

"But I'm going to drive you back to New Orleans."

"And how awkward and uncomfortable would that be for both of us? No, Mark, I made my own plans in case it turned out this way. After I called Terry last night when you were out, I phoned the reception desk and learned I could fly home from Fort Myers. There are buses from here to the airport there. My friend Monica will meet me in New Orleans and drive me down to the service garage to reclaim my car."

"At least let me take you to the bus depot."

She shook her head. "It ends here, Mark. It has to. I couldn't stand it otherwise." *You aren't standing it now, but to draw it out would be worse.* "I can catch a cab at the front entrance to the hospital."

He must have recognized the wisdom in her arrangement, because he didn't argue with her. He fetched her bag from the SUV and silently handed it to her. There were no thank-yous or goodbyes exchanged. Mark, as well as she, must have realized nothing would have been adequate enough.

Clare simply turned and walked away.

He didn't try to stop her.

The days that followed were rough ones for Clare. She felt as if something had died inside her and wondered if it would ever be brought back to life. Time maybe. Isn't that what people said? That only time could cure a severe heartache?

Until then all she could do was battle her dejection. Returning to her classroom helped. That and her friends, who seemed to sense when she needed company and when she didn't, and who complied with both moods.

There was her sister, as well. She came down from St. Boniface to spend the weekend with her. Terry, bless her, never tried to remind Clare how she'd tried to warn her about Mark. Always the nurturing big sister, she simply expressed her concern.

"I could see when you both visited me at the jail how much you already cared for him."

"Foolish of me, wasn't it?"

"Don't punish yourself, Clare. It's easy to fall in love with a guy like him. Do you think you'll hear from him again?"

"Not likely."

"And in the meantime?"

"I'll get on with my life, maybe even manage to forget about him."

"Yes, that's best. Just remember, though, I'm always here for you."

Much to Clare's surprise, there was also Officer Martinez. The dark, handsome cop, who had answered her call the night Roy Innes broke into her house, turned up at her door one evening. He claimed he just stopped by to make sure she'd recovered from the attempted robbery, but when he learned Mark was no longer with her he asked her if she would consider going out with him.

Clare was flattered and told him so, but that she wasn't ready to date again. Officer Martinez was a nice guy, and any other available woman wouldn't have hesitated to go out with him. Only Clare didn't want a conventionally nice guy. She wanted what she couldn't have. A tough warrior, who wasn't always nice but who had her heart and always would.

* * *

She was angry with herself, wondering if she was ever going to shake this hurt, when she came home from school one afternoon to find Lieutenant Mark Griggs on her doorstep.

Clare was astonished to see him there waiting for her. Astonished and not sure whether to be exhilarated at the sight of him or heartsick. There was only one certainty. Seated there, hands on his spread knees, he cut a dashing figure in his boots, camouflaged-patterned combat uniform and the tan beret of the rangers at a rakish angle on his head.

"Mark, what are you doing here?"

He got to his feet, tall and imposing, wearing one of those damnable grins that could make her insides turn over. "Ask me inside, and I'll tell you."

Clare wasn't sure she wanted to do that, not if it meant further anguish. But when had she ever been able to deny him when he was sporting that familiar grin? Digging her key out of her purse, she unlocked the door, preceded him into the house and dumped her purse and the work she had brought home on a chair.

When she turned around, he was leaning against the door he'd closed behind him and casting his gaze around the living room.

"Looks like you've moved in completely."

She wasn't interested in discussing her furnishings. She eyed his uniform. "I guess they've pronounced you fit for duty. You're being deployed again, aren't you?"

Why on earth would he travel all this way just to tell her goodbye? They'd already had their parting. She couldn't take another one.

He looked down at his uniform, as if just now realizing he was wearing it. "You thought because— No, hell, no. See, I was wearing this on base, and I didn't take time to change into civvies before I left Ft. Bragg. All I could think about was getting to you, which is why I drove straight through from North Carolina."

It would have been so easy for Clare to soar into a state of happiness at that moment, but she had been through too much to assume anything regarding this man.

"Are you telling me you suddenly decided you missed me and that you couldn't wait to get to me? Because if that's your reason for being here, it's not enough. I want more than that. I *deserve* more than that."

"Yeah, you do, and I want to offer it to you. And I'm hoping like hell you'll accept it."

"Why this change of heart, Mark? What happened to make you think you had room for more in your life than just the army?"

"A couple of things. Like, for one, understanding that I didn't have to be like my parents, running away from commitment because I was afraid of it."

"And for another?" she pressed him.

"Easy. Easy, but meaning everything. I realized what I should have known all along. Yeah, I love the army, but the army can't love me back. And I want that love, Clare. I need it. With *you*. Everything, marriage, kids, a home."

She was almost ready now to trust him, to go to him and tell him she would gladly provide him with all that. Almost, but not quite.

"What about your argument for relationships that fail when one of the partners is deployed for long periods overseas, or the possibility of being permanently disabled or killed? Not that I wasn't ready to accept those risks."

"The argument no longer applies. There'll be no more combat zones for me. My CO and I talked it over. From now I remain stateside training new recruits to be rangers."

"Are you going to be happy with that?"

"I'll have my career in the army, still be a ranger. With you beside me, that's all that matters. The thing is," he went on, looking anxious now, "could you bear to leave all this? New Orleans, the home and job here you love so much?"

"There are other cities and houses and teaching positions, Mark."

"Are you saying—"

"That I accept your proposal of marriage and all that goes with it? You are proposing to me, aren't you?"

"Oh, yeah. Definitely proposing."

"Then I am saying yes," she said, surrendering fully now to the joy she had so fiercely wanted and finally won.

Mark had been slowly edging toward her all this while. He was close to her now, close enough to wind his arms around her and draw her against him.

"I've been longing for days to kiss this scar," he said, bending his head to tenderly place his lips over the crescent-shaped scar high on her cheek.

"Hey, if it's just about the scar, I don't think—"

"Quiet."

Altering his target, as Clare decided any experienced army ranger would realize the advantage of doing, he got busy kissing her mouth. For a very long and highly satisfying time.

* * * * *

REQUEST YOUR FREE BOOKS!
2 FREE NOVELS PLUS 2 FREE GIFTS!

ROMANTIC suspense

Sparked by danger, fueled by passion

HRS13

SPECIAL EXCERPT FROM
HARLEQUIN® ROMANTIC SUSPENSE

R̲S̲

Harlequin Romantic Suspense presents the third book in the thrilling Black Ops Rescues miniseries from best-loved author Beth Cornelison

Black Ops pilot Jake Connelly battles an escaped convict and a Texas-size blizzard to rescue Chelsea Harris, but will he lose his heart to the intrepid small-town girl?

Read on for an excerpt from

COWBOY'S TEXAS RESCUE

Available March 2013 from
Harlequin Romantic Suspense

A rattle came from the trunk lock, and she tensed. *Oh, please, God, let it be someone to rescue me and not that maniac killer!*

The lid rose, and daylight poured into the pitch-dark of the trunk. She shuddered as a stiff, icy wind swept into the well of the trunk, blasting her bare skin.

"Ah, hell," a deep voice muttered.

Her pulse scampered, and she squinted to make out the face of the man standing over her.

The gun in his hand registered first, then his size—tall, broad shouldered, and his fleece-lined ranch coat made him appear impressively muscle-bound. Plenty big enough to overpower her if he was working with the convict.

A black cowboy hat and backlighting from the sky obscured his face in shadow, adding to her apprehension.

"Are you hurt?" he asked, stashing the gun out of sight and undoing the buttons of his coat.

"N-no." When he reached for her, she shrank back warily.

Where was the convict? She cast an anxious glance around them, down the side of the car, searching.

She jolted when her rescuer grasped her elbow.

"Hey, I'm not gonna hurt you." The cowboy leaned farther into the trunk. "Let me help you out of there, and you can have my coat."

His coat… She almost whimpered in gratitude, anticipating the warmth. When she caught her first good glimpse of his square jaw and stubble-dusted cheeks, her stomach swooped. *Oh, Texas!* He was a freaking *Adonis*. Greek-god gorgeous with golden-blond hair, cowboy boots and ranch-honed muscles. He lifted her out of the trunk, and when he set her down and her knees buckled with muscle cramps, cold and fatigue, she knew she couldn't dismiss old-fashioned swooning for at least some of her legs' weakness. He draped the coat around her shoulders, and the sexy combined scents of pine, leather and man surrounded her. She had to be dreaming….

Will Chelsea find more than safety in her sexy rescuer's arms? Or will the convict come back to finish them both off? Find out what happens next in COWBOY'S TEXAS RESCUE

Available March 2013 from Harlequin Romantic Suspense wherever books are sold.

HARLEQUIN®

ROMANTIC suspense

Willa Merris may be off-limits,
but Gabe Dawson is a billionaire and can break
all the rules to keep her safe...if she'll let him.

Look for the third book in the
Vengeance in Texas miniseries.

A BILLIONAIRE'S REDEMPTION
by Cindy Dees

Available March 2013 from Harlequin Romantic
Suspense wherever books are sold.

A PROFILER'S CASE FOR SEDUCTION
by Carla Cassidy

(Book #4) available April 2013